When **Virginia Heath** was a little girl it took her ages to fall asleep—so she made up stories in her head to help pass the time while she was staring at the ceiling. As she got older the stories became more complicated—sometimes taking weeks to get to their happy ending. One day she decided to embrace her insomnia and start writing them down. Virginia lives in Essex, UK, with her wonderful husband and two teenagers. It still takes her for ever to fall asleep…

REDEEMING THE RECLUSIVE EARL

Virginia Heath

MILLS & BOON

First Published in Great Britain 2020
by Mills & Boon, an imprint of HarperCollins*Publishers*
1 London Bridge Street, London, SE1 9GF

© 2020 Susan Merritt

ISBN: 978-0-263-27297-0

MIX
Paper from
responsible sources
FSC® C007454

This book is produced from independently certified FSC™ paper
to ensure responsible forest management.
For more information visit www.harpercollins.co.uk/green.

Printed and bound in Spain
by CPI, Barcelona

For Emily Lawrence.
Who never fails to make me smile.

Chapter One

∽∾∽∾∽∾∽

Three hundred acres...

'**W**hat the hell do you think you are doing?'

The grubby boy scrambled back to a sitting position and blinked up at him through the thick lenses of his spectacles. When Max had first spotted the lad kneeling on the ground, he had assumed he was a poacher and was about to ride by, not caring if a few of his pheasants were liberated for a poor family's cooking pot. Just because he no longer had any appetite didn't mean the rest of the population couldn't eat and he'd never had a taste for pheasant even when he had enjoyed his food, so it made no difference to him. But as he had crested the small rise near the eastern boundary of his new estate in his quest to fill some time, he spotted all the holes in the ground, the shovels, tools and wheelbarrow, and realised the intruder was digging.

'I asked you a question!' He practically spat in annoyance, aggrieved that he had to make the effort to actually converse or to concern himself with another human being and their peculiar business when he was in no mood for either. The boy's spectacles magnified his dark eyes. They were the oddest spectacles Max Aldersley had ever seen. Instead of arms, the unsightly frame was tied around the back of his head with a bright red ribbon secured in a bow. Perhaps his first guess about the direness of the lad's financial circumstances had been correct if he had to go out looking like that. His gaze drifted to the paintbrush and trowel in the boy's hand, then fixed on the hole he was crouched before. Half-exposed in the mud was a dark object. Spherical, like a pot, which was either being buried or exhumed. All very odd and all entirely unwelcome. All much too much effort. 'Why are you trespassing on my land?'

'My land?' The boy didn't sound like a boy and instantly Max felt his hackles rise in panic at his own curious stupidity. The trespasser stood and his stomach plummeted to his toes.

Now he could see significant evidence that the *boy* was a woman which really made his blood boil. When he had first spotted her scratching around in the mud he had assumed her to be a young man—an easy mistake to make, considering she was dressed in breeches and work boots. Odd work boots. One black. One very definitely brown.

'Oh, hello! You must be the new Lord Rivenhall.'

It was so much easier to be an abomination in front of a man.

Had he known that she was female, he wouldn't have brought his horse so close no matter what she had been doing on his property. But now Max could see the trousers hugged her female form like a second skin and there was no getting away from the fact that the hips which flared from her waist were as unmanly as it was possible for hips to be—more was the pity. Worse, the capacious linen shirt tucked haphazardly into the top of the waistband also did little to disguise the fine bosom beneath. The wench had a body that was made for sin. Unfortunately, there was very little evidence that the rest of her lived up to that promise. Which, all things considered, was probably just as well. His sinning days were well and truly over.

The floppy brown felt hat she wore hid her hair and it was anybody's guess what the strange spectacle affair was all about, but it did a very good job of hiding her features. What the large round lenses did not cover was hidden behind a thick smear of wet dirt. She smiled cheerfully as she idly patted his horse's muzzle with one hand and shielded her magnified eyes from the sun rising behind him with the other.

'We are neighbours, my lord. I called upon you yesterday and twice more last week to introduce myself, but you were indisposed. I am so glad we have finally met. I am Miss Euphemia Nithercott, daughter of Doctor Henry Nithercott of Hill House.'

She stuck out her hand for him to shake. It might as well have been a cobra as far as he was concerned, but he hid the visceral claw of fear of human contact behind what he hoped was a bland, surly mask, ignoring her friendly gesture and her hand to loom taller in his saddle menacingly. 'I have a deep well of loathing for the medical profession.'

'Not a medical doctor. He was an academic, specialising in the translation of Anglo-Saxon texts. Papa was a don at Cambridge for thirty-five years.' She was also still waffling on in the false assumption that her words mattered. When nothing mattered any more and all he wanted was to be left alone. Something he had hoped to be able to do with impunity on this sprawling estate miles from anywhere. Yet here he was, only two weeks in and already burdened with unwanted company.

Max curled his lip, letting her know in no uncertain terms he didn't hold academic doctors in much higher regard either, and watched in relief as she withdrew her hand awkwardly and clasped it in the other one behind her back as her cheerful smile melted from her face under his intense scrutiny. 'He was highly respected in his field.'

Responding with anything sounding remotely like interest would only open the floodgates for more inane chatter. 'Miss Nithercott, this is private property and you have no right to be on it. Leave. Now.'

'Actually, I was just going. However, I do have permission to be here. I am not a trespasser, my lord.' She offered him her best *this is all a misunderstanding* smile and went back to petting his horse. 'Although I understand how you might have been a little alarmed to see someone here so early in the morning. The previous owner of this land, your uncle Richard, granted me access to dig around these ruins years ago. Perhaps he mentioned me to you in his letters?'

'He did not.' As his uncle and his father had been estranged for the entirety of his life, there had been no letters as far as he was concerned—bar the one from his uncle he had read posthumously, months after both his father and the uncle he had never met had both left this mortal coil, expressing sympathy for Max's loss and his bitter regret at never healing the breach. At the time, he had barely registered the loss himself. He'd been too busy fighting for his own life. When he had finally emerged from that agonising pit of hell into the new darkness of his life, he grieved his indifferent father alongside everything else—albeit grieving everything else more. He still grieved it and cursed fate daily for not taking him, too.

'Oh...well... Never mind.' She swatted the detail away with one muddy hand. 'Lord Richard was fascinated by all the things I found and took a great interest in the ancient history of Rivenhall. As you can see...' she made a sweeping motion of the extensive dig site with her arms '... I have found a great deal of important archaeology here. There has been a settlement at Rivenhall Abbey for at least a thousand years and I have been gradually excavating its secrets for the last decade. It is *so* very interesting.'

Max gave the rocks and stones sticking out of the ground a cursory glance. He could make out the odd suggestion of a long-fallen wall here and there, but apart from that there was nothing about the area that she was gesticulating towards so enthusiastically that he found even remotely interesting. Not that he had expected to be interested. He had lost all interest in everything and everyone a long time ago.

'If you would care to dismount, my lord, I

would be more than happy to show you everything I have found so far.'

He would rather gouge out his eyeballs with his own thumbs. Cut off his toes with blunt shears. Curl up in a ball and feel sorry for himself. He hated himself for that, but could not seem to haul himself out of the deep pit of despair he languished in. 'Your permission to dig here is now revoked, Miss Whatever-your-name-is. Pack up your things and get off my land.' His voice was flat and suddenly emotionless as the familiar hopelessness swamped him. 'If I catch you here again, I will set my dogs on you!' He managed somehow to give the idle threat the gravitas it deserved before he quickly turned his horse until his back was fully to her and then began to ride away as if she deserved no more of his consideration, vowing to buy some dogs at his earliest convenience in case she called his bluff.

'You cannot do that! This site is of great historic importance...' He could hear her work boots thump the ground as she jogged after him. Smelled the faintest whiff of rose petals as she came alongside. 'I have to dig here. There is so much still to uncover. Can't you see that?'

He should have ignored her. Should have—but couldn't. He tugged on his reins to bring his mount to a stop and turned to stare at her, then regretted it instantly when he saw the hope in her eyes.

'Go home, Miss Nodcock.'

Please, for the love of God, go home.

'It's Nithercott.' She shrugged without offence, which he couldn't help but admire when he was trying hard to be so very offensive. 'A bit of a mouthful, I know, but it is what it is and there aren't many Nithercotts left in the world. The name comes from Somerset originally, but Papa moved here to Cambridgeshire before I was born. Which was fortuitous for me as I doubt I would have found anything quite as inspiring to dig as Rivenhall Abbey. Let me show you the site… I guarantee you will find *your* history fascinating.'

'I wouldn't place a bet on that.'

'The Abbey goes back to the fifteenth century.' She was pointing to the broken, empty shell of a building in the distance, the one he knew had given Rivenhall Abbey its name. He knew this because he had managed to read an entire chapter of a book about it in his new library the day after he arrived, before he had tossed it angrily aside to stare at his new walls and continue to wallow in self-pity. Something his sister was convinced he over-indulged in. Max agreed, but did not possess the strength or the desire to stop. At the very least, self-pity gave him something to do during the interminable hours of the day. 'Although the earliest parts of the knave are *obviously* Norman. There have been some very interesting medieval finds in and around the Abbey walls. However, it was only when I began to excavate a little beyond the immediate boundary of that building that I began to discover evidence of an earlier settlement here.'

A soft breeze materialised out of nowhere, ruffling the hair from his face, and she saw the scars. Her dark eyes briefly widened behind the ridiculous lenses she wore and for just the briefest moment he saw her smile falter before she politely nailed it back in place. It was a good approximation of a friendly smile, better than most managed when they first encountered his deformity, but still tinged with the awful polite and pasted-on smile of pity he had come to loathe with every fibre of his being. He felt sick to his stomach and ashamed that she had seen it.

Instinctively, he twisted his body and his horse away so that she could see only the undamaged side of his face in profile, then speared her with his most irritated gaze, keeping the hideousness safely out of view even though he knew she had seen it and there was no point trying to fool himself she hadn't.

She was smiling again, trying to appeal to his better nature, and that galled because it was a pretty smile and it did appeal. She was one of those people who spoke with her hands. They were waving wildly, pointing to this and that or making strange shapes in the air while she continued to assault his ears with her chatter and offend his eyes with her femininity while beneath his ribs his heart wept.

'Those walls over there, for instance, are definitely Roman, the size of the buildings suggest that they are the small dwellings of the poorer citizens and I have already amassed an extensive collection of everyday artefacts from the period which paint a vivid picture of what life was like here then. In the last year, I have been digging on this eastern boundary in the hope of finding a temple or villa—something substantial that would explain why there were so many smaller dwellings in such close proximity, but my investigations have only recently taken a decidedly different course from the one I anticipated.' Two magnified brown eyes blinked back at him in excitement through the thick lenses as she beamed up at him. She reminded him a little of a barn owl. 'In actual fact, I believe I am on the cusp of proving that the settlement actually predates the Roman conquest. Lord Richard would have been *thrilled* to know about that. I cannot wait to uncover it all.'

Good grief, the woman could talk. Max had

barely been in her company for a few scant minutes and already his ears were ringing. He avoided conversations now. Had less time for them then he did people. This unwelcome onslaught would need nipping in the bud right this instant if he was ever to get the peace and solitude he craved, as it was quite apparent the academic's daughter cared a great deal about all the holes she had dug and wanted to continue digging them. Something that was entirely out of the question. The last thing he needed or wanted was a woman on his grounds. Or anybody come to that.

'I am not sure how to break this to you…' Sarcasm had become a second language. Another line of defence to hide all the hurt. 'But Lord Richard is *dead*. Which means any agreements you had with him to dig up this land are also *dead*.' As she furiously blinked back at him he noticed her thick, dark lashes were also ridiculously long. Each blink caused them to sweep across the inside of the glass lenses like tiny paint brushes. Max felt himself frown because the sight of them offended him. He was done with noticing attractive details like eyelashes. That part of his life was over and the sooner he accepted it the happier he would be. Then, because clearly she had not unsettled him enough, one muddy finger tugged at the ribbon behind her head and the thick lenses dropped away to reveal a lovely pair of eyes the exact same colour as aged Scotch whisky. They were much too lovely and much too intelligent as far as he was concerned as they stared back at him levelly.

'Get your things and get the hell off my land, Miss Nithercott! I do not want to see you here again.'

She bristled instantly, those insultingly fine eyes shimmering with a stubborn flash of temper which suddenly burned in her golden-flecked irises, and her hands positioned themselves staunchly on her generous hips, drawing his eyes reluctantly to them before he tore them away. 'Now see here...'

Max held up his palm to stop whatever tirade she was about to launch into. He really had no patience for politeness any more, nor did he see the point in it. The need to behave like a gentleman died the exact same day as his face and his dreams.

'We are done, Miss Nincompoop. Take your shovels, and whatever all that other nonsense is, and go. From this point forth, you are banned from setting one foot on Rivenhall Abbey and, as I've already told you, all agreements you once had with the uncle I never knew have been rescinded.' He did not bother to wait for a reaction, instead, desperate to escape, he nudged Drake in the ribs and let the big horse gallop away as fast as he could make it.

Chapter Two

⧼❦⧽

*Dig Day 756: no progress whatsoever due to
entirely unforeseen circumstances...*

Despite her best attempts at being calm Effie
was so incensed, even the pretty two-mile walk
from Hill House to the Abbey had done little to
soften her temper.

How dared he be so rude and obnoxious?

How dared he try to ban her from excavating
the past? When the past was her everything and
she couldn't imagine what she would do with her
days if she didn't have the Abbey and all its hidden
secrets to keep her occupied. What had begun as
a diversion to avoid the despair of her strange lot
in life had rapidly become her salvation. The only
place she truly felt as though she belonged now.

Horrid man! What difference did it make to
him if she dug around the ruins anyway? It was

on the furthest edge of his land, the soil too filled with the deep foundations from a bygone era to be of any agricultural use and a good distance from his house. He had plenty of better acres to ride his big horse in. He was simply being difficult and unreasonable. Two traits she had little time for under the normal course of things.

However, legally Lord Rivenhall actually had a point. He was under no obligation to honour a neighbourly agreement made by his uncle years before because the land was now his to do with as he pleased. There was no written contract—there had been no need of one between friends—and as far as she understood things, a gentleman's agreement died with the gentleman. Unless Effie could negotiate otherwise with their surly new neighbour, Lord Rivenhall was completely within his rights to prevent her from digging up his land.

This prospect angered her even more. How dared that awful man be so…insensitive to the important work that she was doing at the Abbey? Did he seriously expect her to abandon her study just because he said so? She had half a mind to march right up to his front door, demand an audience and give him a piece of her superior mind. Of course, if she did that then she could wave goodbye to any further investigation of the site alongside her purpose and her sanity.

If her father had been alive, typically, he would have urged restraint and caution.

'Effie,' he often said when her frustrations got the better of her or she had rubbed people up the wrong way. 'Appeal to their better nature. Argue your corner using sound logic and reasoning, not emotion. Do your best to find a compromise. Compromise is always key. And remember, as Benjamin Franklin said, *"Tart words make no friends; a spoonful of honey will catch more flies than a gallon of vinegar."'*

He had been fond of learned quotes, probably because he hated arguments of any sort, whereas Effie was more than happy to have an argument if she felt the situation warranted it. The obnoxious Lord Rivenhall warranted it. If he had not been the custodian of the very land she needed to dig, she'd have brought one of her shovels along to clonk him over his thick head with it. Horrid man!

Thanks to him, she was wasting her morning on a wholly unnecessary mission of diplomacy when what she really wanted to do, what she had spent all of yesterday and most of the long, sleepless night impatiently itching to do, was to excavate the rest of the magnificent pot still partly submerged in the ground. Unfortunately, a great well of patience was not a virtue that she naturally possessed.

In all the years she had been digging at Rivenhall she had never uncovered anything which had looked quite like the treasure she had discovered yesterday. Just thinking about it made bubbles of sheer excitement fizz and pop within her. Not liberating it from the soil for further study and not thoroughly digging around its current location would be a tragedy. She paused a few yards from the horrid Earl's front door and forced herself to inhale several slow, calming breaths before she marched into the breach.

'Tart words make no friends.'

Not that she currently had any friends left, but that sad fact had little to do with her occasional tart mouth and more to do with her unique peculiarity, but the new Lord Rivenhall wouldn't know about that yet. Unless the good news had already travelled to him via the gossips or his servants, which in itself made a bit of a mockery of being a recluse.

Hoping her father's often-repeated words of wisdom would calm her, Effie said the phrase over and over in her mind. Not that the house intimidated her. She had been visiting the previous Lord Rivenhall alone since she had been about ten. The old man had always been thrilled to see her and took an active interest in her passion for antiquity. She had had free rein to explore his vast scholarly library as well as dig in the ruins. Right up until his death twelve months ago, Effie had taken tea with him at least twice a week. Unfortunately, this wasn't tea with her father's old friend. It was critical to all she held dear and her fate rested entirely in the hands of his scowling curmudgeon of a nephew.

Out of politeness to the new master, Effie knocked on the imposing front door rather than let herself in through the kitchens as usual. In the spirit of friendship, she also carried a basket of freshly baked cakes for the surly Earl as a peace offering, hoping a few sweet treats and the fine bottle of brandy from her father's old stash might make him more agreeable.

Smithson, the butler, appeared amused that she had done so and even more bemused by the sight of her in a frock, but embarrassment soon clouded his face, his darting eyes saying much more than his mouth. 'I believe Lord Rivenhall is *indisposed* again, Miss Euphemia. Perhaps you would like to leave your basket and I will tell him that you called?' His wary gaze was pleading now, begging her to leave.

Effie had expected this. The village was awash with gossip about how the new owner of Rivenhall Abbey had refused to see anyone thus far. Aside from her, the vicar and his wife had been turned away both last week and the week before when they had called to welcome him to the parish. So, too, had the local magistrate and the physician, Dr Samuels. Although after her run-in with Lord Surly yesterday and his curt *'I have a deep well of loathing for the medical profession'*, she wasn't particularly surprised the latter gentleman had been denied an audience. But he would see her today.

By hook or by crook, he would see her today!

She had even donned a dress for the occasion, something she rarely needed on the long and solitary days filled with digging, but she knew from bitter experience the male of the species always reacted more favourably towards her if she resembled what they expected a gentleman's daughter to resemble. As if the mere presence of skirts and ribbons somehow made her less intimidating or odd. To that end, and because he was new to the parish, she had also vowed to disguise the bulk of her intellect, too. Nothing terrified or aggravated a man more than an excessively clever woman— even if she wasn't in breeches.

She smiled at the butler apologetically. 'No, thank you, Smithson. I shall wait here until His Lordship *is* disposed. Can you please tell him that I have taken root in the parlour and will not be budged until I have an audience with him?'

Smithson nodded slowly, a slight wince on his

face. 'I will try, Miss Euphemia.' Then he leant closer to whisper, 'Although I do not fancy your chances. He is not the most sociable sort and prefers privacy.'

He moved off down the hallway, so she showed herself into the parlour and sat in her preferred seat nearest the large French doors which overlooked the beautiful garden, wishing she was outside working rather than stuck indoors wasting valuable hours on this ridiculous errand.

The butler returned in minutes, obviously agitated. 'I am to tell you that His Lordship is indisposed and will remain so for the foreseeable future, Miss Euphemia. Furthermore, I am to remind you that you have been…' he looked down at his highly polished shoes as he swallowed uncomfortably '…banned from setting one foot on this land henceforth. I am so sorry.'

Effie rolled her eyes, then pasted a cheery smile on her face. 'Thank you for appraising me of His Lordship's position, Smithson. But as I have already stated, I am quite determined to wait.' Because everything hinged on him granting his permission. Effie wasn't cut out for the traditional spinster's life and she certainly wasn't marriage material. Experience had taught her that as well. Her unusually active brain would send her mad if she was forced to embroider or knit, or, heaven forbid, sit through endless polite teas pretending to care about the typical inane nonsense ladies talked about over tea. Her brain needed constant feeding with new knowledge and challenges, not tired, well-worn gossip. 'No matter how long that takes.' She sat primly in her seat, attempting to look every inch the lady for once while poor Smithson visibly paled.

'He is not going to take that well. I am under strict instructions to get rid of you.' And it was patently obvious the servant much preferred to get rid of her, the woman he had known since she was baby, rather than deliver this unwelcome news to his belligerent new master.

Effie shrugged then offered the butler a regrettable smile in apology. 'Then tell him if he wants me gone, I shall be gone quicker if he sees me. And while you are about it, please tell him I believe we got off on the wrong foot yesterday and that I wish to make amends for upsetting him. Tell him I come bearing gifts.' Only the most hardened, rude curmudgeon could refuse both an apology and a present. 'Edible gifts.'

Smithson nodded and she watched his shoulders slump a little as he went off to impart the bad news. Less than a minute later she heard Lord Rivenhall's explosive reaction echo down the hallway.

'Get rid of the blasted woman now! When I told you that I do not wish to see anyone I meant it, Smithson. How dare you come to me and tell me that she will not budge? You should never have let the chit in! Get a couple of burly footmen and throw the wench out.'

Effie knew the house too well not to know his bellowing shouts came from the study. She also knew that she was not going to stand by and allow the man to abuse one of his servants so abominably on her behalf regardless of the need to butter up the new Earl. She stood decisively and marched out of the French doors gripping her basket, determined to take the mountain to Mohammed. The quickest route to the study was outside and around the rose beds to the side. The study also had a pair of French doors connecting it to the garden. His Lordship would certainly not expect her to use them.

Steeling herself to do polite and reasonable battle, she slipped outside and dashed past the roses. Fortunately, the doors were cracked open to let in the fresh spring air. She grabbed the handle and, before she sailed through imperiously, reminded herself of her mantra.

Honey, not vinegar.

'Good morning, Your Lordship.'

The butler gaped at her intrusion. Effie had no

idea how Lord Rivenhall initially reacted because he had his back to her. She watched his shoulders stiffen before his head whipped around. Despite the tousled, long black hair practically covering his face like a shroud, she had the satisfaction of seeing he appeared to be temporarily lost for words.

'Isn't it a lovely morning, my lord?'

'Have you no respect for either etiquette or boundaries, madam?'

'Usually—but I urgently needed to speak you.'

'And you assumed barging into my private study was appropriate when you had already been refused an audience?'

'Desperate times call for desperate measures and I knew you were in because I heard you shouting.'

'If you heard me, then you should already know I have no inclination to suffer your presence, Miss Nuisance.' Lord Rivenhall turned his back rudely and addressed the butler instead as he started towards the hall. 'Show her to the door and make sure she uses it!'

'If you wish to be rude to someone, my lord, I would appreciate that you direct it at me. It is not Smithson's fault that I have refused to leave or encroached on your privacy. And to be clear, I have no intention of leaving until I have said my piece, Lord Rivenhall, so you might as well hear it. Seeing as you are plainly here…' she let her eyes travel around the pristine study until they settled on the completely clear desk. '…and hardly strike me as particularly indisposed.'

He paused mid-stride and slowly turned, clearly unsure of quite how to react to her bold statement. Bravely, Effie smiled, then walked towards the big, mahogany desk and sat in the chair opposite his vacant one to emphasise her intention to remain exactly where she was. Lord Rivenhall did not move from his spot on the Persian rug, piercing her with a glare which could have curdled milk.

'Thank you, Smithson,' she said, dismissing the servant with a smile she did not feel. 'I shall see myself out once I am done. It shouldn't take long.' She fixed her gaze defiantly on her new nemesis. 'Or at least I hope it won't.'

The butler eyed them both warily, then bobbed his head once and swiftly fled the room at a speed that was not at all dignified. Lord Rivenhall let the silence hang ominously, but made no move to approach the desk. Instead, he folded his arms insolently and positively glared at her as he tapped one large booted foot impatiently. Effie decided to take his lack of shouting as a good sign.

'Forgive the intrusion, my lord, but I felt it imperative to apologise for yesterday.'

Honey, not vinegar. Honey, not vinegar...

'With hindsight, I imagine it came as quite the shock to see a stranger digging up your land so early in the morning, so it is hardly surprising we got off on the wrong foot.' For good measure, she wiggled the basket now resting on her lap before sliding it on to the desk. 'I brought fruitcake and brandy as a peace offering. A bottle of my father's finest and one which goes particularly well with our housekeeper Mrs Farley's famous fruitcake. It is her own secret recipe and she guards it with her life—much to the consternation of the rest of the village who would kill for it. But she baked this one yesterday upon my instruction. Just for you.'

'That...was very kind of her...and you.' He practically had to choke out the simple pleasantry through gritted teeth as it appeared to take a great deal of effort—but at least it proved he did possess some gentlemanly good manners and was capable of using them if pushed. 'But wholly unnecessary.' She watched his jaw set stubbornly. 'It changes nothing.'

But changing the subject might give her a few more minutes' leeway. She beamed as if she hadn't heard his latest refusal. Pretending not to hear insults or see the pointed looks was second nature to her nowadays and certainly made life easier than chastising herself for being so unnaturally different. 'What I urgently need to talk to you about is a pot.'

'A pot?' As she had hoped, the abrupt and seemingly bizarre change of topic confused him. 'Why the hell should I care about a pot?'

'Because this is not just any old pot, my lord.' Her cheerful smile was met with open hostility. She could feel the anger at her intrusion shimmering off him in waves despite his statue-like, wary posture. But she would persevere regardless. What other choice did she have? It was only her entire reason for being he was determined to deprive her of. 'This is different. Unique. In the two years I have been seriously digging around the ruined Abbey, I have never seen anything quite like it.' While she apparently had the floor, there seemed little point in pausing. It would only give him the chance to dismiss her out of hand, when he needed to realise first exactly what it was he was dismissing. Whether he wanted to or not.

'I discovered it purely by chance yesterday in the new trench I have started on the eastern boundary. I am not even sure what possessed me to dig there when there are still such rich pickings coming out of the ground near the Roman settlement by the western foundations…'

'Roman? As in Ancient Roman?' Curiosity was getting the better of him, something which clearly disgusted him as he remembered to follow his question with another scowl.

Beyond the scowl, she could not help but notice the Earl of Rivenhall was a handsome devil in a brooding sort of way, when she had been trying so hard to avoid noticing such pointlessly futile if pleasing aspects of the male form. Two dark brows furrowed in consternation over equally dark hooded eyes. A straight nose, strong jaw. The unfashionably dark and windswept hair only adding to his mysterious appeal. Excessively broad shoulders filled his coat and made him appear almost menacing from her angle in the chair below, although why he was buttoned into such a warm coat, the tall points of his shirt collar swathed in a cravat practically tied to the chin when the weather was unseasonably warm was beyond her.

Then she remembered the scars she had seen only briefly yesterday and felt oddly compassionate towards him. Effie had seen similar scars before on a blacksmith in Teversham. They were caused by burns, which must have been agonising to receive, yet while the blacksmith's tight, gnarled scars had been on his arm, from memory and the briefest glimpse of them yesterday, Lord Rivenhall's marred left cheek below the eye had scars which probably travelled down his neck, too. Hence the high collars and the long curtain of hair. And perhaps the open hostility?

She understood what it was like to feel different from others. Most people, in her experience, could be quite judgemental and wary of things they were unfamiliar with—like scars or unusual intelligence. And tactless. As if the person who had the misfortune to be different through no fault of their own was immune to their stares or unsubtle whispers, or, if the people were particularly thoughtless, the insulting words uttered directly to one's face. In all her years on the planet, she had never quite found a way to truly cope with the phenomenon beyond ignoring it. Perhaps Lord Rivenhall's natural form of defence to being different was attack?

'Indeed. This area is teeming with Roman history. We are sandwiched between Duroliponte, the old Roman name for Cambridge, and their English capital Camulodunon—modern-day Colchester. The Abbey was built on the original Roman foundations of what I suspect was once a fort of some sort, judging by the nature of the artefacts I have found. The Normans did that sort of thing a lot and who can blame them? Why waste months digging and laying fresh foundations when there are already perfectly sturdy ones in situ? Colchester Castle and indeed the Tower of London, too, were both constructed on the original Roman foundations and still stand just as strong to this day. They were excellent builders, the Romans. Excellent at everything really. Such an advanced civilisation…' She was losing him with her impromptu, rambling history lesson rather than charming him. She could see his impatience to be rid of her mounting and she had still not told him what she had come here to say.

'Anyway… The pot I began excavating yesterday is particularly exciting. Or at least it has the potential to be. So far, it does not have the finesse expected from a piece of Roman or medieval pottery, appearing to have been shaped by hand rather than thrown on a wheel by a skilled potter. It's rudimentary in construction, practical and lacking in any attempt to raise it from what it was made to be.' All the Roman pottery she had previously found around the foundations of the ruined Abbey bore intricate painted decoration, carved inlays or raised reliefs. Even the very plainest medieval pottery from the site had turned rims and a glazed finish.

'Therefore this pot has to be older. Significantly older.' She paused for effect, offering her most dazzling smile. 'If I am right, it is an artefact of unprecedented importance because we know so little about the people who occupied our islands two thousand years ago. It *needs* to be studied by the Society of Antiquaries. Therefore, you *need* to allow me to dig it up.'

'I need do nothing, madam. This is my land.'

'And I would only be digging on the furthest edge of it. The ruins are a good mile from here. Well out of your way and—'

'No.' His back was towards her again, his big, vexing, impatient feet already heading towards the door.

'But...'

'There is no but, Miss Nitwit. Leave. Now.'

Two years of hard work, everything she cared about, her entire purpose, the only thing she had left was being callously torn away. Unfamiliar panic made her heart race. 'Really, my lord, if I could just explain...' She couldn't allow that to happen. Couldn't contemplate exactly what she would do without it. Aside from drive herself directly to Bedlam. Her rapid, constant thoughts like an itch she could never scratch. 'The site is truly of the utmost historical importance.' And to her personally. It was all she had left. Her future and her sanity. Should she beg? Desperation and fear made her sorely tempted to. Pride made her set her shoulders and apparently took over her vocal cords.

'Your uncle understood all that. But then he was a reasonable and affable man—not a bully.'

So much for honey. 'Frankly, and if I might speak plainly…'

Do not speak plainly. Whatever you do, do not speak plainly. Whenever you do, it never ends well…

'You should be ashamed of yourself for your boorish behaviour both yesterday and today!' And now she was positively dousing the brute in vinegar. 'It is most unneighbourly and without provocation.'

He stiffened and she winced at her forthrightness, yet couldn't quite bring herself to apologise for her outburst. It was unneighbourly. Effie had never been particularly good at remembering either her place or her sex. She blamed that failing on her excessively large brain and growing up with a father who had always actively encouraged her to use it. Nor had she ever had much patience for wilful ignorance or downright unfairness. She had been perfectly polite to him up until now, but that forced politeness only stretched so far. 'Have you no respect for history sir? For your legacy or for knowledge? You do not strike me as stupid. Or anywhere close to being an idiot.' That, she was prepared to concede, was undoubtedly a step too far. Slowly, he turned and beneath the cloak of his hair she saw his mouth was partially open at her insolence. 'So I fail to understand how you can wilfully stand in the way of progress!'

'I am the stupid one? I asked you to leave, madam.' This time his voice was icy calm and, frankly, quite terrifying as he slowly stalked towards her. 'As I am well within my rights as the owner of this property to do. What part of that instruction are you struggling with?'

'I am not easily intimidated, Lord Rivenhall.' It was a lie, she was exceedingly intimidated now that he was stood less than a foot away, but she felt her delivery of the lie had been reasonably convincing thanks to her legendary stubborn streak and unhelpful lack of diplomacy in trying to convince him to see sense. She had never had much patience for blind ignorance.

Honey, not vinegar.

'I should like us to have a rational discussion about the future of the dig like mature and polite adults.' The stubborn streak made her lift her chin defiantly and fold her arms like a petulant, sulky child—although, to be fair, she was only mirroring his stance.

'Then you give me no other choice, madam. If you continue to outstay your welcome, I shall have to remove you forcibly from my premises.' He leaned until their eyes were level, scant inches apart, intent on intimidating her. Intent on letting her know in no uncertain terms he meant business and was heartily unimpressed with both her and her arguments to sway him to the contrary. 'I think I would enjoy that.'

'Am I supposed to be terrified now, Lord Rivenhall?'

Despite all the bluster and noise, all the overtly hostile evidence to the contrary, she somehow knew that this man would not lay a finger on her. Knew that in her bones. How odd, because she wasn't usually one for nonsense like feeling things in her bones. Yet she was so certain he was harmless, her eyes locked on his brazenly as he continued to stare and remained so when he gripped the arms of her chair to lean closer, making no effort this time to conceal the scars marring his cheek. Almost as if he expected her to recoil disgusted at the merest sight of them.

'If you are expecting me to burst into tears and scurry away, then I must tell you that you are doomed to be disappointed.'

He blinked, looked away and hastily stepped back. She smiled again because she could see he was confused by her reaction and perhaps a little uncomfortable with his own attempts to intimidate her, if his sudden inability to look her in the eye was a gauge. He was clearly all bluster. Just as she'd suspected. A lion with a thorn in his paw.

'I need to excavate that pot and will not be deterred from that goal.'

'And I need to be left alone, madam.' His arms were crossed again and he stood far too tall and much too close for comfort. 'Do I need to build a wall encasing my land to keep you off it?'

'You have a lot of land, my lord. If you start building it today, it might be finished in three years and by then, I can assure you, the pot will be long out of the ground.'

However, the rest of the Abbey's secrets would still be buried there—taunting her. Effie tried to ignore the way he overwhelmed her and pretended to look nonplussed while her clever mind ran every possible scenario through to the end in the hope of finding a way to make him see reason and concluded, with her customary rapidity, she had to face facts.

Thanks to her poor efforts at diplomacy, he wasn't going to budge today—in reality, if she continued to push he would only dig his heels in deeper. Something she had quite the knack for making people do even when she tried not to.

He might not budge at all come to that, but the scant remains of the former optimist she had once been and the strategist in her refused to believe she couldn't get him to ever see sense once he listened to her superior and irrefutable arguments. In truth, he really didn't strike her as an idiot. Surely between the pair of them they could come to some agreement—when he had calmed down, of course, and was more agreeable. And there was more than one way to skin a cat or excavate a pot for that matter. The pot was her most pressing priority now that it was exposed to the elements and nature and clumsy horses' hooves. For now, though, it was probably best she retreat and allow the dust to settle, then approach him again when he wasn't feeling so belligerent.

'I can see I have inadvertently called upon you at a bad time, putting you in another bad mood with my irritating over-enthusiasm for the quest I hold dear. Something which was never my intention. Nor was insulting you with my forthrightness. Occasionally, I forget myself and I apologise.' It took a great deal of strength to get those insincere words out without sounding as disgusted by them as she felt. But she managed another magnanimous smile regardless for the sake of the pot. 'When would be a more convenient time for our discussion?'

'Never.'

She found herself smiling ironically. He might well be obnoxiously rude, but at least he was predictable. She could work with that. Or around it. He might not be an idiot, but he was unlikely to be cleverer than her.

According to Papa, nobody was.

Her curse and the root cause of all her problems and isolation—but occasionally it came in handy. 'Enjoy the cake, Lord Rivenhall. And the brandy. I can see myself out.'

Chapter Three

Four hundred and twelve crystals...

Max knew that already because he had counted every damn droplet on the chandelier above his bed twice this week when sleep evaded him. For once, he had someone else to blame for his restlessness. The tart-mouthed, not easily intimidated new bane of his life: Miss Euphemia Nithercott.

He would lay good money she was out there. Since laying siege to his study and frightening the life out of him two days ago, he knew full well she was still digging despite his expressly forbidding her to do so. Annoyed, he threw the covers back and padded to the window, staring sightlessly at the darkness, impatiently willing dawn to break an hour earlier than usual.

He knew she was out there because he had become unhealthily obsessed with checking up on her. Each morning since, as soon as the sun came up, he rode to her haphazard cluster of holes in his ground and each time he had seen as clear as the sparkling crystals on his bedchamber chandelier her dratted hole was getting bigger. Although she was taking her own sweet time about it as only a few inches of dirt had been neatly scraped away from her stupid pot. Why she hadn't taken a shovel to the earth to get the damn thing out once and for all was beyond him. That she hadn't strangely intrigued him.

So much so, the chit had apparently taken root in his thoughts since—although Miss Nithercott was hardly a chit. She was, he estimated, probably nearer thirty than twenty and undeniably all woman. And a damned attractive one at that. The entire time he had been forced to look at her in his own study and inhale the sultry scent of her perfume, his senses had been assaulted with that unfortunate fact. And despite the addition of an entirely respectable pretty dress, his imagination kept conjuring up the image of her lush curves encased in the tight breeches and softly worn shirt he had first encountered her in, when he was certain her femininity had not been tamed by the rigid restrictions of a corset. It was a memory he visited often.

Those errant but ultimately futile thoughts only

served to depress him. Max did not want to contemplate Miss Nithercott's corset, any more than he wanted to contemplate Miss Nithercott. But contemplate both he did with alarming regularity.

Aside from his morning reconnoitres, he had also taken to riding past the ruins every afternoon and evening around sunset, too, and finding no sign of the wench. Which meant she had to be doing her digging in secret in the dead of night like a grave robber, much too close for comfort.

Damn and blast it all to hell! Why couldn't she just leave him alone as he had asked?

Or threatened, more like.

He huffed in disgust and thumped his head against the cool pane of glass. Actively trying to intimidate a woman was a new low, even for him. Max still winced each time he thought about the way he had loomed over her and wished he'd handled the entire situation differently. Been more reasonable, commanding and resolute as opposed to a snarling, panicked mess. But she had caught him off guard and unprepared and he'd lashed out. Lashing out had become a bit of a habit and another thing about himself he had come to loathe. Not that the intrepid Miss Nithercott had listened one jot.

All credit to her, she had neither run nor screamed, or even looked slightly intimidated by his irrational performance. If anything, she had seemed amused, almost as if she saw right through him before she had pierced him with the perfect set down to bring him up short and remind him his behaviour was wholly unacceptable no matter what the provocation.

Am I supposed to be terrified now, Lord Rivenhall?

Words which had haunted him since. Not his finest hour and not a memory he could easily forget thanks to his constantly niggling conscience which ensured he felt heartily ashamed of himself. It was one thing being bitter and twisted and unpleasant to be around, it was another entirely to be a bully to boot. There was never any excuse for that. To have sunk so low as to have attempted to bully a woman was beyond the pale.

Shameful.

He had scarcely slept a wink since.

He'd even given serious consideration to apologising for his ghastly treatment of her—but hadn't. Out of cowardice—pure and simple. Because apologising meant seeking her out, which inevitably meant leaving the sanctuary of this sprawling estate in the middle of nowhere. Exposing himself and feeling vulnerable. Enduring the curious stares. The pointing. The unsubtle whispers about the horrendous state he was in as if the flames had rendered him deaf as well as hideous and devoid of all human emotion.

It also meant having that reasonable discussion she wanted, when he really wasn't up for one of those either. A discussion required extended conversation which he had lost the knack for. It was hard being erudite when you knew all focus was on the ugly scars rather than his sentences and being reasonable might open the floodgates and before he knew it, every Tom, Dick and Harry would assume they could call on him unannounced and engage him in conversation. A prospect which was, frankly, terrifying. Besides, the people of Cambridgeshire were already proving themselves to be an over-familiar lot. At least one new neighbour took it upon themselves to traipse up his new mile-long drive every day seeking an audience. So much so, it was becoming a job of work simply avoiding them. All much too neighbourly for Max's liking. All much too intrusive and overwhelming when what he wanted was to be left well alone to lick his wounds in private and find a way to reconcile himself to his future as he mourned the past.

Not that he was alone now because *she* was out there. He could sense her even though he couldn't see her. Not that he could really see anything tonight. With the moon and the stars obliterated by cloud, it was as black as pitch out there and would be for the next hour at least.

He groaned aloud this time when his conscience pricked. While he shouldn't care, the thought of a woman all alone in the dark bothered him. That she was all alone in the dark thanks to his boorish and disgustingly bullish behaviour bothered him immensely. If something happened to her as a result, he would never forgive himself…

Blasted woman!

Was it any wonder he couldn't sleep?

As he was wide awake and unlikely to get any rest unless he had reassured himself she was quite safe, he might as well take a wander out towards the ruins to check on her. And while he was about it, he should probably grab the bull by the horns and apologise for looming over her, seeing as her blatant trespassing meant he did not have to leave the sanctuary of his new estate to do it.

Less than half an hour later and all his suspicions were confirmed. The new bane of his life was on her knees, using some sort of hand tool as she bent over the pot she was obsessed with. A plethora of lanterns ringed her, casting her face in ethereal light, glinting off her ridiculous glasses and ensuring that even from his hiding place in the trees, Max could see she was smiling.

She did that a lot, did Miss Nithercott, although he wished it wasn't such a beguiling and pretty smile because it drew his eyes to her lips. It also made her dark eyes sparkle, which inevitably pulled his gaze to those ridiculously long lashes when he really needed no reminders of her attractiveness or the sorry fact that she was exactly the sort of woman he would have once been compelled to flirt with. Back in his flirting days when he had adored women with spirit and gumption.

Before...

And there was the rub. Any acknowledgement of his undeniable attraction to her inevitably reminded him of everything he had lost and was trying desperately hard to forget while he readjusted to his life in the skin he had been doomed to live within for ever.

Reluctantly, he tied Drake's reins to a sturdy branch and started towards her. Now that he had reassured himself she was quite safe, he wanted to get his apology over with quickly and get as far away from her as it was humanly possible to be. She unnerved him. Perhaps a tad more than the rest of the world currently unnerved him. He would be quick. Concise. Apologise for the delivery, but explain the sentiment remained the same.

I appreciate you were given certain privileges

*by my uncle on this land, but times change and I
have plans for it now...*

Plans! As if counting the ruined stones she put
so much stock in, in an pathetic attempt to distract
him from his lonely pit of despair, could feasibly
be categorised as plans. He would just tell her the
truth. He wanted to be left alone and needed the
reassuring ring of three hundred acres of empty
parkland to be assured that he was. This was his
land—not hers!

Max was a few yards away when, clearly oblivious to his presence, she suddenly sat back on
her heels and he instinctively darted back into
the shadows, not quite ready to face her just yet.

Coward! My land! Not hers! Just apologise!

She stretched, her back arching, and her bosom
he had tried not to think about jutted seductively
against the soft linen of her shirt as she raised
her arms in the air and rotated her shoulders. The
sight made him forget his lofty purpose and he
simply stared and, to his complete horror, yearned
until he ruthlessly suppressed that pointless emotion. He could yearn all he wanted. No woman
was going to yearn back.

To further taunt him, she rearranged her body to
lie on the ground, her head and arms disappearing
into the hole, her booted feet braced as she wriggled from side to side. The fabric of her breeches

pulled taut on the rounded flesh of her delectable behind. He could hear her little grunts of exertion as she wrestled beneath the dirt and wondered, as he looked his fill, why the blazes there weren't laws forbidding the wearing of breeches by females. Especially females who filled them as exquisitely as the troublesome Miss Nithercott.

'Stop being so stubborn.' She was talking to herself—or perhaps to her beloved pot and with a sigh groped for the discarded trowel on the ground beside her. 'You know you will lose in the end...'

Was it wrong to watch her so intently without her knowledge? Thinking less-than-pure thoughts? Probably—only he couldn't seem to stop. There was something strangely charming as well as alluring about the sight. The stupid pot must mean a lot to her if she was prepared to go to these lengths in the middle of the night for it. Digging by candlelight couldn't be easy.

Guilt pricked again. Because of course he knew this meant a lot to her.

He had seen the panic and desperation in her eyes when she had pleaded with him to allow her to dig and he had ruthlessly ignored it out of self-preservation. Then, determined to impose his will, he had loomed over her, intent on putting the fear of God into her, too.

Which was the only reason he was here.

She was owed an apology and then he would send her on her way with the pot and that would be the end of it. If they never crossed paths again it would be too soon and Max never wanted to have to smell her blasted intoxicating perfume again. Despite several feet of distance, the subtle scent of it assaulted him now. The heady aroma of lilacs and roses. Of lazy summer days and warm summer nights. Why the hell was she wearing perfume while her head was shoved in the mud?

Making sure his hair covered the worst of the damage on the left side of his face, he stepped out of his hiding place and was about to let her know he was there and get the cringing awkwardness over with, when she started to mutter again.

'Come on… Come on… That's it…' Several frustrated yet determined grunts and a great deal of torturous wiggling later a single fist pumped the air as his feet came level with the edge of the hole. 'Yes! Got you!' She scrambled to her knees, grinning, and then promptly shrieked as she spotted him beside her, falling back on to her delightful bottom as she clutched at her heart, the silly lenses magnifying her rapidly blinking eyes.

'Lord Rivenhall! Are you trying to give me an apoplexy?'

'Sorry for startling you…' Although it was

technically she who should be sorry for trespassing again rather than looking irritated at his intrusion as she was now. Of its own accord, his hand reached out to help her up and to his horror she took it. The effect of her touch was staggering because he felt it everywhere as he pulled her to her feet before hastily letting go.

'If I had been holding the pot, I might have dropped it! What were you thinking creeping up on me like that?'

'If your head hadn't been under the ground—*my* ground—you would have heard me.'

And he most definitely should have alerted her of his presence sooner. That he hadn't had been down to damned cowardice again. Alongside the fruitless yearning.

Get it over with, man!

'Actually, I came down here to…er…' Max felt his toes curl with embarrassment inside his boots. 'Apologise for my overly…um…aggressive tone when we last met. And the looming, of course.'

'The looming?'

'Yes. That was unnecessary and I am sorry if I frightened you… Both then and just now. I should have said something sooner, but…' Good grief, he was babbling and feeling more uncomfortable by the second. He'd been staring at her. That's why he hadn't made his presence known sooner. 'But I could see you were busy.'

'How did you know I would be here?'

'Because as you rightly pointed out the other day, I am not an idiot, Miss Nocturnal. Granted you hid the evidence of your clandestine visits reasonably well these past two days—but sadly the pot gave you away.'

'Ah...' She had the good grace to look sheepish as she stared down at her boots through those ludicrous spectacles which did nothing for her.

'Ah indeed. Unless it had begun excavating itself, it did not take a genius to work out you were creeping here under the cover of night to continue doing what I had expressly forbidden you to do.'

'I couldn't very well leave it half-exposed.'

'Couldn't or wouldn't?'

'A bit of both. In my defence, and despite your *looming*, I did intimate I was not going to take particular heed of your warning until the task was finished. You threatened to build a wall, remember.'

'I did.' He rather admired her tenacity and her unapologetic forthrightness. She was an honest trespasser as well as an annoyingly persistent one. 'I also recall threatening to set the dogs on you, yet neither appeared to have worked—because I see you are here. Again.'

'That's because I knew you had no dogs and I would have scaled a twenty-foot wall if I'd had to just to get my pot.'

'You mean *my* pot, surely, seeing as it has come out of *my* land?'

'Semantics. If it is anyone's, my lord, then surely it is the nation's pot, as it is of the utmost national importance? A missing part of our history which provides new avenues for us to study. Whose land it happened to come out of is neither here nor there in the grand scheme of things.' She was smiling again. Teasing him. In a good-natured, not-the-least-bit-intimidated or bothered-by-his-presence way. Nobody had dared do that in quite a while. Not even his sister who had lived to tease him. Before...

The past slammed into him and sullied his surprisingly pleasant mood. Surprising because he couldn't recall the last time he had felt anything other than bleak. To cover the onslaught, he stared down into the neat hole she had dug and the crudely made pot sat proud and whole at the bottom of it.

'Now that your precious pot has finally been liberated, can I assume I am finally to be rid of you?'

'I've removed the last of the soil.' Her eyes dipped, avoiding his, and, more pointedly, the second part of his question. 'Now I need to lift it out.

Which is the tricky bit…pottery is notoriously delicate after centuries in the mud. But I have at least completed all the close work.'

'Is that what the bizarre magnifying contraption is about?' He gestured to the lenses tied to her head and, as if suddenly remembering she was still wearing them, she hastily tugged at the ribbon until they fell to rest about her shoulders like an ugly necklace. Bizarrely it suited her, although to be fair, even sackcloth would suit her.

'Er… Yes. I liberated them from my father's effects, but they kept falling off as I worked. Anyway…' Clearly intent on continuing with the task regardless, she strode to her wheelbarrow and retrieved an old blanket which she arranged like a nest next to the hole. 'This bit could take a while…' She flicked him a dismissive glance. The sort he used to use on his men to great effect when they stepped out of line and needed knocking down a peg or two. It was a bold move when she had absolutely no right to be here. 'But I promise I will be gone before dawn.' When he failed to budge, her brows furrowed in irritation. Another bold response when she was the one entirely in the wrong. 'There is no need for you to stand guard, my lord. I *will* go.'

'But will you come back, Miss Nosy? That is

the bigger question.' One he feared he already knew the answer to.

'Beneath the pot is a large slab—sandstone, I think. Possibly a hearth of some kind, although I haven't found the edges of it yet to discern its exact size. But a hearth would suggest we are currently standing inside an ancient dwelling of some sort, don't you think?'

He stared back at her blandly.

'Wouldn't that be exciting?' The smile died on her lips when she finally accepted he had no intention of smiling back. Then she sighed and finally stared him straight in the eye, her expression achingly sad and the previous excitement tragically missing from her voice. 'There is so much more to uncover here, Lord Rivenhall. Would it be so terrible if I continued my work?'

'Miss Nithercott, I…' Max didn't want to feel suddenly sorry for her. Did not want to feel guilty or cruel for denying her. He wanted peace. Space. Endless open fields blessedly free from people. The wind in his hair and the sun on his ruined skin. 'I came here to be left well alone.' This estate was a poor substitute for the vast expanse of the ocean or the endless horizons he still pined for, but it was all his and he had missed being outside. Was so tired of feeling suffocated by the walls and ceilings he endlessly stared at.

'I would leave you alone. I promise to keep well out of your way. In fact, I shall even hide if I catch the merest glimpse of you. I can continue to dig at night and…' The thought of that had him holding up his palm in defeat, but she misconstrued the gesture and her face fell and her slim shoulders slumped, making Max feel like a brute all over again even though his resolve to evict her was already waning and all his hopes for peace evaporating.

'Please, my lord… This place… This work… It is everything to me. All that I have.' And, God help him, he believed her. 'I beg of you not to take it away.' And suddenly she looked lost and he couldn't bear that because he knew exactly how that felt. He had been lost since the day he awoke in laudanum-blurred agony on that Royal Navy frigate over a year ago and hadn't found any trace of himself in the interminable months since. 'Please…'

Max tore his gaze away from her eyes, hating the desperation he saw in them when he much preferred the sassy and indomitable Miss Nithercott to the one his self-preserving, selfish actions had created. Perhaps with strict boundaries, allowing her to dig her blasted holes wouldn't be the end of the world? But they would have to be very strict boundaries indeed. He did not want to have to see her. Talk to her. Smell her. Even think about her. Or anyone for that matter. He just wanted to be left alone.

He turned to her again, ready to give her a list of stipulations. 'If you promise to keep to the confines of the Abbey…'

'Oh, thank you!' She grabbed his hand again and the rest of his planned list of rigid rules and parameters died in his throat. 'I promise you will never know I am here!'

Max instantly extricated his hand and, because his nerve endings mourned her, fisted it behind his back where she couldn't see it. 'No night digging. I expressly forbid that. It is not safe for a woman on her own to be all alone in the dark.' Not that he wanted to contemplate exactly why she was on her own whenever he encountered her, why she wandered around unchaperoned at apparently all hours of the day or night. Or why there was no ring on her finger. Nor did he want to explore why he had the compelling urge to stand guard over her now, when now was absolutely the opportune time to escape. He'd assuaged his conscience with an apology and had a rational discussion with her and both things had left him feeling off kilter.

She made him feel off kilter.

'I shall escort you home, Miss Nithercott.' Not at all what he had intended to say.

'There is no need. It will be light soon and it will take at least that to get the *nation's* pot out of the ground.' To prove her point, the first hints of dawn whispered in the distance.

'Then I shall bid you a good day, Miss Nithercott.' Before the unforgiving daylight made him more disconcerted than he already was.

Chapter Four

❧❧❧❧

Dig Day 763: hearthstone—if it is indeed a hearthstone—is round!

There was only one metal Effie knew of which did not tarnish underground and that was gold. Although where this ancient Celtic civilisation had gold in Cambridgeshire was anybody's guess. Cornwall perhaps was the closest place, or Wales. Both hundreds of miles to the west—not that she was an expert on British gold deposits. Yet the heavy, perfectly twisted bracelet in the palm of her hand was undoubtedly made of solid gold and completely unlike any other old jewellery she had ever seen or read about.

Judging by the sheer weight of the metal, and ancient provenance aside, it was also incredibly valuable. An inescapable fact which presented a dilemma. While Lord Rivenhall might not care about pottery or hearthstones, precious metal was another matter. It had come out of his land and so by rights it was his. Not telling him she had just uncovered a huge chunk of solid gold was dishonest.

She had to tell him.

Which necessitated breaking her agreement to stay well out of his way. And might irritate him all over again and potentially damage their truce. But what other choice did she have? Right was right, after all, and hopefully he would be reasonable enough to understand that.

She wrapped the bracelet in a handkerchief, tucked it into her battered satchel and set off in the direction of the house.

Smithson was, understandably, horrified to see her and she apologised profusely for putting him in the unenviable position of telling his unpredictable master she needed an audience. However, to the great surprise of them both, Lord Rivenhall apparently took the news well and suddenly appeared in the doorway of the drawing room looking extremely wary.

'Miss Nithercott.'

That he did not invite her to join him in the drawing room or make any move to come towards her was telling.

'Lord Rivenhall, I apologise for disturbing you, but I have found something I need to give you.'

Effie rummaged for the bracelet and held it out. 'It's gold, my lord. A very substantial piece of gold.' The dark eye she could see dipped to the bracelet before fixing back on hers.

'And?'

'And I thought you should have it. It is obviously very valuable.'

The dark eye widened as she walked towards him and offered it. 'I found it a few feet from the hearth all on its own, which leads me to believe it was accidentally dropped or buried, perhaps to keep it safe, much like Samuel Pepys did his Parmesan.'

'I'm sorry...?'

'Pepys...' What had possessed her brain to jump forward fifteen hundred years in one sentence? No wonder Lord Surly looked confused. 'The seventeenth-century diarist? He buried his cheese in his garden during the Great Fire of London.' He was staring at her now as if she were mad, as people were prone to do when she allowed her brain to speak freely without tempering her words. 'Because Parmesan was expensive in sixteen sixty-six. I suppose it still is now, although I cannot say I know the exact price of it...' She huffed out a sigh and gave her odd mind a stiff talking to. 'Anyway, I digress... I suspect this bracelet is of a similar age to the pot. Which would make it at least two thousand years old. Perhaps more. I've never seen anything like it.'

He reached out and took it and she found herself contemplating his hands. They were big, making the substantial bracelet appear almost delicate as he held it. Hands which had obviously seen real work once upon a time, rather than the typically genteel, idle hands of the aristocracy. The strong, blunt fingers were tipped with neat, clean nails which made her feel self-conscious about the state of hers after a long day of digging. So embarrassed, she hid them behind her back and felt compelled to fill the silence. Typically, the only thing she could think to fill it with was history.

'The presence of gold in such an ancient dwelling here indicates that the Celtic tribes which lived on this island before the Roman conquest traded as well as fought with one another—and perhaps even with other tribes across the sea. It suggests a civilisation which was both advanced and thriving. That bracelet is not a crude piece of jewellery either. It takes great skill to smelt the gold, hammer it into a perfectly round cylinder and then twist it with such precision before seamlessly welding the join. Something which contradicts many of the Roman accounts from the time of the invasion which state the Britons were basically savages. No savage moulded that bracelet.

That is a high-status object created for someone of great importance who must have been devastated when they lost it.'

'I thought they buried it. Like Pepys's Parmesan.' He said it with a straight face, but for some reason she got the distinct impression he was poking fun at her.

'I suppose we'll never know exactly who put it in the ground, but we can speculate as to who owned it... The tribal leader, perhaps? Although which tribe is hard to guess. Catuvellauni, perhaps? Or Iceni? Both occupied territory in Cambridgeshire. It is entirely feasible, I suppose—we could even throw the Trinovantes into the mix. They were very...' His head had tilted as if he couldn't quite fathom exactly what it was he was hearing or seeing. A stark reminder of all her differences from the rest of the human race.

'Very...?'

She had started so she might as well finish the sentence. No matter how dull it truly was. 'Very powerful before the conquest. Or at least so I've read in Caesar's account of the Gallic War.'

'You have read Caesar's account of the Gallic War? As in Julius Caesar? He wrote books?'

'The Romans were prolific writers. Without them, we would know nothing whatsoever of our history before they invaded.'

'I had no idea we had a history before they invaded…'

'Most people don't. The records really do need to be translated.'

'So you read them in… What? Latin? Actual *Roman* Latin?'

'Wherever possible. Although some have been lost over time, so I had to…' Why was she telling him all this? When this was exactly the sort of thing that made people give her a very wide berth. 'Um…refer to the Anglo-Saxon histories which borrowed a great deal from the Roman.'

He now had that baffled look which people always got when they realised she was peculiar. No matter how many times she tried to hide it. 'Are you fluent in Anglo-Saxon, too, Miss Nithercott?'

She was. And Norse. She could also get by in Ancient Greek, but her Hebrew was practically non-existent, although, in her defence, she had never had much cause to learn it. 'Technically, the Angles and the Saxons originally had different languages, my lord, but over time they…um…'

'Um…?' Bemusement was rapidly turning into amusement. It was obvious he thought her quite the anomaly. Which, of course, she was.

'They merged, my lord.'

'I shall take that as a yes, then.' The corners of his mouth began to curve into a smile which did odd things to her insides, until the unmistakable sound of a carriage outside turned it swiftly into a frown. 'Smithson!'

The aged butler's grey head appeared out of nowhere. 'I know, my lord. I shall get rid of them.' And with that, Lord Rivenhall disappeared back into the drawing room, taking the bracelet with him and slamming the door.

Effie stood awkwardly on the spot for several seconds until she realised she was in full view of the front entrance and not really in a fit state to be seen by any of the local gentry, who tended to disapprove of her insistence on wearing breeches when she worked. Not that they particularly approved of her in a frock either, but that was by the by. Impending disapproval aside, if they saw her in the elusive and mysterious Lord Rivenhall's hallway, they might feel aggrieved at being sent away and, knowing the way their minds worked, that would inevitably lead to unwanted and entirely unwarranted gossip. When she had promised herself faithfully she would actively try to avoid any more gossip—at least for the next few months.

Until the dust settled.

Because the rector, it turned out, did not take kindly to having the story of Noah questioned during a sermon. Even though, to Effie, La-

marck's hypothesis that new species were created all the time made it entirely improbable the
animals which walked the planet today would be
exactly the same as those which walked down the
gang plank of the ark after the Great Flood several
millennia ago. The ark would have had to have
been at least the size of France to accommodate
two of every species which walked the Earth now!

The congregation hadn't appreciated her comment, either, and she'd been treated as more of a
pariah than usual in the four weeks since which
had made her feel significantly lonelier than she
usually did.

A moment before Smithson opened the door
and exposed her to the caller, she darted into
the drawing room, too. Yet another thing which
seemed to surprise Lord Rivenhall, who had taken
himself to the French doors to stare out at the
garden.

'Do you mind if I hide in here with you for a
minute or two?'

He looked decidedly uncomfortable with the
request. 'Do I have a choice?'

'Not really. At least not till they've gone.' She
smiled to soften the blow. 'Besides, it probably
will not do your standing any favours to be seen
consorting with me, so it's for the best.'

'Why should I not be seen *consorting* with you?'

'Because—and I doubt this will come as a piece of mind-shattering news, Lord Rivenhall— I am a trifle odd.'

'A little eccentric, perhaps…'

It was very decent of him to try to defend her and she found herself smiling at him and meaning it completely. 'Eccentric is wearing breeches and digging holes in the ground, Lord Rivenhall. Odd is when you have a brain which retains every piece of information it happens to come across.'

'Every piece?' He wasn't convinced, although to be fair to him, why should he be? Effie had never even read about another person like her. 'It is impossible to remember everything Miss Nithercott.'

'What proof would you like?' It was probably for the best she get it over and done with. 'Should I recite every monarch from Alfred the Great to King George? I could do it forward and backwards and give you the dates of their reigns. Or Ge Hong's exact and original ingredients for gunpowder from fourth-century China? It's sulphur, charcoal and saltpetre, in case you were wondering. Although rather interestingly, they tended to retrieve the saltpetre from decayed manure rather than mine it back in those days. I've always pondered how he discovered that. What exactly was Ge Hong doing with dung that made him wonder if it might explode? Unless it was a complete accident as so often scientific discovery is?' His square jaw was hanging slack. 'Which neatly leads me to the real crux of my oddness, in that my mind constantly asks questions or speculates and at such speed they often fly out of my mouth before I've given any thought at all as to whether or not it is appropriate to say them. Which inevitably means I either inadvertently offend people or terrify them. And as much as I don't mean to alienate them, I completely understand why I do. It is hardly normal for a person to know all of the bizarre and convoluted things that I do.'

'But not particularly unusual when the person's father is a don at Cambridge who specialises in translating Anglo-Saxon texts.' He had remembered and appeared charmingly smug that he did. 'Hardly a surprise, then, that you have an extensive grasp of history, Miss Nithercott.'

'*Was* a don. He died four years ago.'

'Oh...' She could see that brought him up short. 'I am sorry.' He stared down at his feet awkwardly for a moment and she felt bad for directing their conversation on to a morbid path when she had been rather enjoying it.

'I am afraid my oddity is not confined to just history. I remember everything. Test me. If I've read it, it's in here.' She tapped her forehead.

'Shakespeare's sonnet number one hundred and sixteen.'

'*"Let me not to the marriage of true minds / Admit impediments. Love is not love / Which alters when it alteration finds..."* I've always had a soft spot for that one.' The single dark eyebrow she could clearly see raised, impressed. 'Is it your favourite?'

'It used to be. How many miles is it to cross the Channel?'

'At its narrowest point, just twenty-one. But if one is travelling the normal route between Dover and Calais and in need of a harbour it's twenty-eight. Although that is as the crow flies. If I were being pedantic, and because we can neither fly nor walk to France, it is technically twenty-four miles because we would need to use a boat of some sort to get there and a nautical mile is two hundred and sixty-five yards longer than the standard mile, therefore there are fewer of them.'

His head tilted again and he stared at her for the longest time before shaking his head. 'That is quite a gift, Miss Not-at-all-usual.'

'Or a curse. Depending on how you look at it.' She felt her smile falter. 'Sometimes just listening to my brain is exhausting.' Heaven only knew why she felt compelled to admit that.

'I know what you mean.' His gaze locked and

held with hers, making her wonder if he meant he empathised rather than sympathised. But whatever emotion it was he hastily covered it by looking down. Then seemed surprised to find the ancient bracelet still in his hand. 'Why did you bring this to me?'

'Because it came out of your land and is very valuable. It did not feel right taking your gold.'

'My gold rather than the nation's?'

'I shan't deny it is of the utmost national importance, my lord.'

'Then you had best study it, Miss Nithercott.' He held it out and dropped it into her open palm. 'I should hate to wilfully stand in the way of progress.' Then he smiled, properly smiled, for the very first time and it had the most unexpected effect on her. Her pulse quickened and her tummy felt all funny. Effie found herself smiling back and gazing, perhaps a little winsomely, into his now-twinkling deep brown eyes.

'Excuse me, my lord…' Smithson's head poked around the door, his expression apologetic, as he used the rest of it as a shield. 'There is a lady here to see you.'

'No visitors, Smithson. None. We've been through this. Do not even let her in the front door!'

'I didn't, my lord, but…' The old retainer's eyes swivelled to Effie and back again. 'She is also refusing to leave, my lord, and is currently still on the drive, supervising the unloading of her baggage.'

'She brought baggage?' Lord Rivenhall was practically snarling now, as if he couldn't quite believe what he was hearing.

'She is under the impression she has come to stay, my lord.' Then, his expression turned pained. 'And claims to be your sister.'

Chapter Five

Forty-six intertwined leaves on the Persian and two unwelcome women on the sofa...

Eleanor being Eleanor, she immediately made herself at home and sent the butler for tea. Tea which she couldn't help herself from inviting Miss Nithercott to join them in, knowing full well he would hardly tear her off a strip in front of a guest. Worse, the new bane of his life had a charming smudge of dried mud on her cheek which his fingers itched to brush away. Between that, her breeches and his blasted sister he was in utter hell and the tea hadn't yet arrived.

'You look well, Max. You've caught some sun.'

'I've been riding.'

'That's marvellous! Fresh air does wonders for the soul and you were looking much too pasty.' He watched her gaze wander briefly to the distracting woman sat beside her before knowingly fixing on him. 'The parkland here is so lovely and unspoiled. I'll bet its great fun to gallop across. Do you ride, Miss Nithercott?' His sister gestured to the breeches which were tormenting him. 'Were the pair of you riding this afternoon…or about to before I interrupted?'

He was going to strangle his older sibling. 'She digs, Eleanor. Big holes in the ground near the ruins of the old Abbey.'

'Really? Whatever for?'

'Whatever I can find, Mrs Baxter. The area used to house a Roman settlement so all sorts of things are buried beneath the soil. Oil lamps, coins, pottery. Today I found this.' The bracelet was retrieved from the satchel at her feet and handed to his over-curious, overbearing, meddling sister, who took her own sweet time examining it.

'How fascinating. Is this Roman?'

'Older, I believe. Possibly over two thousand years old—or more. And solid gold. Hence I brought it to Lord Rivenhall as it is technically his seeing as it came out of his land.'

'Miss Nithercott is a historian.'

'An antiquarian, actually. Historians tend to learn about the past from books, whereas antiquarians learn about it by excavating it from the ground.' Miss Nithercott beamed at his sister. 'Historians tend to look down on antiquarians because we get our hands dirty.' She held them up for inspection apologetically and he watched his sister obviously focus on the lack of ring on her wedding finger. 'Hence the breeches.'

'I should imagine it's near impossible to dig a hole in a dress. Or wearing any jewellery.' Subtlety had never been Eleanor's forte. Max made a point of not looking at her hand and instead noticed she was only wearing one earring. Lord only knew what that was about.

'Miss Nithercott has been digging here for years.' Best to clarify exactly where her interest lay before his sister's vivid imagination ran away with her. 'I apparently inherited her along with the house.'

'Even more fascinating…' She shot Max another knowing look. 'Do you live close by, Miss Nithercott?'

'Just across the parkland to the west.'

'How convenient… Alone?' Strangling was too humane for Eleanor. Too swift.

'Yes. Nowadays. But I used to live there with my father. He was an academic. A proper historian who preferred his books to my artefacts.'

'And speaking of artefacts…' Max snatched the bracelet out of Eleanor's fingers and thrust it at her. 'I fear we are keeping you from studying this one, Miss Nithercott.'

Max watched hurt skitter across her features, then embarrassment as she hastily stood. Both made him feel wretched for being the cause, but it couldn't be helped. Better to send her packing before the dreaded tea tray arrived and his sister found a million other ways to ask her if she had a man in her life and then follow it by unsubtly suggesting she might consider him. If she were desperate.

'Yes… Of course.' He hated the false smile she pasted on her face for his benefit, when whichever way you looked at it he had just been hideously rude. 'I shall leave the pair of you to catch up. It was lovely to meet you, Mrs Baxter.'

'And you, too, Miss Nithercott.' His sister made no secret of the fact she was heartily unimpressed with him by over-pronouncing her consonants. 'I do hope we meet again.'

As he rose to see her out, and to apologise for the clumsy way he was practically throwing her out, she waved him away. 'Please do not trouble yourself, Lord Rivenhall. I know perfectly well where the door is.' Was that censure? 'You have pointed me in its direction often enough.' Apparently it was, although he could hardly blame her as he heartily deserved it.

Eleanor waited until Miss Nithercott's delectable bottom disappeared down the hallway—or rather out of his straining peripheral vision. 'I see your manners and surly, belligerent disposition have not improved in the last few weeks Max! You embarrassed the poor thing!'

'You were about to ask if she was engaged.'

'I was about to do no such thing. I was simply being friendly. Something which wouldn't hurt you to attempt on occasion.' The rattle of the tea tray made her pause and they both sat in tense silence while the butler took his own sweet time to deposit it on the table.

'Why are you here, Eleanor?'

'I wanted to reassure myself you were settling in. It has been three weeks and you haven't written. Not even to inform me you arrived safely.'

'You know I hate writing letters.'

'A single, curt sentence would have sufficed!' She inhaled and exhaled slowly, something she did nowadays only to him whenever her temper was close to the surface and she wanted to soften her tone. Max hated that she still felt the need to coddle him. 'I have been worried about you. You left so abruptly.'

'I needed to get away. A change of scenery.' His sister's well-meant fussing and the London house had suffocated him. That morning's newspaper story had been the last straw. 'As you can see, I am perfectly well.'

'Physically, perhaps…'

'Not again, Eleanor!' Immediately Max shot to his feet and paced to the windows to stare out. In the distance, he saw Miss Nithercott walking home across the garden and fleetingly considered chasing after her.

'Yes, Max. Again. You are not yourself.'

'Of course I am not myself!' The anger burned swift and hot. 'Everything I was is gone and I am left with this!' He swept his hair from his face to remind her of the damage the fire had done. 'I lost everything, Eleanor! My life, my purpose. Miranda…'

'Now that you are healed, the navy would have you back in a heartbeat. They only discharged you because they thought you were going to die. We all did. But you didn't and your body has mended. They would give you a ship, Max, if you asked them. They would bite your hand off to give you a ship. And as for Miranda, she was no loss.'

He wanted to howl. Growl at something. Hurl the blasted tea tray. All the placating in the world would not eradicate the hurt. The devastation. The awful reality of that loss.

'I never liked her. Neither did my husband. We

both thought her shallow. And lo and behold—she certainly showed her true colours, didn't she?'

It was a speech he had heard so often he had it memorised. Max allowed her to continue on without really listening. His sister now hated his former fiancée and enjoyed nothing more than castigating her. While her loyalty to him was admirable, touching even, she would never truly understand how he did not blame Miranda one bit for the choices she had made since.

He had released her from their engagement and she had moved on.

Why shouldn't she?

She was young and beautiful and full of life, whereas he was a shell of the man he had once been and not at all the man she had once agreed to marry.

'Are you even listening to me?'

'Can we *not* talk about Miranda? She is in the past.' Everything was in the past.

His sister was silent for a moment and nodded. 'I am glad to hear it… But it is your future which concerns me, Max. Do you have any plans beyond hiding yourself away here?'

No.

'This is a large estate. I thought I might try my hand at running it.' A blatant lie, but Eleanor would not know he had also inherited a battalion of capable staff who ran a very tight ship unless he chose to apprise her. Which he wouldn't. Between the estate manager, the gamekeeper, the butler, the gardener and his new solicitor, they had the entire task of Rivenhall well in hand. All Max had to do was sign things.

'Well, that *is* good.' She smiled as she sipped her tea and he was glad he had given her some hope, albeit false. 'Do you have farmland, too? Tenants?'

Maybe. Probably. No doubt buried in the reams and reams of papers he had not bothered reading because he was indifferent to it all. 'I haven't met them yet.' The only person he had met beyond the walls of his new household was Miss Nithercott. 'There has been a lot to do.'

Like counting the candlesticks in the library or the tassels on the curtains in the study.

'I can imagine… It is vast. Overwhelming, really, to picture you with a house like this. I am looking forward to a full tour later, but I am heartily impressed so far. The parkland looked…'

'When are you going home, Eleanor?'

'I have only just arrived. Are you wanting to be rid of me already?'

It would be cruel to tell her the truth after all she had done for him. 'You have your own life to live, Eleanor. Perhaps it is time you dedicated your time back to Adam and the children rather than worrying so much about me.'

She squared her shoulders, suddenly defensive. 'My husband is perfectly capable of holding the fort for a few days and my children are having a high old time with his mother who thoroughly spoils them rotten. They want to visit, by the way. Soon. They both miss their favourite uncle.'

'I am their *only* uncle.'

'Well, there is that and beggars cannot be choosers, but Thomas and Cecily still adore you. Despite your temporary and irritating belligerence.'

'How many days are you staying?'

'I need to satisfy myself that you are happy, Max.'

Happy! It would be laughable if it wasn't so tragic. 'You need to stop worrying about me. I am a grown man who does not need mollycoddling.'

'You call it mollycoddling. I call it love. Either way, you are stuck with me until I am satisfied.' A nicely, typically Eleanor piece of stubborn ambiguity which promised no clear end in sight. She took another sip of her tea and her expression became nonchalant. 'Miss Nithercott seems *nice*.'

'I hardly know the woman.'

'But surely you must have noticed she is uncommonly pretty.'

Of course he had. He wasn't dead. Unfortunately. 'Is she? It's hard to tell with her masculine attire and dirty face.' He sipped his own tea and held his sister's curious gaze levelly. Eleanor would take any sign of uncomfortableness as proof he was interested. 'Apparently, the locals have little time for her and her obsessive passion for antiquity.' Which struck him as a great shame because she was... Intriguing... Unusual... Ever so slightly hilarious. He had never met another soul quite like her. 'Surely you noticed she is a little eccentric? She spends her days digging holes in the ground, for goodness sake. That is a trifle odd.'

'I find it fascinating. So many young ladies have little between their ears beyond fluff.' But not Miss Nithercott. She could calculate the difference between a nautical mile and a standard one, randomly quote Shakespeare and translate both the Angle and the Saxon languages without skipping a beat. Now that really was fascinating. 'It is refreshing to meet one with a purpose beyond securing a good husband. All power to her, I say.' Eleanor toasted the bane with her teacup. 'Especially if she finds big lumps of gold in the mud. It certainly sounds a more exciting way to spend the time than embroidery.'

Or counting the brass knobs on the sideboard.

Chapter Six

Dig Day 764: four shards of pottery. A cluster of broken but cooked bones. One is most definitely the thigh bone of a chicken. Unsure whether the bigger pieces are from a sheep or a cow. Conclusion—my Celts had stew for dinner...

'Good afternoon, Miss Nithercott!'

Effie had hastily stood and done her best to look presentable the moment she had heard the approaching hoofbeats, but up against the elegant sophistication of the older woman's riding habit she still came up woefully short. Largely due to the morning's light rain, which had caused the sticky peat-filled soil to be more adhesive than usual. She tucked her filthy hands behind her back and hoped Lord Rivenhall's sister wouldn't judge her too harshly.

'Good afternoon, Mrs Baxter. I trust you are well.'

'Very, thank you.' From her seat in the saddle, she gazed past her to nose into the ever-increasing trench Effie had been furiously digging since breakfast. 'Is this where you found the bracelet?'

'Indeed it is. Among other things.' She pointed towards the ruined church. 'Over there has been very fruitful for finding Roman, medieval and the occasional Tudor artefact. Pre-Reformation, of course, as that is when Henry the Eighth turfed the monks off the land and had the Abbey destroyed. While over here, in my most recent trench, the evidence of human settlement appears much older. From the ancient Celtic tribes which once populated this part of East Anglia.'

'Like the Iceni, you mean? Queen Boudicca?' Effie had hoped not to appear surprised, but clearly her face must have given her away as Mrs Baxter grinned rather than appearing mortally insulted at the blatant disbelief at her knowledge. 'Mr Baxter is in the book business, Miss Nithercott. A bookshop in Bond Street, where the aristocrats can purchase their bespoke leather-bound volumes, and a lending library in Cheapside where the masses can borrow them for a pittance. His library has an extensive historical collection which I have been known to make great use of when the mood takes me. I am all for broadening the mind...sometimes. However...' she raised her dark eyebrows mischievously '… I am also a hopeless devotee of the works of Mrs Radcliffe. I know they are far-fetched and a trifle salacious, but I do love a good Gothic novel. Especially if it has a romance in it.'

'My favourite is *The Italian*.'

'You read Mrs Radcliffe?' Now it was the other woman's turn to look surprised.

'I read everything and anything, Mrs Baxter, and find much enjoyment in a bit of escapist fiction.' Back when she still harboured fanciful ideas of love and romance herself, Effie had gobbled up Gothic novels as though they were going out of fashion. But she'd cast them all aside in disgust years ago when she realised they were promising her a dream she was unlikely to ever have. Not when she terrified every man who dared come within six feet of her with her odd brain. 'Which is your favourite?'

'*The Castles of Athlin and Dunbayne*—because it ends so happily with a double wedding.' She sighed wistfully for comic effect, fluttering her hand like a silly dolt with the vapours. 'As does *The Italian*, so I approve of your choice, Miss Nithercott. You should also know I thoroughly disapprove of all novels which end unhappily because the world can be miserable enough at times, I fail to see why we should be forced to consume more misery in fiction during our leisure time. And because I am a shameless romantic at heart and choose to believe love really does conquer all. Is that why you adore the book?'

It used to be. Before realistic cynicism replaced girlish romanticism. 'I adore the way the women characters take control. It gives me hope that one day we mere females might be treated almost equally to males.' The snippiness leaked out before she could stop it.

'Do you disapprove of men, Miss Nithercott?' She appeared horrified at the thought.

'Not all men and not usually.' If one ignored the fact she hadn't met one yet who didn't ultimately disappoint. 'However, you have caught me on a bad day and I find I am now predisposed to be vexed at the entire sex this afternoon on principle.'

'Oh, dear... Dare I ask what has happened to make you so aggrieved at all the poor men on the planet?'

'The Society of Antiquaries of London have refused to read the paper I sent them on Romano-British coinage.' Something they did with great regularity, so Effie knew she should be resigned to it by now. Yet it still galled they could be so blinkered when she was telling them something entirely new.

'Why would they refuse?'

'Because I had the audacity to be born female, Mrs Baxter. The Society neither admits women to their illustrious ranks nor deigns to read anything submitted to them by a woman's hand, let alone publish it in the hallowed pages of their sacred *Archaeologia*. Regardless of the fact I am quite certain I have excavated at least three coins which have never been seen before. Not that they know that, of course, because they haven't read my paper or as much as glanced upon my sketches.'

'That is beastly of them.'

'It is stupid. That is what it is. Near-sighted, thick-headed, narrow-minded, pompous and ignorant prejudice. Thanks to their decision, no other antiquarian will be able to benefit from the knowledge only I currently hold.' None of which was Mrs Baxter's fault. 'But enough of my foolish woes. How are you enjoying Rivenhall?'

'Exceedingly, Miss Nithercott. It is a beautiful house and the grounds are stunning. I think Max will be very happy here.' Mrs Baxter tugged on the reins as her horse began to dance impatiently on the spot. 'And speaking of my brother, we should both very much like to invite you to dinner this evening.'

'Lord Rivenhall wishes to invite me?' All the acting in the world wouldn't cover her disbelief this time. Not when he had avoided her like the plague since he had reluctantly agreed to let her dig around the Abbey and the man had practically thrown her out of his house yesterday before the tea to which she had technically been invited arrived at the door.

Although, to his credit, at least he had disliked her before he got to know her. There was something comforting in that because she knew exactly where she stood. He hadn't been all flirty smiles and charm in the beginning and then standoffish once he realised she was too intelligent for her own good. That was a first and one which allowed her to be herself before him unhindered by the knowledge one wrong word or question would damage their relationship.

'Are you sure?'

'Of course I am sure. We both want to know more about your fascinating work here. Perhaps you could bring some of those artefacts you were just telling me about?'

'I suppose I could...'

'I know he was rude yesterday. He really does not mean to be. The last few years have been... difficult for him and...' For the first time the friendly smile faltered and Mrs Baxter appeared immensely troubled before she waved it away as if it was no matter, leaving Effie wondering exactly what had gone on. 'Well—suffice to say he is not himself and his bark is much worse than his bite. Please come to dinner. I shall be leaving on Saturday and I should like to get to know you better before I go.'

'That is very kind of you—I should love to come.' She felt the loneliness keenest at mealtimes which nowadays, since Lord Richard's passing, were always on her own.

'Splendid… Is there somebody else you would like to bring with you? A fiancé or beau we can invite, perhaps?'

'Neither a fiancé nor a beau, Mrs Baxter.' And pigs might fly.

The older woman beamed. 'Dinner for three it is, then. We eat at eight. Or thereabouts.'

She had ridden off before Effie had had the foresight to ask how formal the meal was going to be. Which meant she had stared too long at the contents of her wardrobe with uncharacteristic indecision as the hands of the clock chimed seven and now had her practically running down her host's drive to avoid being late, clutching her bouncing cleavage in a gown she already bitterly regretted. But in a nod to fashion, and entirely because she had felt uncomfortably dowdy up against Mrs Baxter's effortless up-to-the-minute style, she had donned it simply to prove she was capable of looking more glamourous and ladylike than the average potato sack. Less muddy, too. She had scrubbed her poor hands nearly raw in the bath in her quest to get her nails clean and even press-ganged the maid to do something fancy with her hair. By the time she was done, she hardly recognised the woman in her looking glass and was quietly pleased with her reflection.

However, remorse had set in as soon as she left the house and began walking towards Rivenhall. Only then had she learned the pretty coral silk was entirely decorative and not the least bit practical. It was much too low. So low, that any movement on her part beyond a sedate glide proved too much for the neckline to contain what she had stuffed into it. Gravity was apparently its nemesis. She would have to keep her shawl clamped tightly around her all evening in case the flesh beneath made a sudden break for freedom and proved Newton's third law unequivocally in front of her hosts.

Effie darted behind the screen of a shrubbery to wrestle all the displaced parts of her person back into the gown, then carefully arranged the stupid, filmy shawl she had paired with the impractical gown to cover the vast expanse of skin she had on show before gingerly climbing the steps to the front door without displacing it all again.

* * *

If Max was ever going to get rid of Eleanor in days rather than weeks, he had quickly realised he needed to categorically prove to her he was coping as well with life as he claimed he was. That meant making a good show of going through all the expected motions and masking the bleak hopelessness until her blasted carriage was hurtling back up his new drive bound for London. To that end, he had given her an extensive tour of the house and gardens this morning, then pretended he had urgent estate matters to attend to all afternoon as an excuse to hole himself up in his study and count the books on the bookshelf in between staring at the walls.

By then he had desperately needed the solitude. Attempting to be his old self was exhausting. It had involved making meaningful conversation, showing an interest in his sister's conversation and lying through his back teeth about his plans. And what a plethora of optimistic plans he had conjured out of thin air for her sake. Plans to increase the yield of his fields, stock his stable with the finest horseflesh to breed, to put down roots and live up to his new role as lord of the manor. He even, when pushed, suggested he might soon start to familiarise himself with the local society here in Cambridge. He did, and would continue to do, whatever it took to satisfy her he was finally moving on so she would leave him the hell alone.

Tonight, and no doubt tomorrow, he would also have to suffer the chore of dinner. Eleanor put great stock in the ritual of mealtimes. The communal breaking of bread with others around a table, endless conversation followed by yet more conversation once the meal was blessedly done. Back in London, she and he had looked horns repeatedly with his refusal to play along during his long convalescence and in the dark months since. She wanted him to be civilised and felt those interminable family dinners would aid his recovery and he wanted to be left well alone. By the end, all those meals with Eleanor, her husband and their children only served as a constant reminder of all the things he would never have, leaving him angrier than he might have been if he'd been allowed to take his meal on a tray all alone.

Fortunately, it would just be Eleanor tonight and he already had a plan to escape early, citing his imaginary crack-of-dawn schedule now that he was the lord of the manor. For her sake, and to a greater extent his, he had abandoned her for a second time an hour ago to dress for dinner. Not that his toilette ever took that long, even when he'd had to button himself into his dress uniform and cared about what he looked like. Nowadays, he could complete the task in a fraction of the time and shave blind, so to kill time he had lain in the bath for so long, the pads of his fingers resembled prunes and the water had gone cold.

As tempting as it was to stay put and freeze, dinner was imminent and he had to perform like the brother Eleanor wanted him to be rather than the one she had nursed back to health and still worried about constantly.

Max hauled himself out of the tub and briskly dried himself off. It was only after he had turned to retrieve the fresh clothes he had reluctantly laid out on the bed that he realised the sheet covering the large gilt mirror on the wall had slipped off the frame. Thanks to the lamplight and his nudity, he was confronted with the abhorrent sight of himself in all his glory properly for the first time in months. He instantly felt the bile rise at the ugly, raised and contorted skin marring his left cheek, neck, shoulder, upper arm and chest, like a poorly drawn map of Africa on the cheap papier-mâché globe he'd had in his cabin aboard the *Artemis*.

Sadistically, he stared at himself for as long as he could bear it as a test, silently hoping he could see some sign of improvement to pin fresh hope to, but there was none. The scars were just as big and just as ugly as they had been when he had first seen them almost two years ago. The only difference was the mess was now permanently healed over rather than an agonising, weeping open wound which had threatened to kill him and then cruelly failed to come good on the promise.

Instinctively, he tore his eyes away and snatched up his shirt, shrugging it ruthlessly on before he dared to replace the fallen sheet back on the only mirror left inside his new house. He no longer cared that the old gilt frame was embedded in the wall by several centuries' worth of plaster, or that the glass was Tudor and therefore very rare indeed. As soon as this blasted dinner was done with, he would take a chisel to the damn thing himself and enjoy shattering it into a million pieces rather than witness the awful truth ever again.

Max was still tying his cravat when he slammed out of his bedchamber and, both despairing and fuming, he charged down the stairs to the front door.

He knew it was irrational. Knew he needed to make his peace with it and learn to accept what he could not change no matter how much he willed it. Yet knowing that only served to make things worse. He needed air and space before he was in any fit state to see his sister. At least ten minutes before he could speak, let alone pretend everything in his new garden was rosy. Time to stop the blood rushing loudly in his ears and his heart clanging like a hammer against an anvil in his chest. Before the hovering butler could open it for him, he pulled the door open and plunged through it.

Chapter Seven

Nine circles of hell...

The first Max saw of Miss Nithercott was the startled whites of her eyes as she flew backwards and he only just managed to catch her before the force of his impact sent her tumbling down the unforgiving stone steps. Instinct kicked in and he used both his arms to drag her back to safety, winding himself in the process as she crashed back against him.

As she blinked up at him, he could see her hands curled tightly around his lapels to anchor herself. Just below that, God help him, was one of the most magnificent cleavages he had ever seen. Two perfect rounded mounds strained against the thin fabric and the solid wall of his ribs as her panicked breath sawed in and out. Perfect because they were neither too big nor too small. Encased in soft, peachy skin kissed by the sun. He could feel the press of them through the layers of his coat, waistcoat and shirt. In every nerve ending, too.

Not wanting to be caught staring, he pushed her brusquely to arm's length and tried to gather his wits. Something which proved near impossible when the woman who had made him yearn in breeches suddenly made his body rampant in a dress.

An outrageously sinful, seductive and spellbinding dress.

One which he was suddenly overwhelmed with the need to peel away.

'Oh, Miss Nithercott—are you injured?' Eleanor's shriek brought him back to his senses. She barrelled past and took control, stealing the new bane of his life cruelly from his arms to check.

'No. Just a little stunned.'

'Hardly a surprise when my big oaf of a brother nearly flattened you!' She glared at him for good measure. 'What were you thinking, Max?'

He hadn't been thinking. Just escaping. 'My apologies, Miss Nithercott. I had no idea you were there.'

'No idea!' His sister's hand swatted his shoulder in disgust. 'Did you not hear her knock? Did you not see Smithson about to open the door?'

Unimpressed, Eleanor took Effie's arm and shepherded her towards the drawing room. 'Fetch the poor thing a sherry, Max. Unless you would prefer a brandy Miss Nithercott? Or tea?'

'Sherry would be lovely.'

Max stood rooted to the spot as they sailed past, trying and failing not to notice how the magnificent dress hugged her curves or how the glow from the lamps revealed the shadowy shape of her legs beneath the gauzy folds of her skirt, then slowly released the breath he hadn't realised he was holding.

That was certainly one way to take his mind off the panic.

Usually, when his emotions churned unexpectedly out of control it took a good fifteen minutes to talk himself down. Yet apparently, a brief collision with Miss Nithercott banished all traces of panic in a split second and replaced it with inappropriate lust. He wasn't entirely sure which of his body's reactions was worse. The panic left him fighting for breath and an armful of Miss Nithercott left him breathless.

'Shall I tell the kitchen to postpone the soup for a few minutes while Miss Nithercott recovers, my lord?' Smithson appeared at his elbow, carrying the bane's tattered leather satchel aloft like a tray and the silliest, flimsiest shawl he had ever seen was sat on top of it. A garment so frivolous it was entirely incongruous with the bafflingly intelligent and academic woman who plainly owned it. Without thinking, he took it from the butler to feel the fabric and only just resisted the urge to bury his nose in it when a waft of lilac and rose floated up his nostrils to torture him some more.

'Yes, Smithson. Apologise on my behalf and tell them it shouldn't be too long.' Or at least he hoped it wasn't. Having her back in his house unnerved him. Although goodness only knew what had brought her back again this time. Miss Nithercott was falling woefully short of her promise to keep the hell out of his way and the more he saw her the more unnerved he became.

She was a peculiar combination and one he really did not understand at all. On the one hand she was an unbelievably learned scholar and as such had the single-minded, dogged and bookish characteristics of all the great minds he had ever encountered at the Admiralty or at the society balls and parties Eleanor insisted he attend each time he was home on leave. On the other, there was an undeniable and overt femininity about his new neighbour which contradicted the absent-minded professor aspects of her character. Then—and he would need a third hand for this one—she possessed a quiet, proud vulnerability which called to him. Max was entirely certain he never wanted to have to think about her, yet since the first moment he'd met her he had. Near constantly. Which rattled him.

'Max?' His sister's impatient, clicking fingers wrenched his gaze from the shawl to the doorway. 'Any chance you could pour that sherry before the week is over? Please *try* to be a good host.' And with that, she spun on her heel.

Host?

In the recesses of his mind he heard an alarm bell ringing and because he had a very uneasy feeling, took himself to the dining room. The table was set quite plainly for three.

'Smithson!'

The butler scurried back from the kitchen and skidded to a wary halt. 'Yes, my lord?'

'Is Miss Nithercott joining us for dinner?'

'She is, my lord.'

'And when, pray tell, were you apprised of this fact.'

'This afternoon, my lord. After Mrs Baxter returned from her ride.'

'But before the tea she took with me at four?'

'Yes, my lord.' Blasted Eleanor and her machinations. She had set this up behind his back and purposefully left him in the dark. 'Will that be all, my lord?'

'Could you tell my sister I need a quick word with her, please?' Max fully intended to wring her neck—after she had ejected the unnerving new bane of his life from the premises, of course.

In typical Eleanor fashion she took her time in answering his summons and sailed regally into his dining room looking not the least bit contrite.

'You invited a guest to dinner without my permission?'

'It seemed the least I could do after you had been so rude to her the day before. Besides...' she shrugged, unrepentant '...she is all alone in the world. When I collided with her this afternoon, she was also *upset*.'

Upset? Max hated that that niggled, but asking why the bane was upset or who had upset her would only fuel his eldest sibling's dastardly plot to interfere in every aspect of his life. 'If you wanted her company, you could have dined at her house. Or at the inn. In fact, anywhere but here.'

'Because that isn't the least bit insulting, is it? Not inviting her here only compounds your rudeness by making it appear you are avoiding her.'

'I *am* avoiding her. Miss Nithercott is...' Maddening... Irritating... Confusing... Beguiling... Wearing a dress which made his mouth water '...odd.'

'So are you nowadays, little Brother, so by

rights the pair of you should get on famously. Although to be frank, I don't find her the least bit odd. I think Miss Nithercott is lovely. Refreshing, intelligent and extremely interesting. She is also uncommonly pretty. Surely you have noticed that?'

Noticed! The image of her in breeches had apparently seared itself on to his brain and refused to budge. And now he'd doubtless have the image of her in that gown. Pressed against him and clutching his lapels like a woman waiting to be kissed. 'I have no patience for your flagrant matchmaking, Eleanor...'

'Matchmaking?' The immediate and innocent affront was convincing, or at least it would have been had he not grown up with the manipulative witch who stood piously before him. 'Do not flatter yourself, Brother. I like Miss Nithercott a great deal—but she is much too good for you! Perhaps, I might have encouraged it before you became so bitter and twisted and unreasonably unsociable. But I can assure you my only intention in inviting her to dine with us, aside from repairing any damage done by your shocking rudeness yesterday, was because I should like to further *my* acquaintance with her. Would it kill you to at least play at being a gentleman for the duration of one meal?'

'That I have to suffer your uninvited presence is bad enough, but a guest so soon is...'

He watched the sadness draw her features fleetingly before her temper replaced it. 'Oh, for pity's sake, Max! Go hide in your study with a tray, then!' She had the gall to curl her lip in distaste as if he were the one in the wrong. 'You have become so very good at that.'

'I might just do that!' He had to talk to her retreating back, feeling childish and churlish and thoroughly pathetic for lashing out at Eleanor again when she had stalwartly borne the brunt of all his frustration since the morning they had stretchered him from that ship.

'Good.' She did not turn around. 'And do not be surprised if you feel your cowardly ears burning!'

He waited all of six seconds before the ramifications of his sudden absence from the proceedings piled in. Left to her own devices, Eleanor would have no compunction about telling Miss Nithercott all the sorry details of his recent life and the thought of her knowing his intensely private business and, worse, pitying him for it was entirely unacceptable. He did not want the world and his wife knowing the ins and outs of everything. He most definitely did not want his much-too-intelligent and annoyingly gorgeous new neighbour to know exactly how pathetic he now truly was. And doubtless his wily sister knew that, too.

* * *

'Could you pass the salt, please?'

Self-consciously, from the head of the table, Max did as his sister asked, wishing the lamps in the formal dining room weren't burning quite so brightly and that Miss Nithercott wasn't seated to his left. The very least Eleanor could have done was place the woman on his good side. Now he had to avoid any sudden head movements in case he inadvertently disturbed the camouflaging veil of scruffy hair he hid his deformity behind.

'I think it is outrageous those silly men refused to read your paper, Miss Nithercott.' He had happily allowed the ladies to keep the conversation flowing because he had none. Simply sitting here took that much effort. 'Anyone would think they were afraid.'

'Of course they are afraid.' The bane waved her fork with the same animated enthusiasm as she usually did with her hands when she spoke, wafting lilacs and roses willy-nilly to play havoc with his senses. 'Society might actually crumble if they acknowledge women have brains as well as wombs.' Max did not want to have to contemplate her womb, because contemplating that meant contemplating the route to it. 'We are supposed to remain content as chattels, Mrs Baxter, with no thoughts beyond those fed to us by our biologically superior husbands and no desire above administering to his whims, popping out the fruit of their intellectually superior loins and choosing the menus for his dinner.'

Loins! Wombs! Did the woman have no boundaries? Now his damned head was filled with all manner of inappropriate images entirely unsuitable and not the least bit conducive to digesting the roast beef he was staring at as if his life depended on it. He could hardly flick more than a glance at her without feeling off kilter. The gown she was wearing was too damned distracting and she was a guest, and that in itself was daunting. He couldn't remember the last time he had sat with anyone beyond the tight circle of his vexing sister and her family.

'We are oppressed, Mrs Baxter. In thoughts, in deeds—in everything. The law makes us nought but property to our fathers, then our husbands, we are denied admittance to universities, forbidden from practising medicine or law, cannot inherit titles, keep our own wealth if we marry or sit on a seat in Parliament let alone vote for one. At every juncture society forces us into moulds which we dare not attempt to move beyond for fear of censure. And what is worse is that as women we should seek to empower our fellow women, but instead we are taught to judge them more harshly and in some cases more than the men do. Our society is unforgivingly patriarchal.'

'We clearly need to try harder to work for progress and find some balance.' Not that Eleanor needed any encouragement to take the lead on anything. She had always been a law unto herself. He pitied her poor husband, who for some reason still adored the harridan.

'Hardly progress, Mrs Baxter. If history teaches us anything, then we have regressed.'

'We have?'

'In ancient Sparta women had much greater freedoms than we do nowadays. They were educated and could inherit. They could divorce feckless husbands and still keep their property. According to Plutarch, they held equal status to men. Can you imagine that? And here, Queen Boudicca raised an enormous army and very nearly toppled the Roman regime. She sacked the Roman strongholds of Colchester and London before being narrowly defeated at St Albans. None of her forty thousand men ever questioned her ability to lead.' Miss Nithercott speared a potato and began to wield that, too. 'Then there are the Amazons—if they ever existed, of course, which is still open for debate—who were a famously matriarchal society.'

'Didn't I read somewhere they only had one breast?'

Marvellous. Now he could add that word to the mix as the memory of the feel of Miss Nithercott's bosom against his chest immediately decided to join the overwhelming swirl of inappropriate thoughts in his mind.

'So legend has it, Mrs Baxter—although by design rather than specific mutation. Apparently, they cut one off so they could hold their bows and fire their arrows better. Staggering, really—but they were fierce warriors who hated men and had absolutely nothing to do with them.'

'Hardly a surprise then that they died out,' his sister teased saucily while Max wished he were dead. 'Men do have some essential uses.'

'Oh, the Amazons tolerated them for procreation, Mrs Baxter.' Miss Nithercott's cheeky grin suggested she knew all about procreation. Of course she did. She apparently knew everything. 'They abducted men from rival tribes and used them as slaves after they had mated.'

Max nearly choked on his own potato at her phrasing. 'What else do you do besides digging?' Enough was enough. Wombs and loins were one thing. Mating and talk of procreation quite another. And they still had to eat dessert. His sister beamed, delighted he had finally deigned to join the conversation.

'I like to read. I write. I sketch.'

'Such solitary pursuits. Don't you ever feel lonely?' Eleanor said exactly what Max was thinking. 'Unless you have other family at home?'

'No. It is just me—I am an only child so it is what I am used to and I do not mind the solitude.' Although he was sure her eyes said differently.

'I have never been good with my own company. Growing up I always had Max. A few months before he ran away to sea, I married Adam and had my children. I like the noise and chaos of family, Miss Nithercott. They are my greatest joy. Have you never been tempted to have one?'

Was that sadness he saw in her eyes? Regret? 'To have a family one must first have a husband, Mrs Baxter, and I am afraid that ship sailed long ago.'

Chapter Eight

Dig Day 764: honey, not vinegar...

'Your ship hasn't sailed! You are still young and uncommonly pretty. Isn't she uncommonly pretty, Max?'

Her host grunted in response, making it difficult to know if he either agreed or disagreed.

'I refuse to believe no man has ever offered for you.'

'I was engaged. Once. He died.'

'Oh, that is awful! Am I allowed to enquire how?'

'He was a military man. The cavalry. He was fatally wounded at Salamanca.' Poor Rupert. It still made her sad to think about it even though it had been three years.

'And there has been no one since?'

Nor before. Rupert had been the only man who could tolerate her in more than small doses. 'No.'

'But never say never, Miss Nithercott… Perhaps Cupid might strike again?'

'Perhaps…' And perhaps pigs might fly. 'You ran away to sea, Lord Rivenhall?' Effie deliberately changed the subject. Talking about her marital situation always made her feel awkward because inevitably it led to admitting all the reasons why she was still a spinster and was doomed to be one for ever. 'I did not know you were in the navy. Merchant or Royal?'

'Royal, of course.' Mrs Baxter positively glowed with pride. 'When our father forbade him from ever joining, Max took himself to Portsmouth and enlisted as a cabin boy. From there he rapidly rose up the ranks regardless of Papa's constant and verbose disappointment. By the age of twenty he was already a master and became Captain of his own ship at just seven and twenty. He sailed alongside Nelson at Trafalgar and has earned a huge heap of medals.'

'Very impressive.' Not that Effie's reluctant and mostly mute host appeared to want to talk about it judging by the intense focus he was putting in to slicing his meat. It was obvious he had had no hand in issuing tonight's invitation and wasn't particularly pleased about it either. But for Mrs Baxter's sake Effie would persevere, even though she wasn't entirely sure why the woman had thought it appropriate to extend an invitation when her brother was so against it. 'How old were you when you joined?'

'Twelve.' Again it was Mrs Baxter who answered. 'Our father positively exploded when he realised and immediately dashed to Portsmouth to retrieve him, but Max was already bound for the West Indies by the time he got there. After that there was no stopping him, of course. Max's calling was always the sea. And he looks particularly dashing in a uniform.'

Something she could well imagine. With his height and build and brooding, mysterious presence she could picture him at the helm. Or stood precariously on the yard arm, one hand clutching the rigging while the other shielded his dark eyes as he stared out to sea. The wind riffling his long black hair… Gracious! Where had that come from? Clearly she had read a little too much Mrs Radcliffe last night before bed to be thinking such fanciful thoughts! Thoughts which were most unlike her nowadays. She had ruthlessly trained herself to stop romanticising about attractive gentlemen. Those foolish fantasies always ended in disappointment.

'Are you still in the navy, Lord Rivenhall?' The moment the words were out Effie regretted the question because Mrs Baxter appeared anxious and the surly lord's jaw clenched as his expression clouded.

'No.'

One word. No explanation, but a pointed glare at his sister.

'I suppose it is difficult to juggle the responsibilities of an estate this size and a command a ship at the same time?' She was babbling, and perhaps making an already tense situation worse, but for some reason she felt the urge to pour oil on what she sensed were very troubled waters.

Silence.

Until Mrs Baxter filled it. 'Max was wounded during the naval blockade of the Americas Miss Nithercott. Privateers attacked the ship and tried to scuttle it. He nearly died when…' Her words trailed off at the incensed expression of her brother and she pasted an unconvincing smile on her face before she stared down at her dinner. 'But thankfully he didn't and is all mended now… As you can plainly see.'

Physically, perhaps, but Effie suspected the scars he carried were more than skin deep if the emotion swirling in the suddenly stormy depths of his dark eyes were any gauge. The moody Lord Rivenhall was quite a way shy from being mended. 'From what I have read it was a difficult war.'

'I can assure you reading about it is significantly more pleasant than fighting it.'

She couldn't think of an answer to that and, as

he was back to cutting his food with more aggression than the task warranted, it was patently obvious he did not want one. Effie had no idea where to look so stared mournfully at her plate, too, the awkward atmosphere as dense as city smog on a frigid winter's morning.

'Have you always lived at Hill House, Miss Nithercott?'

Effie grabbed his sister's rescuing olive branch with both hands and for the rest of the meal the pair of them chatted over-brightly about everything and nothing while he did not attempt to say another word.

'Thank you so much for having me.'

After another entirely mute half-hour in the drawing room, Lord Rivenhall accompanied his sister and Effie into the hallway to bid her farewell. She had never been so delighted to be leaving a place in her entire life and felt dreadfully sorry for Mrs Baxter who kept staring at her in abject apology. That they had managed half an hour in the drawing room was a miracle when he had continually glanced at the loudly ticking clock on the mantel every five minutes, making it as plain as day he was sat there on sufferance.

Effie never dared produce any of the interesting stash of coins, brooches and rings from her satchel which she had brought on Mrs Baxter's express instruction and instead gulped down two large glasses of sherry in quick succession while she counted the seconds before she deemed it polite to leave.

She regretted that now.

Those two glasses on top of the dinner wine she had also consumed much too much of during the many awkward silences were making her head spin.

Smithson opened the door and she was almost out of it when Lord Rivenhall spoke for the first time since the main course.

'Where is your carriage?'

'I do not have one. I came on foot, my lord.'

'But it is dark.'

'I know the way home like the back of my hand. I have walked it often enough.'

'But it is *dark*, Miss Nithercott.' Nowhere near as dark as his eyes and his expression. 'We have spoken about the dark. It is not safe for a woman all alone.'

'Perhaps in London, my lord—but here in Cambridgeshire the only thing I am likely to encounter on my way home is the odd fox or badger.'

He shook his head and growled. 'Smithson—have the stable ready two horses and bring them around immediately.' Good grief, surely he did not mean to come with her?

'Really, my lord, there is no need to trouble

yourself or your poor stable master. In the time it takes to saddle the horses I will already be home. Hill House is just across the pasture.' She pointed to the moonlit navy horizon while glancing pleadingly at Mrs Baxter, hoping she would aid in talking him out of it. 'I do not want to be a nuisance.'

'Miss Nithercott, I am afraid I agree wholeheartedly with my brother. What sort of neighbours would we be to leave you exposed to danger? It is best if Max accompanies you home. I should sleep easier knowing you are safe.'

'I could send a message back the second I arrive if it would put your mind at rest.' Although with the housekeeper and maid long gone home she would have to return to deliver it herself. 'Honestly, this is unnecessary fuss when the walk takes less than fifteen minutes.' She seriously considered making a bolt for it, but worried he might chase her. 'And I am not a great fan of riding. Hence my choice to come on foot tonight.'

'Then I shall walk with you, Miss No-common-sense-whatsoever.' A prospect somehow more unnerving than riding alongside him. 'Because alongside the badgers and the foxes are footpads. A man was robbed only last week on the turnpike not five miles from here. Something you would know if you read the newspapers alongside your scholarly books.' A curt reminder, she supposed, that he disapproved of her extensive education, too. Typical, really. A woman with original thought! Whatever next!

'For my own peace of mind as well as my sister's I shall accompany you.' And with that he strode past her out on to the porch, clearly in no mood to take no for an answer and clearly put out at having to do it.

At a loss as to what else she could do without appearing horrendously rude and supremely ungrateful in front of his charming sister, Effie was forced to surrender and ignore the alcohol in her system which was encouraging her to tell him the truth and to hell with the consequences—that he was the absolute last person she wanted to spend another moment with after tonight's performance. He was as changeable as the wind and infuriatingly obnoxious.

'Thank you.'

He nodded and they began to walk down the steps. By tacit agreement, they did this with a good six feet of the cool summer air between them. The awkward silence deafening; the atmosphere so thick you could cut it with a knife.

The front door clicked closed behind them and still he said nothing, apparently content to make her feel uncomfortable for the duration. They were halfway across the lawn when something inside her caused her tenuous grasp on her temper to snap. Probably, she was prepared to concede, fuelled almost entirely by the sherry.

'If it is your mission to make me feel wretched whenever I am in your presence, then you have *thoroughly* succeeded, Lord Rivenhall!'

He seemed shocked at the suggestion. 'It was not my intention.'

'Of course it was. You glare, seethe and grunt at and disapprove of everything, making no secret of the fact you find my company a tremendous chore. Thanks to you I had a dreadful evening—so well done!' He didn't need to like her. Effie was quite used to people not liking her—but would it kill him to be polite? She had been an invited guest after all. 'So did your poor sister, who most certainly did not deserve it! Your appalling behaviour made it awful for the both of us.'

Incensed and humiliated, Effie suddenly stopped dead. 'For the record, I was told *you* extended the invitation. Had I realised it was nothing to do with you, I would never have dared encroach on your precious privacy. Rest assured, I shan't encroach upon it again. You can rot in that house all alone for all I care, because you do not deserve visitors! You are a horrible man, Lord Rivenhall! A rude, obnoxious, churlish…' There really weren't enough insulting adjectives to fling at him. 'Boorish, selfish…'

'And let's not forget glaring, seething, grunting and disapproving.'

'How could I?' Of its own accord her finger jabbed him in the arm. It was as solid as granite and did not yield an inch. 'Are we all supposed to suffer simply because you are angry at the world? You should be heartily ashamed of yourself!'

She was expecting retaliation. Instead, he stared down at his feet. Awkwardly.

'Would it make you feel better to know that I am?' Then he sighed and raked a hand through his long hair. 'You caught me at a bad time this evening. I was not…in any state to receive visitors.'

'Are you ever?' Not really her business and not at all what she should have said at his lacklustre almost-apology.

'No. Never.' He sighed again and stared up at the moon. 'And it's been so long I've forgotten how to do it.'

'You haven't forgotten. You choose to behave like that to push people away.' Again, thanks to the liberating effects of the alcohol, her mouth seemed to be on a mission to bait him.

More silence but she watched myriad emotions play on his face before he nodded.

'You're very perceptive for a genius, Miss Nithercott.'

'And what is that supposed to mean?'

'That all of the excessively learned people I have ever encountered usually know a great deal about things most of us mere mortals cannot comprehend, but have little understanding of things beyond books. Like people and what makes them human.' He slanted her a glance that wasn't the least bit angry for once. 'I meant that as a compliment by the way—before you tear me off another strip.'

'You deserved tearing off a strip. And when you go home you need to apologise to your sister. It is obvious she cares a great deal about you, although heaven only knows why.'

His bark of laughter was sudden and unexpected. 'You are fearless, Miss Nithercott. I have to give you credit for that. Most people tiptoe around me nowadays. Even Eleanor bites her acid tongue and she has always been a relentlessly bossy older sister.'

'Then I would say your quest to push people away has been a resounding success.'

His dark brows furrowed until he eventually sighed. 'Yet I am not pleased by it.'

She did not want to let him off the hook, but compassion and curiosity was already dampening her temper. 'Perhaps you no longer want to be left alone, Lord Rivenhall? Have you considered that?'

Chapter Nine

~~~~~~~~~~~~

One conundrum of a woman...

Max was not the least bit ready to talk about that—or anything so intensely personal—but later he should probably think upon it because he felt she probably had a point. 'A more interesting question is why *you* are all alone? Every time I see you, at dinner tonight, with your head stuck in a hole, even in the dead of night, it is never with anybody else.' They started to walked onwards again. More slowly this time and less than a foot apart. Bizarrely, it felt...cosy. 'Where is your chaperon?'

'I am long past the age when I need one of those.'

'Still—ladies do not usually take to the streets on their own. They always take a relative. Don't you have any aunts or uncles or cousins, Miss Noxious?'

She glanced away and shrugged, yet the shrug

tugged at his heartstrings. 'No. None. The Nithercotts are a dying breed.'

'Then there is nobody? Who checks you are home safe or if you have arrived at your destination?'

'I have servants—Mr and Mrs Farley—and they always know exactly where to find me. If I am not at home I am at the Abbey.' Her eyes sought his again boldly. 'With my head stuck in a hole.'

'Do you like being alone?'

Her mouth opened, then closed and she shrugged again instead. 'I am used to it.'

'That doesn't answer my question.'

'Not many would choose to be alone, my lord, but it is what it is and I make the best of it.'

'By burying yourself in your work.'

'Better that than moping around and feeling sorry for myself.'

'*Touché*, Miss Nithercott.' Max found himself smiling again. The second time she had amused him with her forthrightness in as many minutes, when little amused him any more.

'I apologise. It wasn't meant as a dig. More a reflection on myself. I have, on occasion, allowed myself to dwell on all life's negatives and indulge in self-pity.'

The dead mother. The dead father. And then the dead fiancé.

That could not have been easy. A timely and

poignant reminder that not only his life had been flipped on its head by a cruel twist of fate. 'Losing someone you love is always hard.' Whether that be by death or blatant disgust. 'But as my sister is prone to say, time eventually heals all wounds.' Something Max wanted to believe, but didn't. Some wounds were too extreme to heal fully.

'Rupert was a lovely man. Patient, good natured and could tolerate my company.'

'Tolerate?' What an odd choice of word. 'If you will pardon me for saying, that doesn't sound particularly...' He stopped himself from finishing the sentence.

'Romantic?' She did not seem offended and smiled wistfully. 'It wasn't a love match Lord Rivenhall. I have never been misguided enough to expect that. More a meeting of minds. Rupert was a great friend of your uncle's and, like he, found my passion for history and antiquity interesting. Over time, we formed a friendship and because he was older and wanted companionship and I was sat on the shelf gathering dust, a marriage when he retired from the army seemed a sensible solution for both of us. The campaign to Spain was supposed to be his last. And it was. Except he never came home.'

Every bit of that story depressed him. 'I'm sorry.'

'So am I.' She shrugged again and gathered her flimsy shawl tightly at her neck. 'I was looking forward to leaving my shelf.'

'As Eleanor said, there is no reason why that cannot still happen. You are still young enough and…' Uncommonly pretty, but acknowledging that would make him feel awkward when for some unknown reason Max currently felt anything but.

'I shall be thirty upon my next birthday, my lord. And while I agree my age is not entirely an impediment on the marriage mart, it does not help. However, the greater issue, as we both know, is my oddness. Gentlemen, I have discovered, can tolerate many things, but a cleverer wife than they are is entirely intolerable and I have never been particularly good at hiding it.' Her lovely smile was forced. 'Look—there is Hill House.' She pointed to the shadowy outline of a modest building across the meadow. One solitary lamp burned in a window. Probably the only thing there to welcome her home. 'I told you the walk was short and uneventful.'

She wanted to change the subject. He wanted to tell her he liked her intelligence—liked her, truth be told—but wasn't ready to do that either and sincerely doubted he ever would be. 'I dare say the servants will be relieved you are finally home. I should imagine at this late hour they are longing for their beds.'

'Mrs Farley and her husband live in the village.'

'So there is nobody at home at all?' Max suddenly felt grateful for Eleanor. Even in his darkest moments, she had always been there.

'As I've said, I am perfectly content with my own company.' She was an atrocious liar. To cover her discomfort, she had suddenly quickened her pace, making him jog a little to catch up and when he did she avoided his eyes. 'I am probably speaking out of turn here, but I do not like the thought of you here unchaperoned. It doesn't sit right with me. Perhaps you should hire a companion?'

'A companion!' She laughed. 'I am not in my dotage, Lord Rivenhall.'

'But in the next breath you say you are too old for a chaperon.'

'I am past the need for a chaperon. By a great many years. I think my precious virtue is safe!'

'Of course…because you are a wizened old hag. I think perhaps you need to wear your silly digging spectacles all the time, Miss Naive, because clearly when you look in the mirror you do not see what the rest of us see as plain as the nose on your face.' Her face softened at his inadvertent compliment and her feet slowed a little, but her smile was awkward and, before she said something horribly polite which let him know in no uncertain terms he was barking up the wrong tree if he had misconstrued kindness for anything else, he hastily clarified. 'Trust me—even looking a state in breeches and mismatched boots you need a chaperon. There are plenty of men out there who would be only too happy to take shocking advantage of *any* woman who had the misfortune to be all on her own.'

The awkward smile evaporated and her next words sounded forced. 'Thank you for your concern.'

Clearly he had offended her by criticising her situation. He was about to say something inane and innocuous to fill the tense void and the increasing distance she was putting between them, when she quietly shivered.

'Where are my manners...?' Instinctively Max shrugged out of his coat and wrapped it around her shoulders, then wished he hadn't because it meant touching her and staring down at her face as she gazed up at him, surprised. The ghost of a smile played on her lips, drawing his eyes there and a wave of longing hit him, so intense, he almost gasped aloud. Hastily he stepped back and continued walking, this time more briskly himself because he really couldn't think of a single thing to say.

'Thank you.'

'You are welcome.'

She was staring at him now. He could feel it through the back of his shirt. Through his skin.

Lord help him.

'You baffle me, Lord Rivenhall. One minute you are a beast and then, when I am certain you are quite horrible and want nothing whatsoever to do with you, you surprise me and I see glimpses of affability which make me inclined to allow myself to like you.'

'Affability? Like?' A prospect which bizarrely made him ridiculously happy. 'That *is* worrying. Clearly I need to try harder at pushing people away if that is the case. I can't have you *liking* me. Society might crumble.'

'And visitors might call.'

'There is that. I should probably start being obnoxious again to keep them all at bay.'

'Probably best—if you are truly committed to being a proper recluse.'

'Oh, I am. Entirely committed.' Although he wasn't quite so committed concerning her if the digging and dinner were anything to go by. Or the escorting her home. A proper recluse wouldn't do that either.

They reached a low wall and he found himself helping her over it and much sooner than he would have liked reached her front door.

'Thank you for seeing me home, Lord Rivenhall.'

'You are welcome, Miss Nithercott.'

She opened the door and passed him back his coat, leaning on the frame as he put it back on. As he threaded his arms into the sleeves, he could smell the scent of lilacs and roses on the fabric, feel the warmth of her body in the lining.

'Goodnight, Lord Beastly.'

'Goodnight, Miss Know-it-all.'

'You do realise that insult doesn't begin with an N, like all your others.'

'The K is silent so it doesn't count. As a genius, you, of all people, should know that.'

She grinned and slowly closed the door, leaving him smiling on her doorstep all alone with the sultry roses and lilacs. They kept her with him all the way home.

'What the blazes are you doing?'

Max had fought the inexplicable need to seek her out for three days and had assumed to find her with her head stuck in a hole—not wielding a pickaxe.

'I have been looking for the wall to the dwelling and ironically hit one. Except this one is more modern than the one I am seeking so it has to come out as it's in the way.' She leaned the handle of the tool against the deep wall of the trench and bent to dislodge the stones she had loosened, tossing them out on to an ever-growing pile near his feet. 'Did you apologise to your sister?'

'I did.' She had a nerve reminding him—but he admired it. 'She wants me to invite you to dinner again as penance.'

'If that was an invitation, my lord, it was a poor one.' Another rock clattered on the pile. 'And obviously, for both our sakes, I shall decline it.'

'That's very decent of you.'

'Indeed it is. Besides, not that I care overmuch for etiquette, but it would hardly be proper for me to have dinner with a man unchaperoned.'

'Not that I want you to reconsider my poor invitation, but it would be entirely chaperoned. Eleanor would be there.'

'I thought she was staying only till Saturday.'

'My sister is a law unto herself and has been annoyingly non-committal regarding her departure date. Obviously, as a dedicated and proper recluse, I am counting the minutes till I see the back of her. However, I anticipate I am to be burdened with her presence for at least a few more days unless I can think of a better plan to evict her than boring her to death, which is all I have at the moment.'

'If you purchased some dogs, you could set them on her.'

'And you, too. I cannot deny I've given it some serious thought.'

She grinned and grabbed her pickaxe again. 'They say a dog is man's best friend.'

'Which is exactly why I haven't gone ahead with the purchase. A proper recluse eschews all friends—four-legged or otherwise.' He watched, fascinated, as she swung the pickaxe into the compacted earth and then felt guilty that she was swinging it, cursing himself for the gentlemanly good manners his mother had instilled in him. 'Would you like some help?'

'I can manage.'

'I was never in any doubt of that, Miss Nithercott—but I have the sudden compunction to be neighbourly. You might as well make use of that state while it lasts. It's bound to be very brief.'

'I suppose I could tolerate some help for a short period of time. You could fetch the wheelbarrow and load those stones into it.'

'I could. But I'd much prefer to be in charge of the pickaxe. Unless you fear as a mere man I might not be up to such a complicated task?'

'Be my guest.' She handed it up to him and hauled herself out of the trench. 'Try to aim it at the wall itself rather than the surrounding earth. I don't want to damage the dwelling.'

Chapter Ten

Dig Day 768: progress impeded by an unexpected obstacle...

The last thing Effie expected to see was Lord Rivenhall waist deep in her trench making impressively short work of the wall she had been battling for hours. He'd dispensed with his coat, which gave her an unencumbered view of his broad back and shoulders as he swung the pick-axe with brutal precision. Each time he bent over to toss her more rocks, she was rewarded with the ever-so-slightly scandalous sight of his breeches pulled taut over his muscular thighs and bottom. And he had quite the bottom. She had been surreptitiously admiring it over the top of the wheelbarrow for a good twenty minutes already and was still not the least bit over it.

'Did they teach you how to use a pickaxe in the navy?'

'There is not much call for digging on board a ship.'

'I suppose, as a captain, you mostly stood around giving orders?'

'You have never been on board a ship, have you, Miss Not-a-clue? Because if you had, you would realise what an entirely stupid thing that was to say. The term "all hands on deck" came about for a reason—because there are not enough hands on board to do all of the things that are needed. There are few idle hours. Even when one is the Captain.'

'I read there were eight hundred and twenty crew members aboard the *Victory* at Trafalgar. Eight hundred and twenty-one if you include Nelson himself. Whichever way you look at it, that is a lot of hands. One thousand, six hundred and forty-two of them.'

He smiled and rolled his eyes. 'Well, that was the *Victory* and that was at Trafalgar. If we are going to talk statistics, I should tell you the *Victory* is a first-rate, one-hundred-and-four-gun warship and needs significantly more crew than my humble fifth-class thirty-eight-gun frigate could hold just to fire them.'

'You did not have a crew of eight hundred, then?'

'If only…' He swung the axe back again, the soft linen of his shirt straining most intriguingly against his biceps. 'The *Artemis* was crewed by two hundred and eighty-three. Which only gave me a paltry five hundred and sixty-five individual hands to do all the work.'

'Surely you mean five hundred and sixty-six?' Why had she corrected him, when correcting people always rubbed them up the wrong way.

'No. I *meant* five hundred and sixty-five, because Plumstead, the bosun, lost an arm at the Battle of the Nile and had a hook which he used with impressive precision.' He slanted her an amused glance. 'Which takes the total tally up to two hundred and sixty-seven hands if you include me…standing around and giving orders.'

'You enjoyed that, didn't you?'

'Immensely.'

'Do you miss it?'

His eyes clouded and he nodded. 'Every single day. Or at least I miss the sea rather than the navy. The freedom of sailing into that vast expanse of sky and sea to far-flung places.'

'I've read that sailors—' She clamped her jaws shut, realising in the nick of time what she was curious about was probably inappropriate even though he had paused and was clearly waiting for her to finish. 'Never mind.'

'Ask your question. You know you want to.'

'It's not the sort of question a lady is supposed to ask a gentleman.'

He made a great show of looking every which way before he turned to her, those dark eyes alight with mirth for once rather than annoyance. 'As there is nobody here to hear it, ask it anyway.'

'I was wondering if you had a girl in every port?'

He paused, his mouth opened as if to speak then he clamped it shut again. 'Well, I wasn't expecting that… You say the damnedest things.'

'I'm sorry.'

'My fault. I did encourage you to ask it.' She thought he would leave it at that, but he surprised her. 'I suppose the honest answer is not *every* port.' She could tell by his expression he was recalling one of two of them now and that made her even more curious about him. And those girls. Except she knew that really would be wrong to ask, so instead changed tack.

'Your ship was called the *Artemis*? Goddess of the hunt.'

'I always thought it was a fitting name.' He sighed, remembering, then swung the pickaxe again. 'She was fast, manoeuvred swiftly and was more than a match for any other vessel foolish enough to take her on or try to outrun her.'

'Was?'

He paused and shook his head wistfully, his dark eyes sad for a moment before he turned away. 'She was dismantled after we returned from America. They told me the fire damage was too great to repair. Better to start afresh.' Then the pickaxe came down with such force he sent rocks flying everywhere as she realised she had inadvertently struck a raw nerve.

'You never got to say goodbye.'

'I was probably being given the last rites when the decision was made.' More stones flew as he aimed the blade again. 'I think I received them so many times in the first month I could probably recite them.'

Something which didn't bear thinking about. 'Is that how you were wounded? The fire?'

He nodded curtly, then, jaw clenched, directed all his focus to the task in hand. Obviously hurting. She wanted to comfort him, but didn't know how to. In the end, she decided the best course of action was not to ask a single one of the many questions she desperately wanted to ask. Instead, she did her damnedest to load the wheelbarrow as quickly as he was dismantling the wall, wishing she knew what to say to make him feel better.

* * *

After ten tense, silent minutes, he threw the pickaxe to the ground and kicked the loose stones in the bottom of the trench. 'For pity's sake! I can hear the blasted questions whirring in your mind like a cog, Miss None-of-your-blasted-business!'

'I'm sorry. I know it's none of my business—and I have no intention of prying.'

'Good.'

'And actually, in my case, if I am being pedantic, questions spin in wildly like a top more than whir like a cog.' And so many unanswered questions gave her a headache. 'I cannot stop them.'

'Then ask the damn things, woman, and let's be done with the inevitable inquisition before that big brain of yours explodes!' He started to pace within the narrow confines of the trench, both hands fisted, his expression furious. But for some reason she knew it was at circumstance rather than at her specifically. When she remained quiet, he stopped pacing and glared hands on hips, daring her to speak.

'As you say, it is none of my business.'

'I'd rather you heard it from me rather than Eleanor. Or, heaven help me, idle and misinformed gossip from people with nothing better to do than speculate and fabricate their own answers when none is forthcoming. That used to

drive me mad on board ship. Rumours... Panics...
Fairy tales... If you are going to dig on my land
and make friends with my interfering sister, Miss
No-peace-for-the-wicked, then you might as well
know the sorry truth.'

'All right... How did it happen?'

'We were part of the blockade anchored outside
New York tasked with preventing cargo entering
or leaving the harbour. A stupid waste of time, if
you ask me, and a foolhardy gamble with the lives
of sailors when all the aggrieved parties would
have been better off sitting around a table and
hashing it out like adults instead of playing silly
games to maintain the stalemate for two years.
But what would I know about such things?' The
sarcasm was accompanied by a frustrated shake
of the head. 'I was only there—in the thick of
it—at the mercy of the whims of the government
and the Admiralty three thousand miles away!'

'It must have been hard fighting a war you
didn't agree with.'

'It wasn't a war. Wars have rules, tactics, bat-
tles... Obvious enemies and a clearly defined
cause to be fighting for. There wasn't much evidence of any of that from where I was anchored.
We were fifteen ships in total and it had been a
quiet week. Too quiet. It lulled us all into a false
sense of security. That annoys me the most be-

cause I was lulled, too. Privateers attacked in the dead of night when I was asleep. The first I knew, we were already dodging cannon fire. By the time I got on deck, the ship was on fire. We tried to fight it as best we could, alongside fighting them as well, but the wind sent it spreading to the sails on the mizzenmast. I knew if the mainsail went up then we were done for—a sitting duck—so I climbed the mast to cut it down and managed to set myself on fire in the process.'

'Did it…hurt?' A stupid question, but one which had plagued her since her first glimpse of the scars on his cheek.

'Enough that I wished for death to take me immediately. And perhaps it would have if I hadn't stupidly thrown myself into the sea in order to stop it.' Thank goodness. Effie couldn't imagine how awful it must have been. The pain and fear. 'And very near drowned wrapped in the sail to boot. I think they pumped a good gallon of brine out of my lungs when they fished me out. Although thankfully I have no memory of that.'

But as he recalled it, she saw the horror in his eyes and realised he clearly remembered both the burning and the drowning, and despite the warm sun on her skin she shivered at the thought.

'Does it still hurt?'

He shook his head. 'But I do not feel like my

skin fits any more, if that makes sense. Too tight. Numb in places. Oversensitive in others. It isn't mine.' Anger again—but tinged with something else. Frustration? Sadness? 'It isn't me.'

It isn't me. A strange and upsetting statement which threw up new questions. Questions she knew he wouldn't answer despite giving her permission to ask them. His sister had said something similar when she had assured Effie he wasn't himself. He was clearly lost. Languishing in some strange limbo he was struggling to find his way out of. She understood. After Rupert's death, when she had been forced to resign herself to the fact she would never have any of the things the female part of her craved—like children, or real intimacy with another human being who accepted her exactly as she was—she had had to do a great deal of soul searching to claw her way out of that pit of despair.

Purpose had been her salvation then and was still the only thing which blurred the constant sense of loneliness and otherness she had felt from her earliest memories. Feelings which had intensified as her age had increased and all hope of living any sort of normal life beside someone who wanted her there gradually eroded away with each rejection or daily reminder of exactly how peculiar she was.

Dark days and hopelessness sucked all the joy out of your soul and she suspected Lord Rivenhall's weren't over yet.

'How much of you was burned?' An intensely personal question, but she needed to know. Needed to understand the full ordeal he had been through and perhaps through that him, too. The real him beneath all the bluster and anger. The man whose outer wounds had healed, but who still had a long way to go to be mended.

'In fractions, inches or just body parts? Because if it's fractions, then one physician put it at an eighth. How he came to that figure I do not know. You would have to ask him. The scars run from here...' He pointed angrily at his left ear. 'To here.' He jabbed himself in the ribs. 'Largely thanks to the supremely combustible properties of the fine wool in my *dashing* blue and white captain's coat. At its longest point it is eighteen and a quarter inches. Another helpful physician gave me that hideous number because he felt the urge to measure it. He thought it remarkable. My case remarkable. Because I wasn't expected to survive the night, let alone the six-week sailing home. But survive I did, more's the pity, as I wouldn't wish that first year of recovery on anyone.'

'Why?'

'It was agonising. I spent most of it in a delirious stupor thanks to all the laudanum they forced into me. It was as if I was trapped in a never-ending nightmare involving the fire and the water…' His eyes were bleak now. The anger gone from his voice and replaced by something else. 'Hell on Earth. Then I had to suffer another three months of a different kind of hell as Eleanor weaned me off the stuff after the worst of the wounds had healed over.'

'By then your ship was gone.'

'It was. And my crew and my illustrious naval career with it.' He couldn't disguise the sadness in his dark eyes. 'Alongside my father, who died of pneumonia that winter—not that I was *compos mentis* enough to understand that, let alone grieve for him when he passed. We were never close and even less so after I defied him to go to sea, but still…' He had lost so much. Been through so much. None of it his fault yet he would carry the scars of it for ever. Was it any wonder he was angry at the world?

'Then, of course, I was bullied into six long months of exercise because my muscles had wasted away.'

'Eleanor again?'

He smiled wryly. 'She wanted me to live. I wasn't so keen.'

'And now?' The thought he still might wish for death broke her heart.

'And now… I am here.' He shrugged. 'Trying to find the wood for the trees. Except my sister doesn't think I am capable of doing that by myself.' He bent to retrieve the pickaxe and leant on the handle. 'She thinks I need to rejoin the world.'

'What do you think?'

'I try not to think. Like you, I find my thoughts exhausting.'

'Digging helps. Although it is physically impossible to dig all day and, once I stop, off those thoughts go again.' Effie drew a spiral on her temple with her index finger. 'Spinning wildly. I have to keep myself constantly occupied or they send me mad.'

'I've been counting things. Patterns, forks, clouds…' He sighed. 'It is not a particularly effective method of keeping them at bay. I've been thinking for some time I need another method.'

'If you find a way which works all of the time, please pass it on.' They had something in common. Something real and tangible in common. Something few others would understand and that warmed her. 'I find the nights the worst…'

'When your body is crying out for sleep and your mind isn't done playing with you?'

'You, too?'

He smiled in response and something peculiar happened as she smiled back at him. For the first time in her life she felt a true connection with another human being, although she couldn't put her finger on exactly why that was, other than to feel unjudged and able to be completely herself for a change rather than pretending to be the diluted version she always strove to be in the company of others. Even with her father, dear understanding Rupert and Lord Richard—the three closest relationships of her life—Effie had often guarded her words. Yet with this strange, changeable, complicated man whom she barely knew, but felt she did, she already realised she did not need to do that. More bizarrely, for the first time, her overactive mind was quiet. Calm.

Content.

'Digging might well be a distraction, but it's thirsty work, Miss Nettlesome. I don't suppose you brought any water with you?'

'I did better than that.' She stood and brushed the dust off her breeches. 'I brought lunch. It's in my satchel and I am happy to share it with you seeing that you have practically demolished that pesky wall for me.'

'Then don't dither, Miss Nithercott. Bring it hither from thither before I wither.'

'My name seems to bring you much amusement, my lord.'

'It is such a dreadful name, I feel the near-constant urge to change it.'

'Agreed. It is dreadful. Rare nowadays—but I am not surprised it is dying out. I should imagine all the other Nithercotts were only too happy to abandon it as soon as an opportunity presented itself. The grooms as well as the brides. Unfortunately, my first name is no better so I am doomed on both counts. Euphemia.' She pulled a face as she tugged the food parcel from her bag. 'Euphemia Nithercott... I've always hated it. Such a convoluted, tongue-twisting mouthful. No name should require seven whole syllables. Two would be ideal. Perhaps three at a push. Something innocuous which would help me to blend into the background—or at least try to.' Until she opened her mouth, of course. 'Like Jane Smith or Anne White. Two instantly forgettable names consisting of two perfectly bland syllables.'

'Try living with eight.' He used both his hands to push himself to sit on the edge of the trench. 'Maximillian Aldersley. The ink runs out on the quill before I can finish my signature, which always makes it look untidy.'

They had that in common, too. 'Eight *is* greedy—but Max is nice.' She lowered herself to sit beside him so they could share the food. 'That one syllable suits you.' And now she was sitting much too close. They were almost shoulder to shoulder. She could feel the heat of his body through the soft linen of her shirt. Smell the same comforting aroma of his shaving soap as she had when he had solicitously wrapped her in his coat the other night. Just as it had then, something about it unnerved her and called to her at the same time.

'Then I give you leave to call me Max. Especially as *my lord* doesn't seem to fit any better than my damned skin just yet. It's too new. Too formal.'

'Whereas Captain is *so* very informal.'

'I do not recall asking you to call me Captain, Miss Nit-picker.' He tore off a crust of bread and nudged her playfully with his elbow. Something she was pretty certain no one had ever done before. 'This is the part where you give me leave to call you Euphemia instead...'

'It's Effie.'

'Effie...' The way he said it, his deep voice lingering softly over the vowels as if testing the sound of it, sent shivers up her spine. 'I like it.'

Chapter Eleven

Three eight-foot trenches...

'It's definitely another post hole.'

Effie was gazing down from the edge of the enormous cavity they were currently working on, studying the darker circles in the mud she had just uncovered with her trowel. This slight discolouration, she proclaimed, came about when the wooden posts which once sat in the holes had decayed and altered the composition of the soil. Max wasn't inclined to argue and really did not know enough about digging up the past yet to try if he were. To him, mud was mud, but he was prepared to concede that while one dark circle was coincidence, three the exact shape, size and formation might well prove her hypothesis correct.

'Which leads me to believe this building was either entirely made of wood or, more likely when one considers traditional old English building methods of yore, maybe even wattle and daub. Of course, if that is the case and I am correct in my assumption that this dwelling predates the Roman invasion, it completely contradicts Cassius Dio's account of the ancient barbarian tribes indigenous to this area, don't you think?'

'I think, in order to form an opinion on the fellow, I would first need to know what the blazes Cassius Dio said. Which I don't, by the way, in case you were wondering. I've never even heard of the blighter.'

She smiled and rolled her eyes, totally oblivious to how gorgeous she looked bathed in sunlight. Flecks of copper shimmered in her dark hair where it had escaped its pins. Not that she was really one for pins, preferring to anchor the messy knot to her head with a pencil than spend unnecessary hours ruthlessly taming it with curling irons and fussy styles when she had holes to dig and treasure to find.

There was nothing fussy about the woman stood before him in well-worn breeches and practical shirt and he liked that about her. When she dined with them at Rivenhall, which she had done twice since the first awful meal, she always wore a lovely gown and made more effort with her hair, yet as beautiful as she looked in a dress, it was this Effie he preferred. This one who encroached on his dreams at night and regularly consumed his mind when he wasn't with her. The one he allowed himself just two hours a day with, at random times, always pretending he and Drake happened to be passing by when he counted the minutes until each casual visit.

Max tried to rationalise his obsession using common sense because the facts were undeniable. Firstly, she was a stunningly attractive woman. Secondly, he hadn't had a woman in nearly two years so his rampant lust was only to be expected. And thirdly, she was the only woman in his current acquaintance who he wasn't related to and the only person he had allowed a little into his life since leaving London. Therefore, it was hardly a surprise she had come to feature so much in his thoughts.

However, regardless of all those pertinent and undeniable facts, he had had enough affairs in the past to know there was something unique about Effie which called to him in a way which was entirely different from all those other women. Even his former fiancée, who he was certain he had loved with all his heart.

Yet the way he felt about Effie was different. It wasn't love. Love hadn't felt like this. Nor had simple lust. The first had made him want to pick flowers, then parade Miranda all over town so everyone could see how lucky he was to have won the heart of such a sought-after woman and the second was always short-lived and entirely carnal. While he felt lust for Effie, he also felt affection. Friendly affection because he enjoyed her company. That was new, too. He had never had a female friend, aside from Eleanor and as his sister she didn't count. Max had always been a man's man. Or maybe he had merely been that because there weren't any women to befriend in the Royal Navy? In which case, perhaps that explained his bond with Effie?

Her mind fascinated him. Never in all his thirty-four years had he ever witnessed anything quite like it. The way she worked her way through problems by asking herself questions was astounding, coming to reasoned and substantiated conclusions in minutes when most would take hours deliberating such complicated things. But then most people would have to seek out the answers in books and tracking down the exact piece of research in a book was usually a mission in itself. But if Effie had read it—and lord only knew the woman must have read every book on antiquity in existence—then it was already stored in her cavernous head so she did not need to bother.

'Cassius Dio was one of the great Roman historians. He wrote eighty mighty volumes of the history of the Roman Empire spanning its conception one thousand years before the birth of Christ to the end of the second century. There are other eminent Roman historians, of course, but his work is one of the few which includes their early occupation of our island. He records the Celts as possessing *"neither walls nor cities nor farms".* He describes the tribes as aggressive, warlike and nomadic in nature. Hunter-gathers rather than civilised or advanced enough to grow their own crops. In Dio's books—which are written in ancient Greek, by the way—the Celts are little better than savages who lived in tents without clothes or shoes. But I have always taken issue with that. The English climate is not at all conducive to nudity for at least three-quarters of the year, so unless they were all covered in a thick pelt of hair they would have frozen to death in the winter. And if they were indeed hairy beasties, which not one of the old histories suggests including Dio's, then the Celts wouldn't have painted themselves blue because I sincerely doubt the paint they used would cover dense fur that well.'

'Blue?'

'They used woad as a dye and painted themselves blue when they went into battle to frighten the other side.'

'Gracious! And they used paint instead of clothes?'

She nodded emphatically, causing the loose tendril of hair next to her cheek to bounce in a very becoming fashion. 'I think we can be pretty certain they fought naked because both Julius Caesar and Herodian mention it alongside bold blue tattoos, so I think the paint was used rather like ships use flags...' Her eyes always sparkled when she spoke about something which interested her, which was most of the time. She had the most expressive and beguiling eyes. 'To allow others close by to determine which tribe they belonged to.'

Images of naked, patterned, blue men filled his mind. Then a few naked women wandered in. Followed by a naked Effie with a pencil in her hair. 'Were the ladies nude and blue, too?'

She nodded. 'If they were fighting, it is entirely plausible.'

'Well, that would certainly distract the enemy.' He'd be so dumbstruck he'd be cannon fodder, especially if she was one of the warriors.

The vast wealth of diverse and complicated knowledge crammed into her head was boggling. Sometimes, Max just asked her obscure questions simply to hear her answer. And when she answered, it was never with one simple word. It was long and convoluted, addressing every possible variation and permutation, every existing theory considered, dismissed or upheld with yet more evidence while she argued with herself, until the entire scope of the topic had been explained to him in staggering detail. More often than not, it left him open-mouthed in wonder—but he was always amused, too. There was something about Effie which constantly sailed dangerously close to the ridiculous, which was a place he had always enjoyed. Or at least he had back in the days when he hadn't been so bitter and twisted and he'd had a sense of humour.

'Can I ask you a question, Max?'

'You can always ask me anything, Effie. In fact, I insist upon it. I find your honesty and your undisguised curiosity refreshing.'

'Then that is a first. Most people loathe it.'

'Then most people are daft. What's the question?'

'Are we friends now? I feel as though we are, but I am never entirely sure. And experience has taught me that if I assume, then I am doomed to be disappointed when my perceived friend starts to avoid me.' She said it so matter of factly, but his heart wept for her. It was so ill deserved. Effie was a breath of fresh air, not an irritation.

'I suppose we must be.'

Her delighted smile was like a balm to his soul.
'That's nice. And you don't mind all the questions?'

'I don't want you to ever think you shouldn't
ask questions, Effie. You can always ask me anything…' Which might well open some potentially
awkward floodgates. 'As long as you appreciate
I might not always answer them.'

'That strikes me as very fair. Do you think
Boudicca painted herself blue? I am certain I have
never read any account to suggest she did.'

'Perhaps she was so fearsome, she didn't need
to?'

'Perhaps?' She shrugged as she considered.
'Even so—I might do some research tonight just
to be sure. It will only keep me awake otherwise.'

As clever as she was, and he sincerely doubted
there was anybody on the planet cleverer, she was
also chaotic.

Keeping time seemed to cause her a great deal
of difficulty—no doubt because her mind had distracted her—and she seemed to struggle with the
everyday sorts of decisions which most people
did without thinking. But she was reliably late to
dinner and, when she arrived, would inevitably
have always forgotten something crucial, whether
that be a sensibly warm shawl to go home in as
she had that first fateful night she had dined at

his house and challenged him about his behaviour, the mismatched boots she frequently wore while digging when there were plainly two pairs because some days she wore the brown boot on her left and other days she brought its right friend instead. Or her entire wheelbarrow of tools, as she had this morning. Apparently, she was halfway across the meadow before she realised and arrived at the site after he had ridden past it six times in his quest to *happen* upon her casually, looking delightfully flustered but in matching boots this time for a change.

'If they built a wattle-and-daub structure, driving thick posts deep into the ground as the frame, then the people who built this dwelling were not nomadic at all. Dio was wrong! Or at least he was wrong about the tribes here in Cambridgeshire. They were obviously much more sophisticated than the barbarians he painted them as. Perhaps their paint distracted him exactly as you said... That would make sense. The Romans were invaders so they would only initially see the Celts on the battlefield and formed their opinions based on that!' Her grubby fist pumped the air in triumph that she had worked the problem through. 'Why do people always judge solely on first impressions, Max? Especially when they are invariably always wrong. Take you, for instance. On first impression you were loathsome and now after a few short weeks of acquaintance you are...'

'Tolerable? Invaluable? Wonderful?'

Mischief danced in her eyes while she made him wait for her verdict. 'A little less loathsome, but very handy with a pickaxe.'

'I am touched.' He fluttered his hand in front of his face as if overcome with emotion and she laughed out loud. Effie's laugh was as delicate as she was—in other words, not delicate at all. It was loud and exuberant and refreshingly impossible to fake. 'Such gushing praise will go to a man's head, Miss Never-one-to-beat-about-the-bush. What's for lunch?'

Her face wrinkled as she slapped her palm to her forehead. 'I forgot to pick it up from the kitchen table.'

'You mean there is nothing edible in your satchel? Not even a slice of Mrs Farley's famous fruitcake?'

'Perhaps one of these days you will surprise me and turn up with some food yourself for a change rather than like a sullen bad penny, complaining you are only offering to help because you are so eager to hasten my departure from your land.' They both knew that was a pathetic excuse and he came because digging with Effie was a much more effective distraction from his black thoughts than counting the floorboards in his study. He hoped she had no clue that he also came because he needed to see her.

'Besides…' she wagged her finger '…you're the one with the battalion of staff and the enormous kitchens. If you are hungry, you can take your mind off it with some digging. I need another trench here.'

'But I have to go. I've wasted two hours suffering your presence already.'

'Another two will only hasten my eventual departure from your land and you are so very good with a pickaxe.' She walked saucily to an unspoilt piece of grass and jumped on it then grinned when Max tugged his forelock before going back to stare into their latest trench to contemplate the post hole and ponder its secrets.

Even silent, he could hear her brain working and while he understood that many might find her intelligence intimidating, for reasons he could not fathom because his own official education had stopped at twelve, Effie did not intimidate him. Bizarrely, he understood her.

She was endearing and charming, funny, alluring and irritating all at the same time and quite unaware of all of it. Max, on the other hand, had never been quite so aware of a woman in his life or quite so smitten by one. He couldn't deny the smitten part was a worry, but as he had absolutely no intention of ever daring to act on the attraction for fear of more catastrophic humiliation, he tried to push his concerns to one side and simply enjoy having something other than his own woes to occupy his mind.

'That's three post holes in total so far and all exactly three feet apart.' To make doubly certain, Effie paced the distance again which was always entertaining to watch. She couldn't just pace the distance like a normal person, she had to do a funny half-marching, half-high-kicking pace which she had explained was deliberate as it gave a near exact twelve inches and negated the need to bring a measuring stick—which she doubtless had always forgotten in in the first place. Then she stopped and held one arm out straight like a blade and stared down it. 'But they do not seem to be straight.'

'Perhaps your ancient dwelling is built on an angle?'

'Which would still necessitate a straight wall, Max.'

'They could simply be very bad builders?'

From her expression, he could tell she was already engrossed in trying to formulate a theory, so he rested his forearms on his shovel and simply enjoyed watching her do it. After a long ponder, which for Effie was about twenty seconds, her eyes wandered to the original hole she had found the pot in. 'Unless…'

Then she was off pacing again, only this time from the post holes to the spot he had originally encountered her with her head in the ground. Typically, she checked each measurement twice and then positively beamed from ear to ear. 'I think this hut is round, Max! Exactly like the hearth! And the hearth has to be the centre because it is exactly fifteen feet from it to each of those posts.'

'If that is the centre, then this hut of yours is huge.'

She blinked and her lips parted as she considered it. 'Good heavens! I think you're right! Forget the trench I suggested. We need another one exactly fifteen feet opposite this one to test your theory… Now if my mathematics is correct…' which of course it would be '…a circle of a diameter of thirty feet has a circumference of ninety-four. Gracious—that *is* big!' She tapped her lip and he watched her long lashes flutter in time with her rapid blinking as she calculated with baffling speed. 'And as we already know the post holes so far are three feet apart, then we have at least another twenty-nine post holes to excavate! Or thereabouts as it is not exact but I am assuming the doorframe to be narrower—as doorframes so often are... Why are you staring at me like that?'

At some point his jaw must have dropped without his knowledge. 'Because you are a marvel, Effie. A tremendously odd, tremendously irritating marvel.'

'It sounds as if you had a very productive day and an exciting one.'

When he'd sent word that he would not be home to take afternoon tea with her as he'd promised, his sister had insisted on dinner instead and insisted on inviting Effie. Which meant Max had been subjected to hours of scrutiny as she watched the pair of them—first over the dining table and now in the drawing room as they enjoyed a nightcap. It was subtle, because he had categorically warned his interfering sibling against attempting to matchmake two weeks ago after the first meal the bane had attended, but it was obvious to him she still held out hope romance would kindle and that hope bothered him. So much so he had even considered broaching the subject and having the cringingly awkward conversation with her to set the record straight.

His sister believed Miranda had been shallow and heartless in not marrying him or even waiting until he was properly healed to terminate their engagement. She believed his former fiancée's reaction was unique to her because she was vain and selfish and that another woman wouldn't be so lily-livered about a few scars.

As much as Max wanted to cling to that belief himself, he had long accepted it wasn't going to be the case. His deformity inspired revulsion. He'd seen it first-hand both in Miranda's eyes each time she glanced at him before he released her from the commitment and in the eyes of every man, woman and child since. The constant horrified looks had been one of the main reasons he had imprisoned himself in his sister's London house. On the few occasions she had dragged him out when he was well enough to walk, people pointed and stared. And those were the better reactions. A few crossed the road, others recoiled in horror and one mother had clutched her child towards her and covered his eyes with her hand—no doubt to prevent the poor thing from having nightmares. Never mind the nightmares her extreme reaction had given Max. From that day on he'd taken his exercise in Eleanor's garden and hadn't cut his hair since.

Effie might not obviously recoil in horror, she was much too intelligent and kind for that sort of behaviour, but tolerating his presence or even befriending him was a completely different thing to allowing him to kiss her or caress her and he couldn't imagine her wanting to do either of those things to him in a million years. Not when he couldn't stand the dreadful sight of himself without wanting to be sick on the floor.

'The prospect of a round dwelling is incredibly exciting! Unheard of, even. We'll have to dig a few more trenches to properly confirm it, of course.'

'By *we*, Eleanor, she means *me*.' Max rolled his eyes for effect. 'While she wafts around with a trowel on the last six inches of soft, flaky peat once the hard labour is done.'

As he had expected, she poked her nose in the air and peered at him imperiously down it. 'I managed to dig my own trenches quite well enough before you moved to Rivenhall, so I dare say I'd manage if you stopped insisting on assisting, Max. Not that I ever recall asking you to assist. You took the task upon yourself.'

'That is because Max is still a gentleman beneath his sour exterior, Effie, no matter how much he tries to hide it. Clearly you bring it back out of him.' Eleanor shot him a loaded glance over her sherry glass. 'Isn't that right, Brother?'

'When are you going home, *Sister*? Surely you must miss your poor, put-upon family even if they are undoubtedly glad of the respite?'

'I do miss them. Two weeks is a long time.'

'It is. A *very* long time. Long past time you were off, in fact.'

Typically, Eleanor decided to ignore him to speak to their guest. 'And if your roundhouse is an exciting new discovery, what do you intend to do with it?'

For the first time, he watched Effie deflate as she shrugged. 'What can I do with it? Nothing, I suppose. Although on principle I will doubtless write a paper to torture myself and send it to the Society of Antiquaries which they will, as usual, completely ignore. Then I shall have to wait for a man to make the discovery somewhere else years down the line and get all the credit for it when his work is published in *Archaeologia*.'

'You should get the credit for it.' Max hadn't intended for his statement to come out quite so vehemently. It was so passionate it made his meddling sister pause mid-sip before making a poor show of covering her delighted smile behind the delicate glass as he tempered his voice. 'Your work should be published.'

'It's always been my dream to be published! To be recognised as significant in something at least... That would mean the world.' She caught him staring at her and, as if she realised she had just revealed an important part of herself, shrugged and looked towards Eleanor, pretending feeling insignificant was of no matter when it had to be. Max had felt a lot of things in his life, but being insignificant wasn't one of them. 'But I won't and that is that. My own stupid fault for being born in this body.'

Unconsciously she gestured to her chest and it pulled his eyes there, to the hint of cleavage visible over the neckline of her pretty dress before he wrenched them away. Something which his blasted sister clearly noticed, too, judging by her broad grin visible alongside either edge of her glass.

'Maybe you should submit it under a pseudonym... A male one. I have heard many female authors do that as it is the only way for them to be published.'

'I suppose I could...' She didn't sound keen. She sounded disappointed and rightly so.

'But Effie still wouldn't get the credit.' And that felt grossly unfair. She was so smart she'd wipe the floor with all those fusty, narrow-minded antiquarians. 'I say you should persevere. In fact, I am inspired to write them a sternly worded letter on the subject.'

'You? Write a strongly worded letter!' His sister burst out laughing. 'He would send them a list, Effie, like he sent me whenever he arrived in port.

If that. Max is incapable of creating prose which does not read like a ship's manifest.'

'Then I would send them a strongly worded list, *listing* all the reasons why those lofty antiquarians are actually cretins.'

'That is very kind of you, Max.' Effie reached across the gap between their chairs and touched his hand and he felt it all the way to his toes. 'But entirely pointless. They will not budge. Lord Richard wrote them several letters, but they will not change their rules. If anything, I think the letters annoy them almost as much as my papers do. Perhaps, for the sake of progress, I should try a pseudonym as Eleanor says. At least then others can learn from my discoveries—even if I have to pretend to be Mr John Smith.'

Chapter Twelve

Dig Day 790: sixteen post holes. One spear head. No pickaxe-wielding earls...

Effie retied the ribbons of the glasses around her head and then arranged her belly flat on the bottom of the trench to resume the painstaking task of gently scraping away another layer of soil from the metal object which stood proud above it. It was very likely an axe head similar to the one she had uncovered yesterday or perhaps a tip of a spear. This particular part of the dwelling seemed to have been used for storing weapons and tools because she now had quite a collection. If she focused, she would know the answer before the afternoon was done. The only problem was today had proved itself a bad day for concentration because her vexing assistant had failed to turn up at all.

That was, of course, his prerogative. They never

made any firm arrangements and certainly never discussed times. Max arrived when he felt like it, stayed for only as long as he wanted and then always bade her a good day, making sure she knew he found her presence and her purpose irritating. Rationally, she understood he probably had a hundred better and more pressing uses for his time and it was not as if he had promised to be here to help her—but none of that made her feel less bothered by his absence because since the first day he had picked up her pickaxe three weeks ago, he had always come. In fact, he had not missed a single day in all that time and since they had started on their quest to prove the dwelling was round, he had taken to spending longer and longer with her.

Yesterday, he had worked solidly by her side for six hours despite the hot June sun beating down on them. Not having him a few feet away, asking her questions and rolling his eyes or demanding sustenance, felt wrong.

She missed him.

Worse, she was worried sick about him and had no earthly idea why. But since late morning she had been plagued with a bad feeling which not even the painstaking excavation of a two-thousand-year-old Celtic axe head could banish.

Again, his fault because he was such a closed book.

After their one and only discussion about his

scars, they had never discussed anything too personal. All conversation was limited strictly to the dig or the superficial. Obviously she still had a million questions about Max, concerning both his past and his present and all the complicated pieces in between, all frustratingly unasked because she knew instinctively they would not be welcomed. He had remained entirely true to his word—he never minded the question, but there were a great many he blatantly refused to answer. He never said no outright, but he was an expert at sidestepping them. Yet sometimes, she could see his torment in the fleeting bleak expressions which often skittered across his face or see the swirling unreadable emotions in his eyes which his slightly detached, frequently belligerent permanent mask couldn't always hide.

But seeing as he resolutely avoided asking her anything about herself which could be construed as intensely private, he gave her no way in to probe him and doubtless did that on purpose for exactly that reason. Therefore lord only knew why he wasn't here today and more fool her for allowing herself to care.

Except she did.

With a huff, she tossed her trowel aside and sat up. Her own jumbled thoughts regarding the wretch were slowly driving her mad. Something he would know because he knew more of her than she usually allowed the world to see.

Would it have killed him to send word? Something? Anything? Just to let her know he wasn't drowning in a deep pit of despair all alone.

Then go seek him out.

The obvious solution to her problem had also been there since late morning and was the loudest and most insistent current thought in her head. She had been ignoring it out of pride, knowing doing that would tip him off to the fact that she cared about him. Much more than was probably wise. Max had become her friend, companion and, to herself at least, she was prepared to acknowledge she had developed a teeny bit of a *tendre* for him against her better judgement and entirely at odds with her cynical attitude towards romance. Hardly a surprise when he filled his coat and breeches so well, when he had a voice which made her insides melt like butter and expressive dark eyes which called to her soul.

The wretch.

She absolutely did not want him to know that.

Effie was an acquired taste. She understood that. And understood only too well she was quite capable of sending him running for the hills if she mishandled things by thinking out loud— something she had always done with alarming frequency throughout her life and which managed to damage every fledgling friendship she had tried to nurture. Her inadvertent openness and obvious desire to be accepted was a bit too much and nearly always put people off. It was the reason she was never invited to anything beyond the events everyone was invited to any more and why she had been left on the shelf to gather dust. For now Max tolerated her and that meant the world.

So did his sister…who seemed to enjoy her company and spoke to her in a manner which suggested they were friends, too—or at least she thought they were. Eleanor had asked only yesterday if she could borrow Effie's copy of Mrs Radcliffe's *The Italian* because there were apparently only serious books in Rivenhall's extensive library and she was in dire need of something salacious. Those were the sorts of things friends did…

The Italian!

She could deliver the book! Why hadn't her enormous brain thought of that simple solution earlier? It was perfectly innocent and perfectly believable—meaning she wouldn't have to come off the least bit clinging or needy at all. If anything, it made enquiring about Max an afterthought at the very most and, as long as she didn't look desperate, he would be none the wiser that she cared.

Deciding she had no more time to waste on worrying, Effie rushed home to fetch the volume.

Dashing back across the pasture with it in her hand, within half an hour she was knocking on the front door and less than a minute after that she had been greeted by a slightly drawn but smiling Eleanor, who welcomed her with open arms.

'Effie, how lovely to see you!'

'I brought your book.' Be subtle. 'I was going to give it to Max today, but I haven't seen hide nor hair of him so thought I should deliver it instead of taking it back home. I didn't want you to have to suffer another day with nothing salacious to read.' Undoubtedly too much information, but at least her features felt nonchalant.

'That is very thoughtful. Would you care for some tea?'

Not having any of the answers she had come for yet, Effie enthusiastically nodded and Smithson was dispatched to fetch it. The tray came back with just two cups upon it, which threw up more questions about the new lord of the manor which she had to bite back so hard it hurt.

'How is your quest going?'

'Good. I believe we have located the door and while I cannot conclusively prove the house is round, it's already a semicircle. But we... I...am making progress.'

'Splendid.' Eleanor took a sip of her tea to cover her suddenly uncomfortable expression before smiling over-brightly. 'I am glad it is all moving in a satisfactory direction.'

Effie's bad feeling was getting worse because Eleanor still looked distinctly uncomfortable and her conversation was suddenly stilted when she was normally so open and sunny. Unless Eleanor had decided to tire of her oddness as people— even the kindest sort—tended to do eventually. A prospect which made her chest ache with sadness. 'Of course, things move faster when Max assists me. I missed him this morning.' So much for nonchalant.

'He was indisposed this morning and...' The teacup clattered in her saucer and suddenly Eleanor's face was wretched. 'Oh, Effie—as much as I know he is going to be furious if I tell you, I feel I must because I really have no idea what to do and, so far away from home, nobody else to turn to!' Eleanor was up and pacing, her odd mood doing nothing to calm Effie's now wildly racing heart.

'I hate it when he gets like this. When he withdraws from the world and will not let anybody in... And it's all my fault. Poor Max... I should have handled it differently...'

Fear constricted Effie's throat. 'What's happened?'

'This.' Eleanor reached into her pocket and retrieved a tightly folded sheet of newspaper. She unfolded it and handed it to Effie, pointing to the third announcement in Births, Marriages and Deaths. 'He was devastated when he read it. I could see it on his face. Then he stormed out to who knows where and came back not an hour ago and shut himself away again. He refuses point blank to see me or speak to me about it.'

Effie read it aloud. *'"The Earl of Castlepoint is happy to announce that her Ladyship the Countess of Castlepoint, of Prittlewell House, here on the morning of Saturday last, gave safe delivery of a son and heir..."'* It was a standard announcement with two similar listed directly below. 'I don't understand?'

'She was Max's fiancée. Before the accident. She left him while he was recovering.'

'Oh...' This was the first Effie had ever heard of a fiancée. Her surprise at the news was rapidly overwhelmed by an emotion which churned her stomach. Anger at the woman's thoughtless, callous treatment of Max tinged with overwhelming jealousy that he clearly still had feelings for the woman if this piece of news had caused him pain. *'Oh.'*

'I never liked Miranda.' Eleanor's tone was clipped and her features suddenly furious. 'I always thought her shallow and vain. More concerned with pretty gowns and how full her dance card was than with anything of substance. She went out of her way to ensnare him in the most calculated fashion and I was of the firm belief the only reason she had sunk her claws into him then was because he was a handsome and eligible heir to a wealthy earldom—but I kept my own counsel. When he came home injured, she proved me correct, although it gave me no pleasure to be proved it. He was still bedridden and in agony when she terminated the engagement.'

'She ended their engagement? Then? How could she?' Because such a monstrous cruelty beggared belief.

'Max will tell you he terminated it and technically he did, but only because she put him up to it! Because she couldn't bear the thought of marrying a man who was no longer the dashing naval hero, but a wounded one—regardless of the title and fortune. She was impatient to be the wife of an aristocrat and was not going to allow his inconvenient injuries to get in the way of her desires!'

'That's awful...'

'Oh, but you haven't heard the best of it yet! Within two months she was engaged again—

which completely broke his heart, of course—
and then we had to relive the pain again when she
married a scant few months later. And she had the
audacity to marry in June. The exact same month
she had planned to marry Max because Miranda
had set her sights on being a June bride, too, and
she had no intention of waiting a year until this
summer to do it. In Saint George's in Hanover
Square, of course. The same church they were
to be married in. To rub salt in the wound. And
now this.'

Eleanor shook her head angrily, tears in her
eyes. 'Yet another blow. A reminder of all that
should have been his. He knew she was expecting. Gossip has been rife for months and he diligently reads the newspapers, sometimes I think
simply to torture himself, so I should have had
the foresight to check each one before he reads it
after breakfast. But I didn't think and he saw it,
and he's taken it badly.'

'Poor Max.' Effie's heart bled for him. 'And
what a truly hateful woman to abandon him in
his hour of need.' She wanted to give the witch a
piece of her mind. Right this instant. 'What sort
of a person does that?'

'The sort who cares more for her own social
standing and appearance than she ever cared for
my brother! I have never told him...and I probably

shouldn't tell you…' Eleanor lowered her voice to a whisper '…but a few weeks after he had returned, her visits to his sickbed became more sporadic. At first, I believed her flimsy excuses about being under the weather and exhausted from the trauma of it all—until I realised she was in fact back out in society attending every ball, soirée and tea as if Max did not exist.'

'Oh, my goodness!'

'And he kept asking after her. It was tragic. She would allow a week to pass between visits and when she did deign to grace us with her presence she never stayed very long. That hurt him deeply, but he never said anything. He stores everything inside, you see.' She clutched her fist to her chest. 'And I knew he was worried about it. So one day, I called upon her and tried to appeal to her better nature, citing how much her visits meant to my brother and how I believed they were essential in his recovery and do you know what she said?' Effie dreaded to think. 'That she wasn't cut out to dance attendance on an invalid!'

'But that is atrocious! After all he'd been through… How could anyone…?' She was staggered that anyone could be so unfeeling.

'It gets worse, Effie. I reminded her that the marriage vows stated a wife stand by her husband in sickness and in health and she countered that she hadn't yet taken the vows and wasn't entirely sure she was going to—as she felt that Max was no longer the man she had agreed to marry! Can you believe that?'

'I have no words, Eleanor. None. I am so shocked…' It really did beggar belief. Aside from the dreadful aftermath of his injuries, Max had lost his career, his ship and his fiancée, too, and all because he had tried to save his crew, then had the audacity to survive. Then another dreadful thought occurred to her. 'Had your father died at this point also?'

Eleanor nodded and her expression turned fierce. 'Oh, how I hate that woman and despise everything she has done to my brother. When he first came home he was optimistic and determined to fight, then after things ended between him and that foul harpy he changed. The light dimmed in his eyes and he lost the will to live. I do not think he has found it again since. I blame Miranda for all of it and I do not care if it is small-minded, but I wish her no luck, Effie.' She gripped her hand and her expression hardened with disgust. 'If I ever collide with her again, I swear as God is my witness, I shall spit in her eye!'

'Then you are more civilised than I, Eleanor, because I have never met her or heard of her before today and I already want to wring her neck, then pummel her to a bloody pulp! What a witch! What an evil, malicious, spiteful…' The fury and outrage she felt on his behalf burned hot in her gut and she didn't realise she had leapt from her seat and started pacing until she stopped dead and pointed a quaking finger. 'How far away is this Prittlewell House? Perhaps we should go there right now and give her what for?'

Through the tears, Eleanor smiled, her bottom lip quivering before she enveloped her in a hug. 'Oh, I do love you, Effie! Max needs someone like you on his side.'

That simple, affectionate gesture touched her beyond belief. 'Of course I am on his side. I am his friend. Or at least I hope I am. With Max it is hard to be sure.'

'He plays his cards close to his chest. Too close nowadays but, and if you will forgive the irony, he has been badly burned in more ways than one and finds it so very difficult to trust anyone any more. He never used to be like that. He never used to be so cynical, either, or so pessimistic. But since the accident and after Miranda ran roughshod over his heart, he has built walls around himself which he has allowed nobody to breach. Not even me. It worries me so much.'

'Where is he now?'

'Locked in his study, where I suspect he will

remain for at least a week if his reaction to her wedding is anything to go by. This is a massive setback... When he was doing so well. I was beginning to see glimpses of the old Max. He seemed almost happy again and I credit you with that entirely, but...' Eleanor slumped back into her chair and put her head in her hands. 'We are back to square one again and heaven only knows how long it will take him to get over this latest blow.'

Effie wrapped her arm around her shoulders and squeezed in reassurance. 'If he knew she was expecting, then chances are he was prepared for the news. Today it might have all got on top of him, but perhaps tomorrow he will rally?'

'I was going to go home tomorrow. Just for a few days...' The older woman shook her head before blowing noisily into her handkerchief. 'I am sorry. I shouldn't be dumping all my woes on you, Effie. I was just looking forward to seeing my family... Selfish, I know, but never mind. I am being silly. They will still be there in a few more weeks when hopefully this latest crisis has past...'

And now her heart wept for Eleanor who had stepped into the breach and coped with it all for so long. 'You should still go see them. I can look after Max.'

'No. I daren't leave him. He needs me here. He might not appreciate that, and will undoubtedly disagree with it, but he needs me still. Maybe he will surprise me as you say and bounce back in a day or so.' Her brave expression was unconvincing. 'Once he has stopped lashing out at me, of course.'

'And festering in self-pity.'

'Yes. And that, too. You do seem to know him well.'

'Do you think it would help if I tried to talk to him?'

'I doubt he'll see you, Effie. Or anyone. Not today at least. It's too raw and he won't appreciate the interference. Perhaps tomorrow?'

Chapter Thirteen

Two hundred and twenty-four squares of panelling...

Max stared at the wall and prayed the loud ticking clock upon it would somehow tick quicker and get this damned day over with. He was furious for feeling sorry for himself after all this time and livid that he couldn't seem to stop.

He sensed her before her dark head poked through the study window and he cursed himself for not locking the damn thing the moment he had heard her in the hallway an hour before. How typical she would encroach where she was not wanted! Something he had suspected she would do because the damn woman had no boundaries. Which was probably exactly the reason why he had left it open on the off chance she might come. Heaven help him...

'I found an axe head. A big one. Probably used for chopping wood rather than for battle judging by the shape of the blade. Battleaxes are a lot more showy and this one is nothing but practical. Of course, you would know that if you'd visited the dig site today...but as I can see, you are inordinately busy.' She allowed her eyes to wander to the spot on the wall he had been staring at so intently. 'What were you counting? Cracks in the plaster?'

'Go away, Effie. I'm not in the mood.'

'So I gather.' She balanced one hip on the sill and settled her back against the frame so that he knew she had no intentions of going anywhere and bizarrely he felt inordinately relieved at the prospect. He needed something to be angry at other than his own inability to face facts and he needed Effie. Had been craving her comforting presence since he'd read that damn newspaper this morning. 'But your long-suffering sister is worried sick and...' he sighed and her pretty, insightful eyes locked with his again '...and so was I.'

She was just being kind, he knew that deep down, yet it didn't stop his silly heart from soaring for a moment that she cared enough to be worried about him.

'You might have sent word you weren't coming.

I packed a huge lunch and, with the heat, half it is now thoroughly spoiled and wasted.'

'I never asked you to pack it.'

'No, of course you didn't, because that would have involved you making a commitment and we don't do that, do we? You would much prefer to moan when I haven't brought enough food when you inevitably turn up and still eat more than your fair share.'

Something he couldn't deny.

'Eleanor told me about Miranda.'

'I'll wager she did.' And doubtless rendered him a pathetic, maligned and helpless victim in the process, damn her, when the last person he wanted to be pathetic for was Effie. Even if he was.

'I think it is only fair, before this conversation progresses any further, that I state here and now I already despise her and think you are probably much better off without her.' Max braced himself for the inevitable platitudes and pity. 'Not that I expect you to see that, you silly man. You're not the least bit ready to see sense yet and I am sure you are much preferring your romantically martyred view of it all.'

'Martyred?' That brought him up short. *'Martyred?'*

'When used as an adjective it means to act in

a manner showing affected or exaggerated suffering to evoke sympathy.'

'I know what it means, Miss Nobody-asked-your-opinion. And you are wrong. I seek nobody's sympathy!' The very suggestion was—

'I am not wrong and you know it.'

'You have no right to…' One shapely leg swung over the sill. 'No! Stop…' He stood, outraged, his finger pointed like a weapon, feeling much like King Cnut must have felt when faced with the incoming tide, but still in denial it might roll in. 'I forbid you to climb through that window!'

'Oops.' She shrugged and then grinned as her feet hit the parquet. 'If only you'd bought those dogs you'd threatened, eh, Max? Then you could set them on me for my gross impertinence. Or is this technically trespass?'

He was positively looming over his desk, incensed, but typically his anger did not faze her at all. She sat herself on top of it, uncowed, and stared at him levelly. 'But let's not digress from the topic at hand. We were discussing your martyrdom and how you are absolutely convinced that the lily-livered turncoat Miranda you proposed to is so much better off without you now you carry a few scars that you prefer to punish yourself for getting them rather than be furious at her for not loving you enough for them not to matter. That's the long and short of it, isn't it?'

She hadn't loved him enough. He knew that. He'd always known that. Yet he had loved her enough for both of them and her rejection and her revulsion had destroyed all that had remained of his self-esteem in one fell swoop. 'Get out, Effie, or I swear to God I will throw you out!'

'She wanted someone titled, rich and handsome. The dashing naval hero and sought-after bachelor she could boast about. And now that your accident has left you merely titled and rich you simply do not pass muster any longer. Her rejection broke your heart and spurred you into becoming a recluse…'

'I'm warning you, Effie…'

'And because wallowing in your own self-pity has become quite the habit, you use every little excuse which comes along to justify being a selfish, self-indulgent pain in the neck to everyone who cares about you.' She jabbed him hard in the breastbone with her finger. 'You should be ashamed of yourself, Maximillian Aldersley. Your poor sister is beside herself and worried sick.'

'My sister has—'

'Your sister has done nothing but be at your side for eighteen long months. Come hell or high water. She has sacrificed her time, her family and

I dare say her sanity trying to selflessly drag you kicking and screaming back into the land of the living and she deserves better than this. And so, you near-sighted, stubborn idiot, do you!'

'Coming from the woman who settled for an old man rather than wait for the groom she deserved!' A low blow, but he was floundering. He had expected empty platitudes and unpalatable pity, not an argument stripped bare of both. An irritatingly sound one. Damn her!

'A fair point. But I had to consider practicalities which you do not.'

'Practicalities?'

'The world is not an easy place for a woman on her own. Rupert could offer me a more secure future than I would have had as a spinster all on her own and accepted me for what I am. He was not going to try to change me and, believe me, I have tried changing umpteen times and always failed miserably so that was a huge weight off my mind. I entered into the agreement with my eyes wide open. I knew it wasn't love and so did Rupert. But you thought yours was all about love, and for you perhaps it was, but it wasn't for her and seeing as she has been married to someone else for an entire year now, it is past time to accept it and move on.'

'Move on?' As if it was that simple!

'Are you intent on repeating everything I say, Max? Because I am already finding it tiresome.' She was worse than a bane. Certainly the most maddening woman he had ever had the misfortune to lust after. 'Yes... Move on. Your wounds have healed and, by your own admission, you aren't in physical pain any longer. It is time to let your soul heal, too.'

'Are you an expert on the human soul now as well? Are you going to quote me learned studies? Statistics, perhaps?'

'I am an expert on what your own mind can do to you when it gets bored. *"Idle hands are the Devil's tools."*'

'Good grief, are you seriously resorting to quoting the Bible at me? Is that the best you have, Miss Ninnyhammer?'

'It is Chaucer, actually, I believe. If you are going to take issue with the attribution, at least get it right.' She shot him the saucy smug smile she always wore when she was being insufferably smart, then it softened and she sighed. 'With nothing external to occupy it other than grief or self-pity, the human mind will turn inwards and that is a dangerously slippery slope. Trust me—I know. My mind sends me mad unless it has purpose so I do whatever I can to keep it meaningfully occupied.'

'You dig. Even though nobody cares what you dig up.' He was irritating himself now with the well-aimed but churlish darts.

'Yes, I do. And I persevere. I keep trying. I do not wave the white flag of defeat and give up like the Society of Antiquaries wants me to because their opinion of my work is grossly wrong and one day, by hook or by crook, I shall prove it. It matters. I matter.' She stuck out her chin defiantly. 'I care about it and for now that has to be enough. When faced with adversity, we all have a choice, Max. We can either face it fighting or let it beat us and win.'

Effie was a fighter. She stoically faced every obstacle thrown at her and was determined not to be the insignificant woman society expected her to be. Which made him…what? A coward? The thought left a bitter taste in the mouth. She took his silence as permission to dissect his character some more.

'If I might be so bold as to make a suggestion…'

'As if I could stop you!'

'You might start at feeling angry with Miranda. I dare say that would be quite cathartic as well as wholly deserved, then stop fixating on everything you have lost and the past and start deciding what you are going to do with all the time you have left. Eleanor says the navy would be delighted to have you again. Or maybe you should spend some of your new fortune on your own fleet of ships?' He could feel himself scowl as she poked that raw nerve. Feel the wrench in the pit of his stomach. The call of the sea. The freedom of the ocean. The lure of adventure which had always set him at odds with his father…

'Or maybe do something entirely different? A new challenge, perhaps? You have this huge new estate and a veritable army of tenants. Lord Richard was a good landlord, but he wasn't a forward-thinking one and was most resistant to any new ideas. Experiment with new crops or breed horses. Become a magistrate?'

Each comment was accompanied by a prod of her finger.

'Take up your seat in the Lords and practise politics, perhaps? Study. Travel. Invest in stocks and shares. Speculate. Start a business.' Her finger jabbed him again and he caught it and held it to stop it doing any more damage to both his battered breastbone and his wounded pride. 'You might have a few scars, Max, but you are as fit as a fiddle now and still a man beneath them, and a rich and titled one to boot.' She snatched her finger from his grip to throw her palms in the air. 'The world is your oyster. How I wish I had your choices! Yet you squander them to count the seconds on the clock face and punish those who become rightly exasperated with your self-indulgent belligerence.'

'Thanks for your heartfelt sympathy.' She rolled her eyes at his annoyingly churlish sarcasm and both things galled. What was the matter with him? Why couldn't he move forward? Especially when he felt so mired in the past he was well and truly sick of it.

'You don't need my sympathy, Max. You've had far too much of everyone else's and, frankly, today you don't deserve it. I am livid with you! You made poor Eleanor cry!'

'I did not mean to make her cry...' And now he felt wretched as well as frustrated and betrayed. Somehow more wretched than he had when he had read that damn newspaper and been slapped in the face with Miranda's happiness.

'I know. You were hurt and you lashed out. But you cannot keep doing that. It is unfair.' He abhorred mirrors nowadays, even metaphorical ones, but she was holding one up to his face regardless and making him evaluate what he saw. It wasn't pleasant. 'Now she doesn't feel as if she can go home tomorrow...'

'She never mentioned she was going home?' He

wasn't being fair to Eleanor. Not by any stretch of the imagination.

'Well, she isn't now and wild horses will not drag her from here on the back of this no matter what either of us say. But she had thought you were making progress and felt she could risk taking a step back. The poor woman misses her family.'

'And I feel guilty for keeping her from them. It is one of the reasons I left London in the first place. That and the constant mollycoddling.' And the pity and the platitudes. The staring and pointing. The newspaper story confirming blasted Miranda's confinement. 'This morning was a shock and I handled things badly.'

'It wasn't a complete shock, Max. You knew she was with child and were probably counting the days until it arrived.' Effie was much too intuitive. Clearly she saw right through him. 'You live in Cambridgeshire now because you claim to be tired of London, yet diligently read the London newspapers—and not, I'll wager, only for the important news if you were concerning yourself with the birth, marriage and death announcements.' She did more than see through him! The blasted bane could read his mind!

'One doesn't have to be a genius to work out you were actively looking for the notice.' Which, of course, he had been. 'Which beggars the question as to how you intended to deal with the news, Max? Or did you just accept today's tantrum as a given and had no plans beyond that?'

A few months ago—hell, a few weeks ago—he'd have bellowed his denial from the rooftops. Yet the anger he usually felt at the mere mention of Miranda or his scars or his behaviour had apparently fizzled out because it was the bane who had done the mentioning. 'I live from day to day, Effie. I do not think or plan beyond that.'

The absolute truth. Admitting it aloud gave him palpitations, but in a strange sort of way. Admitting it to her also made him feel less alone.

'Understandable given what you have been through. You have been grieving so many things—' She reached across the desk and lay her palm over his hand. Something about her touch made him feel instantly better too. 'But mourning officially lasts a year, Max. Any more is unhealthy. It's time to cast aside your widow's weeds.'

She was right. He knew she was right—but the prospect of doing it was daunting. 'I am not sure I know where to start.'

'We both know you have already started. Your mind is craving purpose again and once that begins, everything else gradually follows. Your soul will not repair itself overnight—but it will mend, Max. I promise.' Her hand squeezed his and he suppressed the urge to turn his palm and lace his fingers with hers where they belonged.

Belonged? Where the hell had that stupid thought come from?

'Go and apologise to your sister and invite her lovely family to visit.' She stayed his instinctive rejection with her finger on his lips and he forget everything he had intended to say. 'For the sake of her soul, my Lord Recluse—not yours. And then, if you still need some purpose today, I have a pickaxe urgently awaiting your attention.' She severed the contact and slid off the table, leaving his lips tingling and a comforting puff of roses and lilacs in her wake which surrounded him like an embrace. 'I happen to know Mrs Farley's fruit-cake won't have been spoiled by the sun because it is steeped in enough brandy to preserve a corpse.'

She was right about everything. He knew and felt strangely humbled by her insight. Yet he also felt afraid. Looking forward terrified him, but there was nothing positive to be gained in con-stantly glancing back. Not when the die was cast and, as much as he might wish it, he couldn't change it. But perhaps with Effie's help he could move forward. He wanted to.

So wanted to.

'You know I am putty when it comes to Mrs Farley's fruitcake. Why didn't you mention it sooner? It would have saved you the lecture.'

'Where would the fun be in that?' Rather than open the door, Effie left via the window she had arrived through. She smiled and was less than a few yards away down the garden when he realised he wasn't at all ready for her to leave.

'Wait...' She turned on the path, her dark head tilted in question, the copper in her hair shimmering in the sunlight. The bane of his life and the balm to his soul. 'Was this all a ruse to get me to do your dirty work, Miss Not-above-knavery-to-get-her-own-way?'

She beamed, then shrugged, unrepentant, before sashaying away. 'You have half an hour, Max. Then I am eating all the fruitcake myself.'

Chapter Fourteen

Dig day 798: no progress whatsoever, thanks to three interminable days of torrential rain. But the sun is out now. Which is just as well...

Effie was no stranger to remorse.

When one frequently spoke or acted without thinking, which she did as a matter of course most days, remorse reliably often followed. However, this dose was niggling worse than usual because it hadn't come about because her mind had raced ahead before her mouth caught up, it had come about by telling a lie.

A big, fat and dishonest lie which she wasn't entirely sure what to do about.

The rain had had a bearing because she hadn't been able to dig for days, which in turn meant she was all alone at home with her noisy brain going slowly mad. And with idle hands, the Devil had apparently made use of hers.

Although in her defence, not that she could really defend the indefensible, she had not set out to lie. With nothing better to do, she had resorted to busying herself by properly organising and expanding her notes on the dig site, which had rapidly turned into another research paper to send to the Society of Antiquaries. She then followed it by writing a heartfelt letter, passionately explaining the significance of her find and pleading with them to at least read the paper. Then, in a moment of uncharacteristic dishonesty borne out of sheer frustration at their continued and stubborn blatant ignorance, she had taken Eleanor's advice and *not* signed it Miss Euphemia Nithercott.

Instead, she'd used a pseudonym.

One she was certain they couldn't ignore.

Maximillian Aldersley—the Tenth Earl of Rivenhall.

Then, before she thought better of it, she had dashed out in the downpour and managed to get it to the post office just in time to make it on to the mail coach. The first pangs of remorse had twanged as she had watched it be spirited away. Two days on and they were still twanging because she had no idea how to break the news to Max. Or if she actually should. There was every chance they would recognise the handwriting, or the location of the dig site, and realise exactly who had really sent the letter and send it back unopened like they always did.

But what if…? She already knew Max wouldn't take it well.

As if her thoughts had conjured him, two large booted feet appeared at the top of the trench she was crouched in.

'I am in hell, Effie. Utter hell and I blame you for it entirely. It is a sorry state of affairs when a man looks forward to suffering hours of your incessant talking in a muddy trench doing back-breaking, menial work, simply to get some peace.'

'Your niece and nephew have settled in, then?'

'Indeed they have. Alongside their nanny, their father, his mother and one blasted puppy who hasn't stopped yapping since it arrived. Of all the puppies in the world, what possessed my brother-in-law to get them that one? It is a menace.' It all sounded idyllic to her.

'Perhaps it's nervous. A change of scenery can do that to an animal. Or so I have read. What do your family think of Rivenhall?'

'The brats seem to love it. Which is a concern as already I am terrified they will never leave now that Eleanor has lured them here upon your flawed instruction.'

'You did not have to take my advice.'

'Yes, I did, or I'd never have heard the end of it! So I justifiably blame you entirely for the death of my peace and, thanks to the rain conspiring with you *and* Eleanor against me, what is left of my blasted sanity.'

'It wasn't meant to be for your sanity. It was entirely for Eleanor's.'

'The trouble with my sister is when you give her an inch, she takes a mile. Just like you, as a matter of fact. Give me a crew of men to manage any day over a couple of meddlesome and manipulative women.' He huffed out a sigh, looking thoroughly put upon, gorgeously windswept and distractingly all manly. So much so, she was constantly having to remind herself she was a committed cynic regarding men and a pleasingly broad pair of shoulders, strong back and sinfully pert bottom did not alter the fact that Max was as male as the next man and, by default, inherently doomed to disappoint her in the long run. Even if he was her friend and she was unwisely fond of him. 'Did I tell you she spent the week preparing the nursery? And trust me, it is a little too prepared for a short visit from the brats.'

'But not too prepared for *many* short visits. Eleanor said you are their favourite uncle, so it is only natural your niece and nephew would want to spend time with you—and only proper you should have the facilities to welcome them.'

'I am their only uncle, so it is not as if either of us has a choice in the matter.'

'Regular visits from them will be good for you. Little people are good for the soul.' So, apparently, was confession. She had to tell him what she had done even though she knew he was bound to explode in outrage.

'And little feet, I have discovered, also make a great deal of noise on those old oak floors. So do little paws for that matter. I blame you for both.' He crouched down, bringing his distracting muscular thighs level with her eyes. 'Your trench appears to be filled with bilge water. We can't dig that until it dries out.'

'I know.' She tapped the wooden pail sat half-full beside him. 'I thought it might aid the drying if I removed most of the water but it's proved futile. As fast as I remove it, it fills up again. Clearly, man can drain the Fens all he wants, but the moment they are fed with a little rain they return to type and flood. I blame the peat beneath the soil. There seem to be more old peat bogs around this dwelling than over by the Abbey... But then I suppose the Abbey needed to be built on solid foundations and a wooden house would not.'

Stop procrastinating and tell him. Fall on your sword. Beg for mercy.

'Are they all as bad?'

'Fortunately, thanks to your covers on the other side of the dwelling, those trenches seem to have avoided the worst.' Max had predicted the storm several hours before it had happened and then appropriated every piece of oilskin, canvas and wood at Rivenhall to cover the most important trenches which had yielded the most finds thus far.

'Then let's work on them while the weather holds. It is bound to rain later. Just look at that sky.' He pointed upwards at the single paltry, dark cloud in the sky.

'It is not going to rain, Max.'

'I might not know my Iceni from my Catuvella-uni, Miss Naysayer, but like any good sailor worth his salt I know my weather and I smell another storm.' He offered his hand to haul her out and then frowned in disgust when he saw the state of hers. 'Good lord, you are filthy! I mean, you are always filthy so I'm used to it, but that is a new level of muddiness, even for you. Yet despite the mud, I can still see you are wearing odd shoes. How hard is it to match a pair of shoes, Effie?' He walked off, shaking his shaggy dark head and leaving her ankle deep in water.

'Don't mind me. I can get myself out.'

'Probably best.' He returned with the wheelbarrow which he deposited next to one of the covered trenches while he watched her clamber up the sticky mud. 'Did you have the foresight to bring a towel?'

'Of course not. But I brought cake.' His favourite, as a sweetener in the hope it would make him less inclined to hit the roof when he learned she'd used his name without permission.

'Mrs Farley's...?'

'Well, I certainly did not bake it.'

'Did I tell you I am thinking of marrying that woman? What she can do with a humble currant and a bag of flour is a miracle. Is she single, perchance?'

'Not yet. But Mr Farley is seventy-seven and as such could feasibly turn up his toes at any moment. Mind you, at seventy-six, so could she.'

'If you are expecting me to baulk at that, I should warn you, I've always been partial to an older woman.' He had bent over to remove the pegs from the canvas protecting trench sixteen, allowing her to admire his spectacular bottom unencumbered. 'There is an earthiness to them which is...' She could hear the wistful smile in his voice and groaned aloud in mock disgust. The disgust might be false, but the pang of irrational jealousy felt very real.

'I have no desire to hear about your many conquests, Max—old or otherwise.'

'To be fair, seventy-six is a bit old. I always drew the line at late forties. After that, gravity tends to have taken its toll.'

'Ugh!'

'And how old was Rupert? Eighty? Ninety?'

'Fifty-nine.'

'Fifty-nine! You really were going to marry an old man! I assumed, when you said he was older, it was by less than twenty years. But fifty-nine, Effie…?'

'You sound as though you disapprove.'

'Of course I disapprove. What sort of a marriage would you have had with a man old enough to be your father? When you are so full of life…' His voice trailed off and she watched him shake his head in disbelief before his big hands spanned her waist and he effortlessly lifted her into the trench. Which once again put her eyes level with his distracting buff-clad thighs and reminded her of the hard muscles which pleasingly upholstered his strong arms and broad shoulders.

I am a cynic! A weak-willed and easily waylaid one.

'I told you—it wasn't a love match. It was more a marriage of convenience. He wanted a wife…'

'What for? To bring his slippers? To polish his ear trumpet? To keep him company in his dotage?'

'And I wanted…' To feel part of something. To feel like a woman first rather than an oddity. Feel a baby grow in her empty womb. Watch it grow. Love it with all her heart and never be lonely again. She shrugged, not wanting him to see how depressing it was to know her one chance at having what every other woman of her acquaintance took for granted had passed her by and she would never know what any of those longed-for things felt like '…more than what I have now.'

'I know—you wanted the security of marriage because life is *so* difficult for a woman on her own. I understand that—' He didn't look like he did. 'But those same securities would also come with a younger man. Could *still* come with a younger man. Preferably one still with all his own teeth. You were selling yourself short, Effie, and that is so sad.'

'One cannot sell oneself short if there is only one bidder, Max.'

He scoffed as he rummaged in the wheelbarrow. 'Do you seriously expect me to believe you were Miss Never-been-kissed before you met my uncle's decrepit friend? Because I won't have it. Oddness aside, you scrub up well.'

She decided to take that as another compliment because his tone had sounded flatteringly incredulous and despite being a little back-handed, it still made her tummy go all fluttery. 'Hardly never. In fact, as long as I disguise my natural self from the first moment I meet a gentleman and talk about superficial things like the weather, they have always seemed rather eager to kiss me initially.'

'So why the blazes didn't you marry one of them?'

'Getting them to kiss me has never been the problem. It's getting them to want to continue kissing me after they discover the truth about me that's always been the struggle. They seem to forget I am a woman the moment the real me slips out of my mouth...' She paused, waiting pathetically for another compliment which never came while he continued to rifle noisily in the wheelbarrow with more concentration than she felt it warranted in view of the gravitas of what they were discussing. Then, in a moment of pathetic weakness and to her abject horror, she accidentally said what she was thinking out loud into the void.

'I think I emasculate them.'

She saw his body stiffen before he turned, lips parted, and she realised she had shocked him. She found her hand slicing backwards and forward. 'I didn't mean by actual castration, Max.' Another poor choice of word when his groin was mere inches away and she was now thinking about it. The size, the shape, the form... 'I meant that their desire for me withers...' Good grief, the inappropriate words were coming thick and fast now! 'I mean it deflates...' It was like a disease of the jaws! It was his fault. His shaving soap, his arms, his thighs and the intimate proximity of his masculine parts were scrambling her wits. 'What I mean is...his *desire*, not his...um...desire.' To compound her misery she found her finger was pointing south and felt her face combust.

Laughter rumbled in his chest. 'You are blushing! Like a beetroot.'

'Only because you have the wrong end of the stick!' Suddenly every word coming out of her mouth sounded hugely inappropriate to him as well as her if the second bark of laughter was any gauge. 'And by stick I meant stick and not...'

She could see the amusement dancing in his dark eyes. 'And not?'

'Sometimes I loathe you!'

'Only sometimes? I must be slipping.' He passed her a trowel and when she snatched it out of his hand couldn't stop himself from grinning ear to ear. 'In case you were wondering, I understood your initial statement perfectly, Effie. Without the need for all your hilariously inappropriate descriptive clarification. Your big brain makes them feel emasculated in the inadequate sense rather than the literal.' To vex her he also pointed south, his lips twitching as he struggled to hold the laughter in.

'Then why didn't you just say so and put me out of my misery, you wretch?'

'Where would the fun have been in that? I thoroughly enjoyed watching you flounder and that unflatteringly blotchy blush was the icing on the cake.' He snorted again when her hands automatically sought her cheeks to feel the apparently unflattering blotches for herself.

'You're a miserable, reclusive curmudgeon. You're not supposed to have fun. And certainly not at my expense when I am one of the few people who can tolerate you.'

'That's true.' He jumped into the trench beside her making the six-foot-by-three-foot space feel overwhelmingly small. 'I shall try to curb the urge in the future. Although to be fair, it would be much easier to do if you stopped giving me good reason. You are the one who used the words wither and castration in the same sentence and then dug yourself a bigger hole trying to correct them.'

'You know the words fly out of my mouth before I've had time to consider them.'

'Then try breathing in between them, Effie, darling.' He was too tall. Too broad. Too everything while smelling sinfully too good. And he had called her darling, when no one had ever called her darling, and the endearment sounded wonderful on his lips. It all had a devastating effect on her pulse. 'It might help prevent unnecessary embarrassment in the future.'

'Good advice.' And because it was and she was more mortified now than just embarrassed, and because he already had his back to her, she inhaled deeply and slowly blew it out. She didn't usually allow herself to be so flustered with a man. Not any more at least. She blamed the fact she was today on three long days of not seeing him despite knowing full well he had always had the power to fluster her. Although bizarrely, as much as Max flustered her, he also liberated her, too. With him, she gave her big brain free rein and never pretended to be anything but what she was. He was her friend. Which was lovely and she should be content with that seeing as she had never had many of them. Except increasingly she wasn't.

'Do I intimidate you, Max?' So much for breathing before she thought aloud.

He paused and she held her breath, unsure she truly wanted to hear his answer, but desperate for it all the same.

'No.'

'Why not?'

Another pause. Strangely loaded and significant this time as his answer mattered so much to her. 'Because it is hard to be intimidated by a woman who cannot match a pair of shoes.'

Had he tempered his words? Sidestepped the question as he was prone to do when he did not want to honestly answer? Was he placating her, or worse—paying her lip service because he was kind beneath the bluster? He didn't seem intimidated ever—but then their friendship had always been strictly platonic. Perhaps that had a bearing? Or was she reading more into the pause and his answer than he had ever meant because her feelings for him weren't entirely platonic any longer and probably never had been? The feminine part of her was attracted to his physicality and the temporal part was attracted to the man beneath. Was she trying to read more into his words because she wanted more than friendship? Did he?

Of course not! This was all Eleanor's fault. Because Eleanor had set her reading Gothic novels again and the unrealistic romance in them was doing strange things to her cynical brain and reawakening her curiosity of men. Every heroine looked remarkably like her in her odd head and every hero bore a striking resemblance to Max. This was exactly why she had stopped reading the rubbish!

Max had never flirted with her. Or flattered her with effusive compliments. Never given any clue that he saw her as a woman as well as an irritant. All clear signs he did not reciprocate her foolhardy blossoming feelings.

But then again, after everything he had suffered, after his fiancée's cruel rejection, would he?

Too many questions crowded her mind, none of them she was brave enough to risk asking out loud. In case one slipped out and royally spoiled their friendship for ever, she bit down on her lip and tried to focus on the task in hand. Behind her, Max happily did the same although she sincerely doubted he was similarly plagued by questions concerning their unlikely but complicated relationship.

Did she intimidate him?

What sort of a blasted question was that to ask hot on the heels after he had only just discovered there had been multiple idiots who had apparently kissed her in the past. Idiots who were too stupid not to want to do it again! Because to his way of thinking, asking if she intimidated him was merely a polite way of asking if she emasculated him, which would be laughable if everything about Effie didn't remind him hourly exactly how masculine he truly was.

The most masculine part of him was still reeling at the sight of her all flustered and damp in that worn shirt and those damned form-fitting breeches. And she had a smear of mud on her cheek, which he'd had the devil of a job not brushing away the second he had seen it. The only way he could stop himself was to pretend he did not want to hold her muddy hand when he had stupidly offered to help her out of the trench, because in that precise moment, had he hauled her up, he would have hauled her into his arms and likely scared the hell out of her.

What baffled him, what he still couldn't wrap his head around, was how those idiotic men had found the strength *not* to kiss her because he was severely struggling with it.

Every day it got harder and, to make it worse, the urge wasn't only fired by her pretty face and mouth-watering figure, but by her mind. The more he got to know her, the more he wanted to know her in every sense of the word. His unwelcome infestation of visitors aside, the past three days had been interminable because he had missed her. He'd even ridden twice in the pouring rain in the pathetic hope he would still find her here, tenaciously digging despite the foul weather. The linen shirt plastered to her skin and rendered translucent…

And those thoughts were not helping his discomfort at all. What had possessed him to work in the same trench as her? Mere inches away, but still too many miles apart for his liking.

Blasted torture!

Clearly he had a masochistic streak to have chosen this, rather than the other fifteen trenches he had dug, just to be close to her?

Annoyed, he thrust the trowel into the soft mud wall in front of him and felt the tip of it strike something solid. Even though he knew it was probably a rock, he still took the time to remove the soil carefully from the surface exactly as Effie had taught him.

The edge of whatever it was seemed large and curved like a wheel and, because he did not possess her patience or want to alert her to the fact he might have found something and then have to suffer her leaning over him while he worked, he discarded the trowel and began to tug away the earth with his fingers. Then he hit peat and that happily crumbled with the merest touch.

Little by little, the object quickly revealed itself until Max had uncovered a foot-wide crescent. But unlike a wheel, it wasn't hollow, nor did it have spokes. He swiped his hands over it to clean away the mud and then stared in disbelief at the tiny spot of ornately tooled metal he had clumsily uncovered.

'Effie...'

His tone must have alerted her to his discovery, because like a shot she at his side and staring in disbelief. 'Good heavens...'

Suddenly crouched next to him, her fingers joined his as they frantically removed the dirt. A task made easier by the moisture left in the ground from days of rain, the removal of years of compacted earth with the pickaxe only days before and the fresh drops which decided to fall from the sky to soften the peat it sat in. In no time and oblivious of the rainfall soaking them through, they had unveiled a perfect circle, obviously an ancient shield, the centre decorated with a proud riveted disc around which swirling patterns had been pressed into the metal.

Max stepped back to allow her smaller, more nimble, gentle fingers to prise the embedded edges from the earth, then watched transfixed as it was suddenly and miraculously free with hardly any effort and she lifted it.

'I cannot believe it is completely intact.' She laid it reverently on the grass on the top of the trench and ran her palm over the pattern as the rain that had started again hammered down on it. 'Unless the peat somehow preserves things better than normal soil?' She tugged free the hem of her shirt and used it to clean away as much muck as she could and then just stood and stared at it in wonder. 'It is beautiful... Truly beautiful... Obviously bronze by the patina and lack of rust... The workmanship exquisite.'

'So much for the Celts being savages, then? The man who used this had excellent taste and knew one hell of a blacksmith.'

She slowly turned to him, half-smiling, half-agog. 'You are right... The man who owned this was someone special, Max. This shield is a statement. Purely ceremonial, I'll wager, and a mark of his status, exactly like the gold bracelet. Both are incredibly special objects and it is too coincidental to find two such treasures in one small space.'

'Do you think it plausible this wooden hut belonged to a king?' If the Celts even had kings.

'Perhaps... Which would make this dwelling...' Awe turned to excitement as she beamed, then launched at him, wrapping her arms around him in an exuberant hug while jumping up and down. 'Oh, Max! This is wonderful! Wonderful! You've found something wonderful! He's someone important! Someone hugely important! That explains why his house is so big!'

'Do you think?'

'It has to be! He is an eminent chieftain or a king!'

'Or a queen like that Boudicca you and my sister are so fond of. That bracelet is too small for a man's wrist. And then there is that comb you found. Big, hairy, blue men wouldn't bother with a comb...'

'Wouldn't it be wonderful if this was a woman's house? A different sort of woman than society understands today, of course.' Much like Effie herself. 'But one who mattered once. Someone important...' Her hands clutched at his waistcoat as she beamed and bounced on the spot. 'You've found something amazing, Max!' Caught up in her excitement he looped his arm around her waist and laughed, picking her up and spinning her around in the confined space as best he could until they were both giddy. 'You've found something amazing!'

'We found something amazing, Effie.'

We...

He liked the sound of that on his lips. Liked the feel of her arms locked around his neck. The feel of her lush body in damp fabric plastered against him. The sight of her bedraggled hair and the way it dripped rainwater on to his face. The way that rainwater spiked her long lashes and dewed her lips.

He felt his heart beating against her ribs.

Felt his chest rise and fall in time with hers.

Lost himself in the depths of her beautiful, expressive eyes.

Then forgot all the reasons why he shouldn't kiss her and simply did, sighing against her mouth as he gathered her close. She tasted like the outdoors. The sea air. The vast horizons he had sailed towards, filled with promise and wonder. Smelled of lilacs and roses and rainwater. Felt like utter perfection in his arms.

As if she had been made for him. That was his last rational thought before he lost himself.

Until the sound of rapidly approaching hoofbeats broke the spell and the pair of them jumped apart and blinked at each other, stunned.

Chapter Fifteen

❦

Three too many people at dinner...

It was like being under a microscope.

He was going to kill his sister for practically forcing this invitation on Effie, especially as she had made sure she hadn't given her either the time or space to sort it all out since the awkward moment she had arrived like the cavalry in the carriage, intent on rescuing them from the rain. Eleanor had taken one look at the pair of them, grinned like a loon and doubtless started plotting that very same instant.

They had taken Effie home, where she had been pressganged into returning to Rivenhall, his sister stubbornly refusing to take no for an answer and, in case she changed her mind, had dispatched her carriage again to fetch her to be certain. And early to boot, which was probably why their obviously uncomfortable guest was wearing one blue sparkly earring and one red, when the lovely gown she had paired them with was green.

Tonight, Eleanor had crowned herself queen of the knowing looks, which she shared much too frequently with her husband, Adam. Adam, to his credit, was attempting to make conversation with his mother to fill the painful silences while Max wished himself invisible, the blasted meal over with so he could finally have some privacy to talk to Effie and clear the air.

Assuming, of course, that he could clear the air. It was entirely feasible she was furious at him for taking liberties and this almost guaranteed she bitterly regretted it. She hadn't been able to look him in the eye since, which was no mean feat when she was sat directly opposite him at the table thanks to his blasted sister's blatant matchmaking and was soldiering through her dessert with such speed she clearly wanted to be gone. Frankly, he couldn't blame her. If he'd had somewhere else to go and hadn't felt obliged to support Effie in Purgatory, he'd be atop Drake right this minute galloping towards the furthest point on any map just to escape. Scotland had never appealed more. Or Dublin. Or even France, despite the bitter war with Napoleon.

But alas, he was stuck, hoisted by his own petard, and desperate to make things right again. To that end, he had a little speech all worked out to avoid the inevitable ritual humiliation, which largely blamed the heat of the moment and the excitement of the find for kissing her like a starving man feasting at a banquet and giving his meddlesome sister all the ammunition she needed to royally embarrass the pair of them. Because Eleanor might not have witnessed the actual kiss, but she had certainly seen the two, large, muddy handprints on Effie's breeches like the mark of Cain damning him for all eternity and announcing to the world that he had been the one to put them there.

To make matters worse, it had, in all reality, been the briefest of kisses. Seconds rather than minutes, yet intensely significant all the same. If he was going to be shot for a wolf rather than a lamb, then at the very least his damn sister could have postponed her unwelcome rescue a little longer so he could have prolonged the experience before it all came crashing down around his ears.

'Surely the Society of Antiquarians will have to take you seriously now you have found the shield *and* the bracelet, Effie?'

She shot him a very furtive, very awkward look before she answered his sister. 'One would hope.

I have certainly never read about anyone finding anything similar.'

'It's staggering, isn't it, to think that people lived here—at Rivenhall—two thousand years ago and that their belongings still exist even though they are long gone?'

'I suppose even then this was the perfect sight for a settlement. The Fens would have been fertile hunting ground with an excellent source of water. It was why the Abbey was built here in the Middle Ages. The church and the aristocracy always built on the prime spots...' Her eyes wandered again to his and swiftly dipped. As if suddenly remembering the events of the afternoon was too awful to hold them.

'You need to write that paper, Effie! Write it and submit it and we shall all march on their offices if they dare to send it back again! We could carry placards and protest outside until they relent.'

She smiled at his sister weakly, then glanced at him again, looking entirely horrified this time before she stared dejectedly at her empty plate. 'Maybe they will read it this time without the need for all that fuss.'

'I think we should make the fuss regardless. It will serve them right!'

'Forgive my wife, Effie,' said Adam, smiling

in apology. 'She's always had a radical streak. But she is right—you do need to write about your discoveries. But if the blinkered society of crusty old men will not publish it, I know a few publishers who might.'

Eleanor beamed at her husband. 'He does, too, Effie! Wouldn't it be better to write a whole book which will be read by hundreds rather than an academic journal like *Archaeologia* that is only seen by a select few?'

'I suppose…' Her eyes only made it as far as his chin this time before she tore them away.

'Just think of it… All leather bound with gilt lettering. Sat in bookshops and on library shelves all over the country as well as mine. It would certainly be a splendid way to thumb your nose at those crusty old antiquarians.'

'Would these publishers baulk at an academic history written by a woman?' Max saw hope blossom in her lovely eyes briefly before Adam unwittingly and insensitively quashed it.

'They do not need to know you are a woman. We can give you a male pseudonym or just use your first initials rather than your Christian name to muddy the waters. There are ways around these things.'

These things being all the same ludicrous things the idiots at the society used to obstruct her at every turn. 'I think it should say Euphemia Nithercott and be damned!' Without thinking Max slapped the table so hard the crockery rattled, which garnered another swift knowing look from his sister to her husband. 'It's Effie's work and she should get all the credit.' She almost smiled at him.

'Thank you, Max.'

'She should—but I am a realist.' He was going to strangle his brother-in-law. 'Even if we could find a publisher who would use Effie's name, the general public will not buy a serious history book written by a woman. And the academic establishment will be up in arms. It would be a bit different if she were writing fiction. That market is much more forgiving of female authors—for the right sorts of books, of course.'

Oblivious of the damage he had just done to Effie's dreams, Adam hammered one final nail into the coffin. 'Or you could publish the work in your father's name. An academic of his gravitas would guarantee it was taken seriously for sure and doubtless it would fly off the shelves.' He patted her hand and Max found himself fuming at the gesture. Not out of jealousy, but sheer outrage because despite being well meant—Adam Baxter did not have a mean bone in his body—it was both paternalistic and patronising while completely diminishing all that she was. 'We'll find a way around it, Effie, I promise. But first you need to write the thing.'

'I suppose…' Her usually animated eyes and tone were flat and Max's heart broke for her. How demoralising must it be to hit barricade after barricade on your quest to move a single step forward? How galling must it be to be continually put in your place by men who possessed less than a quarter of Effie's intellect? He had never been so ashamed of being a man in his entire life.

'I think it's time we left the ladies for our port, don't you, Max?'

This was the absolute last thing he wanted to do when all the light had dimmed in Effie's eyes and he finally understood with perfect clarity what she had meant when she had said he had numerous choices and she had so few. The world was made for men and brutally unfair to a woman as brilliant as her. 'Perhaps we should stay with the ladies tonight?'

'Absolutely not.' Eleanor's eyes were dancing. 'We have urgent gossip which must be shared and dissected. Isn't that right, Effie?'

A statement which caused her to visibly pale. But as trapped as he was, she, too, stood and trailed after his sister and Adam's mother like a condemned prisoner on the way to the gallows.

The two parties split at the door and he decided it was telling she did not look back. Before he and Adam turned the corner to his study, he heard Effie's voice in the distance. 'I shan't be a minute. I need to visit the...'

'Yes, of course.' Eleanor this time. 'Sherry or cordial, Effie?'

'Sherry, please.'

Then silence. A silence Max couldn't afford to ignore. He hastened Adam into the room and pointed him in the direction of the port decanter, then briefly excused himself to answer the call of nature, determined to clear the air and tell her he, too, would march outside the offices of the blasted narrow-minded antiquarians because their dismissive treatment of her was entirely unacceptable.

He was prowling in the hallway when Effie reappeared and instantly blushed crimson. 'Ah...' Her eyes dipped to the hands which had suddenly clenched in front of her, so tightly her knuckles were white. 'I hoped you would hang back... We need to talk... Urgently as a matter of fact... There is something important I have been meaning to tell you all evening... You see, the thing is, I might have inadvertently...'

'I know. And you really do not need to worry.' He waved away whatever damning words she was about to utter. Rejection was always best handled with indifference. Largely because his foolish pride couldn't handle outright rejection. It was bad enough from everyone else—painful in the extreme, in fact—but hers had the power to seriously wound and he wasn't entirely sure his battered heart was up to that.

She seemed relieved. 'You know?'

'It was inevitable…' He smiled. Nonplussed. Or as nonplussed as he could smile when his throat had constricted with pain. 'Wasn't it?' The masochist in him willed her to deny it.

'It was a moment of madness.'

'It was.' Max shrugged. Hoped he appeared blasé and unbothered. 'I shan't hold it against you.'

'Oh, thank goodness!' Her breath came out in a whoosh. She was obviously and unflatteringly relieved. Like receiving a last-minute pardon while the executioner was sharpening his axe type relieved. His heart shrivelled, then wept at the sight. 'I've been so worried about telling you. I was certain you wouldn't take it well… I am not entirely sure what I was thinking, but at the time… Well, clearly I wasn't thinking and acted on impulse rather than giving the matter serious thought…' Each word slashed like a blade, but he kept his expression light. Something which took every bit of his strength to accomplish. 'As you say, a moment of frustrated madness…'

'It was just an exuberant display of excitement borne in the heat of the moment, Effie. Perfectly understandable after we had just unearthed that magnificent shield. I have never found anything before and now I understand what you see in it. Digging up treasure is a heady feeling. A heady feeling indeed...' He was in danger of laying it on a bit thick. 'Let us blame the shield for our stupidity.'

'The shield?' She blinked and her cheeks heated some more. 'Stupidity? Are you referring to the kiss?'

'It was hardly a kiss, Effie. More a bumping of faces in the tight confines of the trench. And quite obviously a big mistake.'

'A mistake?'

'Are you going to repeat everything I say now?' He attempted a playful smile which physically hurt to keep glued in place while he waved the perfect kiss away with a dismissive flick of his suddenly lead-like hand. 'It's best forgotten, Effie. In fact, if you hadn't brought it up, I probably would have forgotten all about it already—what with all the excitement of unearthing actual buried treasure and all...' Something about her expression bothered him, but he couldn't put his finger on what. Because nerves were getting the better of him, he ploughed on regardless, mindful he was babbling like a country maiden attending her first ball at Almack's, desperate to convince her he was perfectly nonchalant with her obvious bitter regret and disgust. 'It's funny really when you think about it.'

'Think about what?'

'Me and you.' The feigned laughter sounded pathetically hollow to his own ears, so he sincerely doubted she was even slightly convinced by it, but he persevered. Wishing he were dead. 'A hilarious joke...' Except he wanted to cry it was all so tragic.

'It is?' Her expression was now as bland as the cream plaster wall behind her and he really could not read her. Awkwardness and hurt turned to uneasiness and abject humiliation, making him want to howl at the moon rather than stand in front of her denying all the feelings he could no longer deny to himself.

'Well, of course it is. We are friends, Effie. Nothing more and nor could we be, thank goodness.' Talking hurt. Swallowing was impossible thanks to the crushed glass which had suddenly materialised in his throat. His palms felt clammy and he wanted to run. 'The fact we are friends is bizarre enough, don't you think? What with you being the bane of my life and all...'

'The bane.'

'In a good way.' The ground felt unsteady

under his feet as he realised, too late, he had made a hash of things. Somewhere between blaming the excitement of the shield and perhaps a wee bit before he had called her a bane out loud, he had grievously insulted her. She made no attempt to mask the upset on her lovely face.

'Can banes ever be good?'

'In your case, exceedingly.' He knew he had to fix it, but had no earthly idea how without telling her that he cared. For her. A great deal. 'Not every man can boast a bane quite like you, Effie.' Without the benefit of either a trowel or a shovel he was apparently digging the largest hole he had attempted in a fortnight. A deep, cavernous pit which was taking him straight to hell. 'You are unique.'

'Unique?'

'Yes—different. Totally unlike any other person I have ever met before, nor likely will ever meet again...' He paused before the truth tumbled out, before he confessed he found her attractive in every sense of the word—mind, body and soul— but she misconstrued his silence completely and instinctively backed away as if he just slapped her.

'An oddity, then.' There was no misinterpreting her expression now. She was angry. Two chocolate eyes glared back at him stormy.

'Not in a bad way.' Five pathetic and lacklustre words which he would have chiselled on his gravestone as penance after she murdered him for them. 'Not so much an oddity in the odd sense, more odd that you are so...' Maddening, lovely, entertaining, necessary, entirely perfect from your magnificent big brain to your mismatched earrings. 'Errr...uniquely you.'

'If you will excuse me, Max, your sister is expecting me.'

He caught her arm as she barged past and she stared at his hand as though it were a snake. 'I am not articulating myself very well, Effie. You see, the thing is...' Perhaps the best solution was to simply start all over again from the beginning, leaving out all the bits which might let her know he had fallen for her hard. 'What I meant to say was...'

She tugged her arm away and peered at him down her nose. 'I understood your initial statement perfectly, Max. Without the need for all your inappropriately descriptive clarification. Like everyone else you see my big brain first and not the woman! And there I was thinking you were different from everyone else!' Then she stalked off towards the drawing room, leaving him standing there wondering how he had managed to make a bad situation so much worse without even trying.

Chapter Sixteen

Dig Day 801: it is still raining. Thank God!

'Is everything quite all right, Miss Effie? Only you don't seem yourself.'

Mrs Farley placed another cup of tea on the desk alongside a slice of fruitcake. Fruitcake which instantly reminded her of him. Dratted man. 'The rain is getting me down. It has barely stopped in a week and I am eager to get back to the dig site.'

A big fat lie.

For the first time since she had seriously picked up the trowel after Rupert's death, Effie was actively avoiding the ruined Abbey. Or rather she was actively avoiding a certain irritating gentleman who technically owned it and wasn't in any hurry to reacquaint herself with him after he had kissed her senseless and then likened it to a mere bumping of faces in a confined space, before calling her the bane of his life and reminding her she was peculiar.

It was entirely his fault she had been staring out of the rain-soaked window feeling sorry for herself all day rather than finishing the detailed sketch of the Celtic spearhead lying in front of her. The sketch she had promised herself she would finish today to add to the expanded paper she was writing, which doubtless nobody would read anyway so what was the point? Thanks to Max, everything felt futile and her thoughts were sending her mad, largely because they all revolved around him in some way.

She hadn't been able to concentrate on anything except Max.

In her pocket his lacklustre note of apology seemed to burn against her thigh, reminding her she was a fool. She did not need to read it for the six-hundredth time to know exactly what it said or feel aggrieved at the dull and impersonal prose. Prose which read more like a list than a heartfelt apology, the penmanship atrocious and all in all it only served to rub more salt in an already painful wound.

Dearest Effie
I am sorry I offended you.
I made a hash of things.

Please allow me to clarify so we may clear the air.
Max

Clarify! When he had been insultingly quite clear enough! And as to making a hash of things, she wanted to shake him by his annoyingly broad shoulders and scream that he had made more than a hash! He'd run roughshod all over her feelings, behaved exactly like everyone else, when she had convinced herself he was different and, if the constant dull pain behind her ribs was any indication, he had also broken her heart and certainly wounded her spirit.

Her own stupid fault, she supposed, when she knew his predicable and unoriginal reaction was bound to come eventually. If only he hadn't kissed her, then perhaps she wouldn't feel so awkward about things. It was hard to brazen it out and behave as if it was no matter when she had clung to him like a limpet, thrust her body against him like a wanton and kissed him back as if her life depended on it.

Which in those scant, reckless and significant moments it had.

On top of being a thoughtless and huge disappointment rather than the man she had stupidly convinced herself he was, Max was also the best kisser she had ever had the misfortune to bump faces against.

Effie was furious at him. And furious at herself for allowing the instinctual female part of herself to make a complete fool of her again, when she had long worked out that books and digging were better than men and she had made herself perfectly comfortable on her dusty shelf after her last hope of leaving it died with poor Rupert on a battlefield across the sea. Damn Max for giving her false hope!

Frustrated, she snatched up the rusty spearhead and stabbed it in the cake, then sprung out of her chair to pace. Pacing had become her only source of exercise these past few days thanks to both the weather and her cowardice. In the gaps between the showers, she convinced herself to go out and then talked herself out of it each time in case she encountered him. She had refused every single one of Eleanor's invitations to visit Rivenhall, too, citing the paper she was eager to write and pathetically using the weather as the perfect excuse to get it finished without distraction. And when Eleanor had called upon her yesterday to see how she was getting on, Effie had lied and said the words were flowing and perhaps they would become a book after all and then feigned uninterested nonchalance whenever the other woman had dragged the name Max into the conversation. Which she had tried to do with alarming frequency.

Although she had hinted he was miserable, too, although she had no idea why, but suspected it was something to do with what Eleanor called their *tiff* and that knowledge had made Effie feel slightly better. He deserved to suffer. The thought of him blithely carrying on oblivious when she felt absolutely wretched seriously galled. She was glad he realised he was in purgatory, because she was quite determined to make him stay there. They weren't friends any more as far as she was concerned and, as he had plainly stated, there was no chance of them ever being anything more than friends, ergo they were now nothing to one another beyond acquaintances. She would maintain a cordial and polite distance because she still needed to dig on his land. But on principle she would refuse any and all assistance from him in the future because she didn't want to be within ten miles of the dratted man—let alone ten feet.

Once she stopped avoiding him and the ruins like the plague, of course, because she still wasn't the least bit ready to have to face him.

Mrs Farley poked her head around the door. 'You have a caller, miss. From the big house. Shall I show him in?'

'Him?'

'I didn't ask his name. But he's big and brooding and soaking wet.'

Effie's stomach plummeted to her toes. 'Tell him I am indisposed, Mrs Farley.' What was good for the goose was good for the gander after all. And she wasn't ready. Might never be ready if her bouncing nerves and aching heart were any gauge.

'Tell her I will wait, Mrs Farley!' The deep voice came from the room beyond. 'Until Miss Nom de Plume is disposed.'

Nom de Plume! Oh, dear…

Max's dark, dripping head appeared over the housekeeper's shoulders, an opened letter scrunched in his raised hand and his expression as stormy as the sky outside. 'And then tell her I intend to wring her manipulative, duplicitous, libellous neck!'

'I can explain…'

'Explain what? That you wrote to the Society of Antiquaries pretending to be me? That you submitted a scholarly paper without my knowledge which they are about to publish in my name?' As Mrs Farley reversed in subtle retreat, he stalked in and tossed the letter on her desk.

'Or that you invited them to come to *my* house, Effie! At their earliest convenience no less! To join me at the dig!' Then she saw more than anger in his eyes. She saw fear. 'I can't have people in my house, Effie. Strangers... How could you? I am not...' As if he realised he was showing her so much more of himself than he intended, his expression hardened once more. 'I am not having it!'

As angry as she was with him, she wanted to hold him and comfort him. The fear was all to do with his scars. All to do with the wicked Miranda's rejection. She was certain, but knew he would never admit that. 'I am sorry, Max... I didn't think.'

'You are damn right you didn't think!' He tapped the folded letter hard with one blunt-tipped finger. 'It's about to go to press, Effie! They were so excited by *my* amazing discoveries, they wanted to rush it into this quarter's *Archaeologia* with all haste so the entire antiquarian community can learn from *my* work!' His fists clenched as he began to pace, prowling her small study like a caged tiger about to pounce. 'What if they all decide to come on the back of it? A pilgrimage of complete strangers, lining up at my door... All ready to stare and gawp!'

More proof that it was the way he looked which lay at the heart of his self-imposed isolation.

'I really am going to have to build that blasted wall, aren't I? And get dogs.' He looked so lost. So desolate as he paced, she instinctively went to him and grabbed his hand to anchor him to one spot long enough that she might be able to penetrate his own destructive thoughts obviously whirling in his complicated head.

'I will make it right, Max.' His eyes went to where his fingers had laced with hers and simply stared. 'I promise… We shall send another letter admitting to my deception and that will bring it all to a crashing halt.'

'It is too late… They are already on their way, Effie. I am to expect them tomorrow afternoon…'

'Then I shall be there tomorrow afternoon and I shall tell them the truth to their face.' His eyes finally rose to meet hers and he nodded. 'I dare say they will be so furious to learn it is me— the most persistent and irritating bane of their life—they'll order the edition delayed or, at the very least, every copy of that journal destroyed as a mark of protest before they can send it out. Rivenhall's secrets will remain exactly that—secret. I promise…'

Her hand reached up to touch his face and he leaned into her palm. Then immediately pulled away when her tingling fingers had sought his hair and he had given her an intense and troubled look she couldn't begin to decipher.

Other than it was troubled and she was the cause of it.

Feeling instantly awkward at indulging in such an obviously affectionate gesture when he had made it plain days ago he did not reciprocate the feeling, she glanced at her offending append- age, cursing it for having a mind of its own, then shoved the guilty hand behind her back in case it was tempted to go wandering again. Which it was.

'Thank you, Effie.' He was backing away, put- ting several feet of distance between them. Dis- tance which felt more temporal than physical. Significant again, as so many odd moments with Max so often were. 'I shall see you tomorrow evening, then...'

'Stay.' She didn't want him to leave. Despite all her anger at him, all her hurt at his cutting unin- terest, she couldn't bear him going just yet when he was clearly upset and she had caused it. 'You are soaked through. Have some tea... I'll fetch some towels.'

'No.' He couldn't meet her eyes again. 'Point- less. I'll only get soaked the second I leave.' He gazed longingly towards the door and she felt her throat tighten at the blatant rebuff.

'Mrs Farley made fruitcake.' Why was she practically begging when only minutes ago she had wanted to give him what for? Pathetically, she gestured towards the desk where the house-keeper had left a slab of his favourite confection and was horrified to see the rusty spearhead still sticking out of it. The sight of it seemed to bring Max up short, too, because he blinked at it, then at her and shook his head emphatically.

'No, thank you.' Too polite. Too formal. He couldn't meet her gaze. All very explicit signals he had misinterpreted her comfort as an attempted seduction and was plainly eager to run for the hills at the hideous prospect. 'Adam and the children are returning back to London shortly and I promised Eleanor I would be there to say goodbye...'

'Of course.' It was staggering that a second rejection from him could hurt as much as the first, when the first had been so cutting and decisive she really no longer harboured false expectations or ridiculously girlish hope for more. Yet it did. Max had made it obvious he did not want her in a romantic sense—she'd already had that spelled out loud and clear—but clearly he no longer wanted to be her friend any more either and, as much as she had fantasised about stepping back from the relationship to serve him right for disappointing her, knowing he would be nothing but relieved at the news was an awful blow.

'I will send the carriage tomorrow.'

She found herself bobbing a stiff and painfully

awkward curtsy in the wake of the new parameters he had set, when she had never curtsied to him before. 'That is very thoughtful of you.'

He bowed and hot tears prickled at this new starched formality. 'Good day.'

No, it wasn't. It was one of the worst. For the first time in a month she was categorically relegated back to being the annoying and peculiar oddity again, when for a while, with him, she had cast off those shackles and just been Effie.

'Good day to you, too…my lord.'

'Oh, I understand perfectly, little Brother! You hold all of her hopes and dreams, the fruit of two years of her labours and the power to help her in the palm of your hand and intend to crush it into dust. And I refuse to be a party to it!'

Max had known it was a mistake to confide anything to Eleanor because she always took the opposite stance to his, and always had, purely to vex him.

'Then make yourself scarce. Or better still, I'll saddle you a horse right this minute and you can follow your family back to town. I dare say you'll have caught them long before they reach the first posting inn!'

His sister's cup clattered in her saucer, sending tea sloshing over her skirts and the floor. 'I might

just do that! Because I am thoroughly sick of you
and your dark moods! And thoroughly sickened
by what you are about to do to poor Effie!'

'Poor Effie!' How typical she wouldn't take
his side. 'Poor blasted Effie used my name without my permission...' And invited strangers into
his sanctuary. And crushed his stupid hopes in
her fist, too. He was still reeling at her reaction.

'Tell me, Max if she'd have asked, what exactly would have been your response?'

'Well I'd have...' Said no. 'Counselled her
against using a pseudonym. Especially mine!'

'You're a two-faced coward, Max Aldersley!'

'Two-faced? *Two-faced!*'

'You heard me. What happened to the table-
thumping advocate of last week? The one who
was adamant Effie should publish her work because it was an outrage that she couldn't?'

'She should publish her work. As *her.* Not as
me.'

'Fiddlesticks! This has nothing to do with her
borrowing your name and everything to do with
the invitation she extended to the stuffy antiquarians who continually thwart her at every turn. You
do not want them in the house!'

He couldn't deny that part bothered him the
most. It might not have last week when he had
vociferously thumped the table—but last week

she hadn't trampled over the tender new shoots of his self-confidence and withdrawn herself entirely from him like a tortoise hiding in its shell.

'You just want to be left alone.'

'I don't want every Tom, Dick and Harry overrunning Rivenhall once that article gets out...'

'You don't want anyone to see your ugly scars, Max!'

He recoiled as if slapped at the harsh comment, because, even in his darkest days when his skin had been a bloody and festering mess, Eleanor had never once openly acknowledged he had scars which others found abhorrent.

She pointed at her forehead hard. 'I do have some idea how your thick head works! That's what you think of them, isn't it? Unseemly? Unsightly? You don't want people staring or whispering behind your back... You don't want to see their shock.'

'By shock you mean disgust, surely?' If they were going to finally speak plainly, then he'd speak plainly and be damned. 'Recoiling in horror in case this mess is contagious! Crossing the street... Covering their children's eyes.' Eleanor had been there that day and yet neither of them had mentioned it at the time or since. To all intents and purposes, they had both been oblivious to it all because that was the easier option. More civilised. A denial of the truth—all pretence and all damn lies. 'Of course I don't want strangers in my blasted house gawping at my face, Eleanor! This is the one place where I can avoid all that humiliation!'

His sister's anger dissolved at what he knew was a bereft and hopeless expression. 'I understand your reluctance Max. I know the last eighteen months have been awful and the behaviour of some people hurtful in the extreme, but the scars really do not look half as bad as they once did… and you do need to come to terms with them.'

'Easy for you to say.'

'They are not going to get any better, Max, no matter how much you hope they might. They have been the same for months. Is it your intention to hide away for ever just because of a bit of…?'

'Gnarled and hideous skin?' He had no patience for whatever diplomatic adjectives she was scrabbling for.

'You are a long way off hideous, Max.'

'And a long way off handsome.'

'Is that what bothers you the most? That you are no longer as handsome as you once were? When only the shallow and superficial would ever care about such nonsense.' They both knew she was alluding to Miranda. 'Effie isn't like that at all. I doubt she even sees the scars now that she knows you.'

He scoffed, disbelieving. Wishing it were true, but accepting that it wasn't. 'You really need to take off those rose-tinted spectacles, Eleanor, and face the harsh facts...'

'You need face the harsh facts, too, Max. If you pursue this course of action out of self-preservation, you will only end up pushing her away in the process. This decision will ruin things between you.'

'How many times do I have to tell you there is nothing between us?' At least not any more. 'There never was.'

'I have eyes, Max. I can see how much she means to you.'

'We are friends.' *Were* friends. Before he'd acted on impulse and ruined everything with one short, ill-considered and life-altering kiss. 'Just friends, Eleanor.'

His sister smiled maternally and reached across the table to squeeze his arm. 'Friendship is the perfect foundation to build love upon... Tell her how you feel.'

'Out of the question.' The words had flown out before he had considered the gravitas of them. Typically, his sister grasped them straight away and leapt on them.

'Maybe she feels the same? Have you considered that?'

'She doesn't.' There was no point in denying it when he'd already let the cat out of the bag. Eleanor would never let it go unless he killed her romanticised and forlorn hope stone dead, just as his had been.

He watched her face fall and saw the sympathy in her eyes. 'You've told her already, then?'

'Not in so many words.'

'Oh, for goodness sake, Max. Then how could you possibly...?'

He held up his palm and tried not to show how thoroughly wounded he was by Effie's latest rejection. 'I am not some gauche and inexperienced virgin, Eleanor... I do know when a woman isn't romantically interested in a man.'

They tended to react to an unwanted kiss with obvious discomfort as a rule, then hastily retreated, and in case he was in any doubt she felt disgusted at the prospect, her response this afternoon had confirmed it. She had inadvertently touched his scars and, when he had pulled back—filled with longing and foolish hope that to her they really didn't matter—she had stared briefly at her palm as if they had burned it hideously, too, before she fisted it behind her back and he'd watched her erect a sturdy and prickly fence around herself to keep him well away. He still felt nauseous thinking about it because that hideously polite and distant curtsy had almost killed him. And he certainly did not want to contemplate exactly why she had stabbed the fruitcake.

'Perhaps you used to have a good gauge on women—but I suspect your view of such things has become skewed since Miranda...'

Max leapt out of his seat to show his sister their conversation was done. He was not going to rehash the demise of his engagement on the same day as he had buried his blossoming dreams of Effie.

'Maybe the enforced proximity of this unwelcome visit is exactly what you both need to sort things out. Why don't I have some rooms readied for your guests in case you change your mind before tomorrow?'

Enforced proximity would kill him for sure. 'The long and short of it is...' He sucked in a calming breath and decided to bite the bullet in as brief and as matter of fact a way as he could without entirely humiliating himself in the process. 'I've completely and thoroughly murdered the friendship between Effie and myself.'

'Murdered is probably a tad exaggerated...'

'Trust me. It really isn't. It's been dead for almost a week already.'

'Which is why you are actively avoiding her.'

He hadn't entirely avoided her. He had sent her a heartfelt note, a tenuous olive branch suggesting they talk about it all, and she had ignored it. Doubtless she had only been polite yesterday because she was so eager to have her research published, although it hadn't lasted long.

Eleanor's expression was filled with pity now and he suppressed the urge to dash away from it so he could curl up in a ball somewhere and lick all his latest flayed, open wounds in private. 'Prolonging the agony of it all to continue the acquaintance is…is…' Emotion strangled his vocal cords and threatened to overwhelm him, so to cover it he walked to the window and stared sightlessly out for several moments before he could choke out a response. 'It would be…unbearable, Eleanor.'

Her silence said it all. It stretched for a good minute before she spoke again.

'Can it be fixed?'

'No.'

'Are you certain? Only you've come such a long way these past weeks, Max, and I credit your *friendship* with Effie as the cause. Maybe you have misread things? Or panicked unduly? If you loathe yourself, I should imagine it is very difficult to believe another would see beyond the things you hate about yourself. Maybe she just needs a little time… Or wants to be wooed a little.'

Wooed! He would laugh at the ridiculous suggestion if it weren't all so tragic. 'It cannot be fixed.'

'Most things can be fixed, Max—it all depends on how badly you want it and whether you can both be bothered to take the time and trouble to do so.'

'We would *both* have to want to fix it, Eleanor.' And she didn't.

'Would you like me to intervene? I could talk to her and…'

He shook his head. 'Absolutely not! I want no interference.' No more humiliation. 'I've made my decision and so has she.'

'Very well…' He felt his sister's hand rest on his shoulder. 'All I know is—whether it be as a friend or otherwise, it is plainly obvious Effie cares for you a great deal, too. And you will regret crushing her dreams, Max. Because if you do, then whatever you have or might have is as dead as a doornail for sure and it really will be too late to resurrect it once it is done.'

Chapter Seventeen

Three antiquarians...

With a disapproving Eleanor noticeably absent from the drawing room, Max and Effie had sat in brittle silence in the half an hour since she had arrived until the sound of the most unwelcome carriage in the history of carriages could be heard on the gravel outside. There had been so many confusing and conflicting things he had wanted to say to fill the awkward void, he didn't trust himself to say any of them without coming off as either entirely desperate or entirely pathetic. She simply looked drawn and miserable and he blamed himself for both, thanks to his sister's persistent and unyielding argument that he was crushing Effie's dreams regardless of the fact that it was the bane who was largely in the wrong because she had gone behind his back.

'They're here.'

He had never heard her voice sound so flat or so resigned. Where had all the fight and bloody-minded determination he associated wholly with her and secretly admired gone today? A stupid question when he already knew the answer.

Crushed in his fist.

But was self-preservation in this case selfish as Eleanor believed? Max had been mulling it over for hours and still wasn't sure which of them was right. All he knew was how he felt and that was thoroughly wretched. He loathed himself—inside and out. And the silent woman before him certainly did not look as if she had any desire to be wooed. She could barely look at him.

'I suppose we should go and greet them... Get it over with...' He would support her in that at least. And defend her if they dared to diminish her achievements simply because of her sex. And even do his damnedest to get them to publish her research under her name exactly as he had originally promised—because a promise was a promise no matter and he couldn't bring himself to break his to her now he had pondered things long and hard.

'Yes... Of course. The sooner it is done, the sooner they will be gone.' And so would she and his world would be plunged into darkness again.

Max led the way, supremely conscious of her behind him, inhaling his last whiffs of her perfume and wishing he could turn back time to the second he had uncovered the shield and sent things spinning so catastrophically out of control. They arrived at the front step as the high-sprung carriage came to a halt and, before the footman could get to it, the door flew open and a grinning, short and rotund man jumped out with his pudgy hand outstretched.

'Lord Rivenhall!' Still beaming, the gentleman pumped Max's hand enthusiastically. 'I am in awe, sir! Complete awe! In all my years of research I have never read an essay so thorough, so compelling or so well written! And the attention to detail in those sketches! I cannot wait to see your magnificent pot in all its glory, examine that bracelet or cast my beady, eager eyes over your roundhouse… What a day this is! What an honour it is to meet you!'

'Er…thank you.' His eyes darted to Effie in the hope she could shed some light on the identity of man, but she seemed to be doing her level best to blend into one of the columns behind Smithson or melt into the flagstones. 'And you are, sir?'

The slightly older man chuckled and slapped him on the arm as two more gentlemen alighted from the carriage. One reed thin and slightly

pompous looking as he cast his critical eyes over
the estate, the other so beige and nondescript he
would be impossible to pick out of crowd. 'Probably should have started with the introductions
first, shouldn't I? Sir Percival Egerton at your
service, my lord. A devoted antiquarian both man
and boy and, aside from digging the ground for
buried treasure much like your good self, I also
edit *Archaeologia* for my sins. As soon as your
paper found its way to my desk, I knew I had to
meet you.'

He stepped aside and swept his arms out to encompass his painfully thin colleague who made
no attempt to smile and stared at him down his
long beak of a nose, his eyes drifting immediately to Max's scars before he deigned to look him
square in the eye. Openly judging him as men of
supposed good breeding so often did and clearly
of the belief he had every right to.

It was exactly this which made Max instantly
dislike him. Undisguised disgust at his deformity
aside, he'd met many men of his ilk in the Navy.
All usually sat behind an ornate desk at the Admiralty, making sweeping opinions and decisions
about things they knew little about and refusing
to budge from them no matter what the cost. Give
him a man who had worked his way through the
ranks any day over one who believed he was born

only for the highest. 'This is Francis Brighouse, the Marquess of Denby, and one of the society's most active and respected Fellows.'

Was it his imagination, or did Sir Percival's cheerful smile suddenly look a trifle strained? The pompous Marquess merely inclined his head and didn't bother to speak, so Max did the same, but made a point of smiling slightly as he did so to show the fool he wasn't the least bit intimidated by Lord Denby's superior title or attitude or blatant distaste. 'Welcome to Rivenhall.' It would be a cold day in hell before he tacked the words *my lord* to any remarks to this arrogant blue blood.

'And beside him is our honourable secretary, Lord Whittlesey.' Sir Percival's smile was definitely pasted on this time, which was telling. 'He was the one responsible for sifting your paper out of the plethora which find their way to us each month, so you have him to thank for our over-enthusiastic imposition.' And doubtless was similarly responsible for returning all of Effie's previous efforts unopened. Already loathing him and sorely tempted to just punch him and be done with it, Max shook his proffered limp hand and tried not to curl his lip in distaste as he did so.

The bland man doffed his hat and inclined his beige head, his eyes latching on to Max's cheek like a limpet and not leaving. 'Lord Rivenhall.'

This was all as hideously awful as he had expected and he felt his toes curl in shame inside his boots while the angry acid churned in his stomach. 'Lord Whittlesey.'

'We are all three of us thoroughly thrilled to be here to see it all!' Although only Sir Percival looked thrilled, Max noted. The other two now looked fashionably bored and vaguely suspicious, as if they had no intention of gushing about Effie's magnificent discovery until they had clapped eyes on it themselves and satisfied their own sanctimoniously superior eyes it was not a big sham. 'It is jolly decent of you to have invited us. Can we visit the site today? I am beyond eager to get started.'

Max responded with a bland smile. As much as he wanted to contradict the man and explain they had been dragged here under false pretences—or at least under a twisted version of the truth—he would not humiliate Effie by doing it out here in front of the servants.

'I, for one, am eager to see how one can *accurately* discern wooden post holes when the said wood is allegedly two thousand years old and will undoubtedly have rotted away centuries beforehand.' Lord Denby smirked at Lord Whittlesey and in that instant he realised these two sanctimonious nay-sayers were here solely to find cause to discredit Effie's work not celebrate in it as it was due. They were the brakes on Sir Percival's enthusiastic carriage and unlikely to give her a fair hearing no matter how well written and researched her paper was or how vociferously he supported her cause.

Which did not bode well. For either her or him.

'They are quite discernible—I can assure you. If you know how to properly discern them, that is.' He could look down his nose, too, especially as he topped the skinny windbag by a good four inches and was probably twice as wide. 'I suppose that is what makes this discovery so unique. To an *amateur's* eye all mud is merely mud.' Max smiled to soften the edges of his blatant insult, pleased that the buffoon bristled regardless. 'It takes *real* skill and intelligence to find what nobody else has managed thus far. Wouldn't you say, Lord Denby?'

'I shall reserve judgement until I see it.'

Max felt his eyes drawn to where she still stood rooted to her spot behind the pillar, saw her defeated posture and miserable expression as she stared down at the floor awaiting his judgement. It tugged on his heart as her reality slapped him in the face. If it was this hard for a man to be taken seriously, and he was already beyond frustrated by the lofty lord's scepticism, then he couldn't imagine what each day was like for Effie. Each knock back. Each disparaging dismissal because a woman wasn't supposed to succeed in a man's world.

And there I was, thinking you were different from everyone else!

Her words, spat in anger, came back to haunt him because he suddenly realised he, too, was no different from the men currently looking down their noses. How could he possibly be any different if he actively lent a hand to scuppering all her dreams as well? When he knew more than anyone how unbearable it was to lose all hope and all purpose. All she wanted was to see her work published. How could he not help her do that?

'And see it you shall.' Although doubtless he would bitterly regret the decision in the coming days. 'But not until tomorrow—' out of the corner of his eye he saw Effie's head whip up in confusion '—as we have been plagued with a week of rain and the ground will need at least another day to dry out. Tonight, you may examine the artefacts we have found thus far instead and marvel at our magnificent discovery.' Without thinking he threw out his palm to encompass Effie, hoping she would come to his aid.

'We?' Sir Percival followed his gaze and suddenly beamed from ear to ear.

'Yes... We...' He was thinking on his feet now,

lost in the ocean with no compass to guide him, but certain he needed to change course. 'Allow me to introduce you to my…um…' He turned to her, smiling, hoping she could see the panicked message in his eyes and nobody else could. Hoping her quick brain would come to both their rescues because his was floundering. 'Miss Effie…'

'Jones!' She stepped out of the shadows and slanted him an odd glance. 'Miss Effie Jones, Lord Rivenhall's assistant.'

'You have a female assistant?' Lord Denby seemed affronted by the idea and he addressed Max rather than acknowledge her. Something which made his blood boil until the fool spoke again and vaporised it into shooting steam. 'I have never heard anything so ridiculous! Is there a shortage of good manpower here in Cambridge?'

'It is her talented hand which drew all the sketches.' He would give Effie as much credit as he could without arousing their suspicions, just to vex this arrogant arse. 'I am afraid I cannot draw for toffee.'

'Still—with the finest university in the country practically on your doorstep, I fail to see…'

'A pleasure to make your acquaintance, Miss Jones.' Sir Percival stepped into the breach. 'And may I say, what magnificent sketches they were, too…' He wasted no time bowing, clearly thoroughly attracted to Effie, and took his time over kissing her hand. Something which filled Max with irrational jealousy, which he covered by turning to his stony-faced but rapidly blinking butler.

'Smithson, fetch my sister, will you? As I placed her in charge of getting the *rooms* ready.'

'Of course, my lord.' Smithson nodded slowly. 'But first I shall have the tea and sandwiches sent to the drawing room immediately... Or perhaps something *stronger* to revive your guests after their journey while their *baggage* is brought in and I *speak* to Mrs Baxter?'

In that moment he could have hugged his astute butler. 'Yes Smithson. See to that immediately... Gentlemen—if you will kindly follow me.'

Effie wasn't entirely sure what was going on, but certainly wasn't about to contradict Max when he had apparently had a last-minute change of heart. She was trailing after the men to the drawing room when a very flushed and slightly out of breath Smithson intercepted her. 'If I could borrow you for a moment, Miss *Jones*?'

'But of course.'

Regally he closed the doors with a bow, sealing the gentlemen inside and then dragged her by the arm down the hallway and into the library where Eleanor was impatiently waiting.

'Well, this is all unexpected, isn't it?' Although Max's sister did not look the least bit fazed. 'But exciting, no? Some emergency covert machinations are required while Max keeps them occupied in the drawing room. Fortunately, the spare rooms were only cleaned yesterday after my family left, so it shouldn't take the maids long to put fresh linens on the bed. I shall tell Cook we are four more for dinner tonight and pray she can rustle something suitable up at such short notice. If she can't, we shall ply them with wine and brandy and hope they don't notice.' She paced as she thought, ticking things off on her fingers.

'Smithson, you sort out the tea and inform my brother I shall be with him as soon as possible. I shall assist him in stalling them with small talk until we can dispatch them to their bedchambers to rest before they dress for dinner. And, Effie— you need to dash home and gather up all your artefacts and I'll have them all laid out in here as if they have always been here. This room will make a better museum than the study. I shall have the carriage dispatched to meet you there, as I suspect that will be quickest, and then you can bring it back and sneak it all in while the gentleman are safely ensconced in their rooms.'

'Good idea!' Effie was about to bolt out the door when Eleanor stopped her.

'And if you are to be Max's assistant, you should pack a bag, too, and I'll have another room prepared for you.'

A prospect which made her panic far more than lying to the antiquarians did. 'There really is no need when I only live across the pasture...'

'There is *every* need if we are to convince them of this ruse! You are the expert, not he, and my brother is bound to come unstuck left alone with them for three whole days! It will be much safer if you are staying here—at their beck and call and ready to intervene at a moment's notice. I fear you must be his shadow, Effie. Because Max is doing this all for *you* now, isn't he?'

There was no arguing with that, because the logic was entirely sound, but logic did nothing to calm the enormous butterflies now flapping in her tummy or the nerves which were bouncing all over the place. But as sound as it was, it still did not explain Eleanor's brother's sudden and unexpected about-turn. 'I suppose... Although I should really speak to Max first and see what he—'

'There's no time for that! I shall apprise Max as soon as I have dispatched your guests to their rooms while you go and fetch absolutely everything you think he might need to convince them he is not an impostor.' Eleanor steered her to the door and practically pushed her through it. 'And, Effie—make it a big bag as you will need both your digging clothes and suitable attire for dinner each evening. Something pretty and formal. That oozes all your feminine wiles... Like that lovely coral silk you wore to our first meal together? That is very becoming and guaranteed to distract them from asking too many questions.'

'Do we want to distract them?'

'We do until we have a proper plan!'

Chapter Eighteen

Dig Day 802: be careful what you wish for...

A little over three hours later, and entirely flustered, Max's packed carriage finally turned towards the Rivenhall stables. Having no idea which artefacts to bring, she had brought them all and the tightly packed trunk contained enough clothes for every eventuality and far too many for just three days.

Not wanting to cause a scene or inadvertently put her foot in it, she intended to creep back into the house through the kitchens in search of her bafflingly changeable host or his sister so they could brief her on the plan. She hoped to God there was one, because with all the excitement and the packing and the panicking, she certainly had no clue what to do next and no earthly idea what exactly Max thought he was playing at. One minute she was the devil incarnate for taking his name in vain and the next she was his assistant and about to move into his house.

But as the carriage slowed, the man himself was waiting for her, looking more anxious than she had ever seen him. It was Max who opened her door, his expression thoroughly relieved.

'Thank the Lord! Blasted dinner is in an hour and I am in over my head here.' His big hand engulfed hers as he helped her down, then remained clasped around it, sending her already racing pulse galloping at the contact. 'We need to talk, Effie. Urgently.'

She certainly agreed they did. She had absolutely no idea what was going on.

He tugged her to the quietest corner of the yard.

'The first thing you should know is your antiquarians are happily settled in their rooms and have been for the last few hours...' He glanced down at their intertwined hands, appeared startled that they were indeed intertwined and hastily severed the contact.

'The second thing you need to know is I think I've managed to convince them that I know what I'm talking about when I really haven't a clue. Although that is more to do with Eleanor's gift of the gab and ability to charm the birds from the trees than my solid grasp on antiquity. It might also have something to do with Smithson's liberal hand with the brandy. But...' He huffed out a breath and ran a very agitated hand through his long hair, looking thoroughly mortified.

'But?'

'Lord Denby is the worst kind of snob and took real issue with me having a female assistant. In fact, it seemed to cause him a great deal of consternation and he simply would not let it lie... I'm sorry, Effie...' His dark eyes were filled with remorse on her behalf.

'All par for the course in my world, Max. Women are supposed to be decorative, not intelligent...' Something about the way he stared down at his feet made her panic. 'Do I need to leave?' Because that would be the absolute icing on the cake. Not only would she be denied the recognition for the discovery—something she had resigned herself to the second she had signed his name on the letter—but now that Max had relented and was apparently going to play out the façade created by her poorly considered pseudonym, she was to be denied the opportunity to witness it even as a spectator. 'Is the prospect of a woman at the dig so abhorrent to him?'

'I'm afraid it's worse than that.'

Worse! Oh, dear.

'Thanks to Eleanor...' He cleared his throat,

his eyes darting to hers, then flicking away. And behind the curtain of hair he was suddenly hiding behind, she was almost certain she detected what looked a lot like a blush.

'I am really not sure how to tell you the next bit, so I'll just say it straight out… In view of his persistent and fixated outrage at your involvement with the paper…she told them you were my fiancée.' He winced as he said it, as if he was waiting for her to hit the roof and seemed genuinely surprised when she neither said nor did anything beyond blink. Because frankly, after the million and one thoughts, questions and scenarios to career through her mind these fraught past few hours, that certainly had not been one of them.

His next words came out in an embarrassed tumble. 'To be fair to Eleanor, it did seem to do the trick and Lord Pompous backed off and immediately directed his over-active scepticism elsewhere.'

'I am to play your fiancée now?'

'Obviously, I demanded to know what the hell she thought she was about when I finally got her alone and she quoted you as the inspiration for her spur-of-the-moment solution, stating that men like Denby would not question a lady's diligent support of her betrothed and would be seen as natural because… Er…' He was delightfully awkward now and most definitely blushing. Which was a first. She had never seen him so flustered or uncertain. And she had never heard him stammer. 'Because in his eyes, as my fiancée, your place should be by my side regardless... What with women being chattels and all, with no thoughts beyond those fed to them by their biologically superior menfolk and no desire above...um...administering to his—or in this case my—whims.'

Her words. Almost exactly.

'And that worked?' She found herself smiling at Lord Denby's utter stupidity as well as Max's charming awkwardness. 'He can cope with me assisting you as long as we are engaged—but not because you engaged my services as an assistant?'

'That is the long and short of it, yes.' He slanted her a wary glance. 'Eleanor has appointed herself our chaperon... For appearance's sake, of course, rather than... Are you angry?'

'Not in the slightest. Thank goodness Eleanor thought of it.' She watched the tension dissolve in his broad shoulders and suppressed the sudden urge to run her hands over them. 'Are Sir Percival and Lord Whittlesey similarly placated?'

'As Lord Whittlesey's sole purpose, as far as I can make out, appears to be to agree unquestioningly with everything Disapproving Denby says and as Sir Percival seemed crestfallen to learn that you were spoken for, I'd say so. He seems to have taken a bit of a shine to you, by the way.' Max seemed to be watching her reaction to that intently.

'It will tarnish. It always does.' She hoped her words sound blasé rather than bitter because Max was being nice. 'What is our plan for tonight?'

'We'll eat, then show them the artefacts. I shall propose a very early night so that we can head to the ruins early.' His gaze suddenly swept the length of her and he winced again at her now thoroughly crumpled day dress. 'Eleanor is insisting it is to be horrifically formal, so you'll probably have to change. Once the carriage is unloaded, it can take you back home to do so.'

'No need. I brought every decent gown I own and…' His words finally permeated her brain. 'Did Eleanor not tell you she invited me to stay?'

His mouth settled in irritated flat line. 'She neglected to apprise me of that fact. I wonder why?'

Effie did not need to wonder, but now felt hideously embarrassed to be put in the awkward position of defending herself and Eleanor—who was only being practical.

'She insisted. She believed you would need me here…to be your constant shadow in case you were put on the spot.' She watched his jaw clench and his dark eyes harden. 'If it is a problem, I can just as easily take it all back home...' She instinctively turned towards the carriage in time to see the last of her baggage disappearing towards the house with the butler marching behind it.

'Smithson!'

The butler halted at Max's bellow, then swiftly changed direction. 'Yes, my lord?'

'What were my sister's *precise* instructions regarding Effie's luggage?' His arms were folded, one booted foot tapping impatiently.

'To take the artefacts and documents directly to the study and her trunks to the Rose bedchamber, my lord.'

'And when were you given this instruction?'

'Several hours ago, my lord. Just after we dispatched the carriage to fetch Miss Effie.'

'I thought as much.' He huffed out a sigh of complete disgust. 'Kindly show Miss Effie to her room, would you, Smithson?' Then he stalked towards the house without so much as a backwards glance.

Max was going to murder his blasted sister! And he'd enjoy doing it! Despite having strict orders *not* to interfere, she hadn't been able to stop herself. Now Effie was ensconced in a bedchamber just across the landing from him in the family wing and would be playing the part of his fiancée for the duration!

Utter torture and not a damn thing he could do about it.

With a growl he tossed his second ruined cravat aside and snapped open a third, because to compound his misery she had also insisted dinner was a formal affair, ostensibly to impress the stuffy antiquarians, but he was now of the firm belief it was also to parade Effie in front of him in a beautiful gown in the hope temptation would spur him into acting.

Well, the joke was on Eleanor because Max would be tempted if she was wearing a blasted sack, but he'd already acted and wasn't about to risk acting again under any circumstance, so she could have saved them all the trouble! Once bitten, twice shy.

And devastated at the result.

How the hell was he supposed to sleep knowing *she* was just across the hall? And in the Rose bedchamber, no less. The one which he presumed his uncle's wife had used when she was alive because it was the feminine mirror image of his. The one his sister had been using since her arrival, but had suddenly vacated out of the goodness of her manipulative heart. No wonder his sibling had gone to ground. She knew damn well he'd be fuming!

Keelhauling was too good for Eleanor! Walking the plank was too good for Eleanor! She had gone too far this time! As soon as these three dreadful days were over with, he was sending the manipulative meddler back to London with the biggest flea in her ear and banning her from returning for at least a month! It was predominantly her fault he felt so awkward in his own skin. Hers and the gawping antiquarians. And the smitten Sir Percival, whom he did not trust to not flirt with Effie despite her being fictitiously betrothed to him. Max wasn't entirely sure he could cope with anyone flirting with her in his presence, let alone an eccentrically charming, similarly scholarly and as passionate an antiquarian as Sir Percival Egerton. Even if he was exceedingly short and round.

Although, apparently, being short and round did not prevent Sir Percival from wooing and he'd said as much.

'Too bad she's all yours, old chap, else I'd be after her like a shot.'

And no doubt he would be, too, once the truth came out or if Effie was similarly tempted. They were, intellectually speaking, basically two peas in a pod.

But if she was tempted by a man six inches shorter than her and as round as a cricket ball, would she be so easily repelled by a few scars? Scars which had healed and were never going to get any better. He glanced at the covered mirror still embedded in the wall and seriously considered taking a quick peek at his reflection to see if he might pass muster.

Perhaps if he only glanced at himself in profile it wouldn't make him queasy? Just to check his cravat was tied correctly and he didn't look ridiculous in the bronze-silk waistcoat his meddlesome sister had laid out in the absence of a valet. Because Max could not bear the thought of showing the full extent of his hideousness to another— even if that other was a servant paid to suffer it.

Gingerly, he walked towards the mirror and making sure he was stood with his right side to the wall, he moved just the edge of the sheet to one side. The waistcoat wasn't too bad and his cravat was straight if a little boringly tied. The black coat his sister had also selected fitted well around the shoulders.

So far so good. And probably best if he left it there.

Except for some reason he couldn't.

He let his eyes move upwards.

Good grief, his hair had got long! So long it practically touched his lapels. And since when had it decided to curl? As there was no way he could envisage facing anyone without it to hide behind, he supposed it wasn't too bad. It wasn't as if he could grow a beard instead. Thanks to the burns, he no longer needed to shave the ruined side of his face and half a beard would be both pointless as well as ridiculous.

He risked tilting his chin slightly and was amazed the pasty invalid he had come to expect was no longer present. Thanks to all the digging he had a tan. Not as deep and as brown as his skin was prone to turn in the hot sun of the Caribbean or during the summer heat around the horn of Africa, but the good side of his face was golden and it looked healthy enough. And he didn't feel sick at the sight of it.

Yet.

Perhaps he should risk a proper look? See if Eleanor was right and the damage wasn't entirely hideous. Perhaps if he learned to accept himself as he was, a bit of his old self-confidence would return and then maybe…

And perhaps he was simply just chasing windmills and should leave well alone. He pulled the sheet back down, but stayed where he was. Then practically jumped guiltily out of his skin when Smithson rapped on the door.

'Mrs Baxter has sent me to remind you that, as the host, you are expected downstairs immediately to be there to greet your guests as they arrive. Which would be in five minutes, my lord, so you are in grave danger of being late.'

Max had forgotten he was the host. Like so many things, he was grossly out of practice with social etiquette and dreading this meal because he couldn't escape it. He used to be a charming and much sought-after dinner companion, so he supposed the skill must still be there somewhere. Buried deep inside and probably in dire need of an airing, but he would attempt to locate it for Effie even if he was still furious at his sister.

He found Eleanor in the drawing room, thankfully alone. 'What the hell do you think you are playing at?'

'I am sure I do not know what you mean?'

'Inviting Effie to stay? Putting her in the Rose room? Making her my fiancée was one thing—I was prepared to give you the benefit of the doubt on that one—but the rest smacks of blatant matchmaking when I warned you not to interfere!'

She gave him a withering glance and then rolled her eyes. 'Inviting her to stay was basic common sense and you might as well know I've told her to be your shadow for the duration, too, Max, as leaving you alone with those men is bound to be problematic.' It galled that she had a point. 'And as for the Rose room, surely, as your fiancée, it would be expected she be given a room to reflect her new status in the household?'

'I doubt the antiquarians will waste their time wondering which room she is sleeping in.'

'Then you underestimate Sir Percival.' Not what Max wanted to hear. Her voice dropped to a whisper as they heard the distant sounds of movement beyond the door. 'Surely you noticed the passionate glint in his eye when he first saw Effie?' He had and he didn't like it. 'I shall be keeping my beady eye on him and reminding him she is spoken for.'

'Thanks to your interference. Make sure that is the last of it, too.'

'As if I shall have the time! I knew I should have readied the room and the house for guests before they arrived. Thanks to you, I am chasing my tail. It is a miracle I have managed to pull together a proper dinner for this evening. Make sure you keep them all thoroughly occupied tomorrow. We do not want any of them seeing the butcher, the baker and the candlestick maker traipsing into the house with emergency supplies. I am expecting you all to leave promptly after breakfast and not to return until at least luncheon.'

Then she turned on her heel and sailed to the door in time for Lord Denby and his snivelling crony, Lord Whittlesey, to walk through it. 'Gentlemen! I trust your accommodations are to your satisfaction…'

Max put himself in charge of dishing out the drinks, much to Smithson's blatant consternation, to ease himself into hosting, keeping one eye on the door for Effie. Sir Percival entered next and made straight towards him.

'I have been reading your essay again, Riven hall, and it has thrown up so many questions.' Oh, dear. 'For example, how can you be entirely sure the bracelet in particular predates the Romans rather than be something from a later period? Only some medieval jewellery is sometimes impressively ornate.'

'When you see it after dinner, I am certain it will alleviate any doubts.' A fudged answer, but the best he could manage on his own. 'And if that doesn't convince you, the shield we found last week will.'

'A shield, you say? A partial?'

'Intact. Solid bronze and really quite magnificent.'

'Oh, you are a tease, old chap! How am I supposed to compose myself at dinner when I'm as excited as a…?' He paused mid-sentence and suddenly gaped over Max's shoulder, the ancient shield clearly forgotten. *'I say!'*

Max followed his dumbfounded gaze to Effie, who was a positive vision in red silk. So lovely it made his heart pound and his mouth go dry. Before he could reconnect his brain to his feet and move towards her, Sir Percival had wasted no time.

'Miss Jones—how lovely you look.' He bent low over her ungloved hand and kissed it.

That kiss galvanised Max into action and, imbued with the most peculiar and inescapably proprietary feeling, he went to claim her. Not caring, for once, what anyone thought but Sir Percival, who needed to learn she was most definitely not on the market.

Chapter Nineteen

Dig Day 802: no progress and, more worryingly, no plan...

'Good evening, my darling. Don't you look ravishing.' A flirty Max was not something she had ever seen before, let alone experienced, and it completely scrambled her wits. Or perhaps that was simply the way her nerve endings danced when he lingered over kissing her hand, then curled it possessively around his arm. He anchored it in place with his warm palm as he escorted her into the room as if they were a real betrothed couple. It was such a solid arm, too, one which should have made her feel secure, when in fact it did anything but. He lent down to whisper in her ear and his warm breath sent tingles shooting down her neck, bouncing down her spine towards places which really had no place making their presence so apparently known in polite company. 'Your earrings match for once. I am impressed.'

'So do my shoes.' Was that her voice? It sounded strange. Too squeaky. Too breathy. Obviously flustered. She quietly exhaled to try to slow her racing pulse. 'Thanks to the maid Eleanor has assigned me, I even have proper hairpins.'

'Which is sad, because I much prefer the pencil.' He kept hold of her arm as they reached the others. 'Gentlemen, may I introduce you again to my fiancée, Miss Effie Jones. The very best assistant a man could wish for.' He squeezed her hand reassuringly as he said this and nearly all of her residual disappointment in him from the last week disappeared. He was attempting to give credit where credit was due as well as playing along with her charade. Nobody had ever done either before, for either the sake of her work or simply for her.

Lord Denby grimaced, or at least the half-hearted attempt at a polite smile when his eyes were so obviously not attempting the same came across as a grimace. 'You draw very pretty sketches, Miss Jones.'

Pretty! She wanted to stamp on his sanctimonious foot. As if he sensed that, Max took charge. 'I believe dinner is about to be served. Shall we?'

Miraculously, as if they had rehearsed it in advance, Smithson simultaneously opened the big double doors to welcome them all into the formal dining room. As the ranking peer, technically Lord Pompous should have walked through the big double doors first, but Max strode forward regardless, slanting her a heady glance which told her he had absolutely done it on purpose just for her when the disgruntled Marquess was forced to trail behind.

He solicitously escorted her to her chair and gave her hand a final squeeze of reassurance before he let go. Eleanor had done a splendid job of the table, which was fit for a royal banquet. The silver shone, the tall and ornate candelabra twinkled and there was a stunning arrangement of both flowers and fruits as a centrepiece which included a pineapple—the most expensive and rare of fruits. Lord only knew where she had found one on such short notice. Max was seated at one end, with Lord Denby and the mostly silent Lord Whittlesey, and she had been placed at the other flanked by the friendly faces of Sir Percival on one side and Max's sister on the other.

As their host, Max made a toast welcoming them properly to Rivenhall on behalf of the both of them, which was another thoughtful touch, and then the soup was served.

'Your fiancé was telling me you found a shield last week, Miss Jones?'

'We did indeed, Sir Percival…'

'Oh, do call me Percy. Sir Percival is such a mouthful.'

'We should be delighted to drop the formalities, *Percy*. At least at this lowly end of the table. Please do call me Eleanor and this is Effie.'

'We did indeed find a shield, Percy—well, Max did actually—and it is magnificent. I've searched through every research book and through all my back copies of *Archaeologia* and I cannot find any record of anything similar.' She did her best to describe it while he listened intently, interrupting only with the most pertinent and sensible questions. It was obvious he was a true antiquarian in every sense of the word—knowledgeable, curious and with an enthusiasm which matched hers, but which seemed sadly lacking in the other two gentlemen from the society.

'It has entirely altered our perception of the dwelling as it is so fine and so ceremonially decorative, I am becoming more convinced that we have stumbled upon the house of a tribal leader or an individual of great import. Max is convinced that person is also a woman because there have been several feminine items—like the bracelet alongside personal items like a comb and a rather delicate cloak pin.'

'Really? How wonderful! A queen rather than a king. Your very own Boudicca.'

'Obviously, it is too soon to be anything beyond speculation at this point, but certainly worth bearing in mind as we excavate the rest of the site. But the shield is breathtaking... I really cannot wait to show it to you.'

'And I cannot wait to see it!'

'Then why don't the pair of you quickly pop out before the next course is served?' Eleanor leaned forward conspiratorially. 'I doubt the other gentlemen will notice as they seem thoroughly engrossed in their own conversation.'

Effie glanced down the table where they were indeed engrossed. As if he sensed her staring, Max's eyes suddenly locked on hers and held for a moment, making her pulse quicken, before he returned his concentration to Lord Pompous on his right. He was different tonight. Every inch the Earl. Commanding and confident and effortlessly in charge despite the superior and snooty peer sat beside him. 'We can't. Leaving would be rude...' And it would leave Max entirely exposed exactly as Eleanor had warned.

'It is only rude, Effie dear, if we are being very formal and we have already decided to eschew that here in the cheap seats. Five minutes will not hurt.' She glanced at her brother, then back at Effie before nudging her in the arm. 'Go. Everything is well in hand here. I shall make suitable excuses and have a footman fetch you before the fish arrives. I dare say we shall cope without you.'

'Well, if you are sure...' She stood, intending to slip out quietly, but as soon as she did, every other gentleman around the table immediately stood, too. Then Percy appeared behind her and pulled out her chair, then offered her his arm.

'They will only be a moment.' Eleanor waved their unconventional departure away and ushered them all to sit. 'Tell me, Lord Denby, what kindled your interest in antiquity?'

Lord Pompous was only too pleased to answer, allowing the pair of them to leave without the slightest objection, but as Effie walked through the door on Percy's pudgy arm, she could feel Max's eyes boring into her back. She turned and there they were. Dark, intense and swirling with an emotion she could not decipher, but which thrilled her nevertheless.

'Could it be part of a quernstone?' Percy was running the flat of his hand over the fragment of obviously carved, curved sandstone she had pondered since she had dug it up a few days before she had found the pot and just a few scant inches from the hearth. He was in no hurry to leave the library despite the other two gentlemen being obviously ready to move on to the port because, thanks to Max, it was Effie who was holding court.

'I suppose it could be…' She stared at the object as he examined it, taking in the worn narrow grooves on the flat side. 'It certainly has the look of something which could grind grain into flour… If it is, of course, it entirely contradicts Dio's accounts of the tribal Celts as hunter-gathers.'

'Indeed it does. Because this would suggest they grew crops rather than gathered. And were savvy enough to be able to make bread.'

'I believe they reared animals, too—rather than hunted.' She was enjoying discussing things with Percy, whose knowledge was gloriously extensive and his mind quick enough to keep pace with hers most of the time.

'As if such a thing could be effectively proved,' Lord Denby scoffed from his throne in the corner, having made sure he took the largest and grandest chair in the library the second they had entered the room as a mark of protest, no doubt, for Max's lack of deference earlier.

'Actually, my lord, I believe I… *We*…' her gaze automatically flicked to Max, who nodded his encouragement as if she had not just slipped up and excluded him from the discovery while she had been waxing lyrical all on her own for at least half an hour '…we have found evidence of pastoral farming.'

Effie hurried to the stewed bones she had placed in a labelled leather pouch and gently tipped them on the table. 'We found these by the hearth alongside some shards of pottery, so have to assume they are the remnants of a meal. The last meal they ate at the round house, else why would it have been there? Although that beggars the question as to why they left in such a hurry. An attack, perhaps? Herodian, Dio and Tacitus commented on the bloodthirsty nature of the tribal fighting. If a rival invaded their land, won the battle and then destroyed the houses, then any survivors would have been forced to flee. Unless there were no survivors…'

There were so many possibilities, all racing through her mind as she briskly considered the merits of each.

'Or perhaps an epidemic ravaged the settlement? If whole villages were abandoned and disappeared as a result of the Black Death in the fourteenth century, it is entirely conceivable similar things happened many times beforehand, too. It is not as if they chronicled their history like the Roman scholars attempted to do. I have found no evidence of the existence of any written language…'

She was being too intelligent. Too peculiar. Her odd mind jumping ahead much too fast because Max was there and she couldn't seem to stop herself lapsing into her true self around him and Percy also made her feel comfortable. 'Anyway…' she smiled at the beaming academic as she focused back on the contents of the table '…these here are definitely chicken bones and I believe these others are from a larger grazing animal such as a sheep or a cow.'

'They could just as easily be from a wild boar or deer hunted in the forest, Miss Jones.' Doubting Denby was not the least bit convinced. Hardly a surprise when, so far, he had not been convinced of any conjecture or evidence Effie had put forward. He had, however, conceded a few of Max's points, but as Max hadn't committed the shocking crime of being born female or being able to quote all the pertinent Roman histories of the Celts to the letter, it went without saying that in Lord Denby's cynical and prejudiced eyes, he *must* be the more informed than she could possibly ever be. It was hard not to show her frustration at his persistently blinkered outlook, but once again she bit her lip. Without Denby's support, her discoveries would never make it into *Archaeologia* even with Max's name on them.

'Well, that one is definitely from a cow.' Max

winked at her as he pointed at the fat, stubby bone in the centre of the pile, dashing in to save her as he had so many times this evening already like a knight in shining armour. 'Which, as Effie says, *is* a grazing animal which has been kept for thousands of years by all manner of ancient civilisations. Didn't the Egyptians keep cows? Even the Book of Genesis mentions the creation of livestock for man to rule over. And technically, that was only on the sixth day… A ridiculous number of centuries before our Celts put beef in their stew.'

'Are you an expert on butchery as well as antiquity and theology, Lord Rivenhall?' Lord Whittlesey had not said much all evening, unless it was to add fuel to Lord Denby's current contrary argument.

'Have you ever been on a gunship, Lord Whittlesey?'

'I have never had cause to, Lord Rivenhall.'

'Well, that explains your ignorance then. I sailed with His Majesty's Navy for twenty years and butchery is one of the many skills I learned on deck. We always set sail with a plethora of animals on board to feed the crew—cows, pigs, sheep, chickens and occasionally even the odd goat. So I think I am more qualified than anyone else in this room to state, and without any doubt whatsoever, that that bone comes from a cow. And if I am not mistaken, I will even be so bold as to identify it as a rib. Whereas this...' he pointed to another fragment, looking quietly triumphant as well as the most virile and manly man around the table '...looks a lot like the tail. Clearly our Celts were as thrifty and creative with their rations as my cook was on the *Artemis*. I do hope they boiled it to death before they served it as the tail can be horrendously tough.' And with an entirely smug, male smile which suited him immensely, he stood. 'That's quite enough antiquity for one day. Time for some port, I think. Followed by a spirited game of billiards if any of you gentlemen are inclined to wager.'

'I'll wager every penny, brick and stick of furniture I own in exchange for your beautiful and brilliant fiancée.' Percy had been an outrageously delightful flirt all evening. Effie already adored him.

'Then prepare to sleep on the streets when you return to London, my good fellow.' Max shot her a heated glance for appearances' sake, which her instantly needy body refused to believe was entirely for appearances. 'Because I have no intention of ever parting with her.'

Chapter Twenty

❧❧❧

One smitten portly rival...

The pair of them were already as thick as thieves. Max had no right to be jealous—but he was. Jealous and frustrated at the way the pair of them so obviously got on. In fact, it was causing him so much consternation, he sincerely doubted he would be able to sleep at all. He'd been pacing the rug in his bedchamber for at least half an hour since thoroughly thrashing the scoundrel at billiards and hadn't yet managed to remove more than his waistcoat he was so aggrieved.

And Effie was probably annoyed to boot.

Perhaps it had been churlish to put a stop to the discussion when she was clearly in her element and impressing the hell out of her beloved Sir Percival as well as making steady inroads into the snooty Lord Denby's terminal scepticism. But it was the obvious rapport she had with blasted *Percy* which was gnawing away at him. The fellow was an outrageous flirt and needed to be closely watched. Something he had found impossible to do when the pair of them had slipped out of the room before they had finished their soup!

And Eleanor, who frankly should have chaperoned the pair of them as she was supposed to, had stayed and pandered to Lord Denby's ego until the fish arrived, clearly oblivious of Max's frequent and pointed looks reminding her that the pair of them were all on their own. In the end, rather than entrust a servant in case there had been some funny business which required avenging, he had gone to fetch them himself and found the pair huddled together in the library oohing and ahhing over the shield like a new-born child in its crib. Their child! Quite forgetting it was the same blasted shield Max had discovered!

There had been no further opportunities for Flirty Percy to waylay her after that. Max had made sure of it! For the next few days he intended to stick to him like glue whenever Effie was around because Eleanor was an abysmal chaperon.

The soft tap on the door was followed by her whisper. 'Max... Are you still awake?'

'Is everything all right?' She had gone to bed
hours ago. He knew because he had counted every
minute since. Jabbing balls with his cue as if each
was Sir Percival's grinning round head.

'Are you decent?'

For a moment he thought about hunting for his
cravat to retie it around his neck to hide the scars
and then decided there was no point. His sister
was right. They weren't ever going to get any better and Effie already knew all about them. If she
hadn't baulked at the feel of his cheek, which was
the least damaged part, then what difference did
it make? And if her taste ran to intelligent short
and stout men anyway... He heard his own teeth
grind and decided he wouldn't care. He was what
he was—and if that wasn't good enough, then it
would be a cold day in hell before she would ever
know how much that hurt.

He answered by throwing open the door, daring her to be horrified. And then sincerely wished
he hadn't.

She was stood in a billowing nightgown. A
nightgown made up of so much fabric it should
have been perfectly decent. Except it was anything but. The scooped neckline framed the slen-
der arch of her neck and showed much too much
perfect skin. The long, floaty sleeves were finished in filmy lace which partially obscured her

hands until one burrowed free to fiddle with the ends of her dark plait which hung to her waist.

The diaphanous, gauzy fabric, which might well seem sensible and sedate in daylight, was rendered partially translucent in the soft candle-light, forcing him to see the sultry curve of her hips and the legs which had tormented his dreams since the very first day he had encountered her dressed in those breeches. He wished for those muddy breeches now. Another layer to prevent his mind reeling at the thought of what was under that soft muslin. He watched her eyes wander to the covered mirror, saw her clever mind decipher why it was covered, saw the flash of pity and dreaded her next words.

'There was no time earlier to talk about tomorrow...' He almost sighed aloud at the unexpected reprieve from the conversation he never wanted to have. 'What with the dinner and antiquarians and billiards. So I waited up.' She edged in, chewing nervously on her bottom lip, oblivious of how beautiful she looked or how her innocent gesture made his blood heat. 'I didn't want you to be unprepared.'

Unprepared was the perfect word, because he had been totally unprepared for the sight of her like this. Supremely conscious of his big bed behind them, turned down and waiting, and the hideous scars on his face, which rendered all hope for the bed null and void, Max nodded tightly, hoping he didn't look as overwhelmed as he felt. He could barely breathe, let alone speak.

The air around him was suddenly heavy with the heady scent of lilacs and fat summer roses. With things unsaid and hopes unfulfilled. He knew they were best left unsaid. Knew he needed to be thankful she was his friend and not keep foolishly wishing for more. For everything.

Everything?

The truth slammed into him and left him unsteady. She was his everything.

Good lord, he was doomed.

She stared down at her feet, forcing his eyes to her pretty bare toes poking beneath the hem. Another unwanted reminder of what lay—or did not lie—beneath that ridiculously feminine and romantic nightgown. 'So where should we start?'

'Er…' He'd like to start by hooking his fingers beneath the ribbon at her shoulders and sliding the seductive garment slowly down her arms until it puddled around those dainty toes. 'Perhaps…er…we should begin with a potted history of the Celts?'

Max tried to focus. Really he did. But as much as he didn't want to let her down on the morrow, her presence sat primly on the *chaise* by the

window was too distracting and completely overwhelming. With nowhere else to sit other than
beside her, Max was perched on the bed. Wishing he had been emasculated so that his masculine parts would stop reminding him he wasn't.
Wishing his heart wasn't so full it felt as though
it might burst at any moment.

'Then you are convinced Lord Denby will disapprove of what we have done.'

'From what I can make of him so far, very
probably. He is a bit of a...'

'Pain in the arse?'

She giggled and he inexplicably felt ten feet
tall. 'I was going to say traditionalist—but I much
prefer your assessment. Yes, he is and he does
seem to have a fundamental problem with me, so
I am afraid it is going to be down to you to justify the way I have done things and prevent him
from attacking the ruins like the advancing army
of Attila the Hun.'

'Lord Denby is a lot of foul things, but an Attila he isn't. He doesn't have the physical strength,
for one thing. Did you notice how much padding
he had in his jacket? I doubt he's ever wielded
a pickaxe. To be honest, I'm surprised he didn't
struggle with a spoon. He has unpleasantly thin
wrists for a man.'

She smiled. 'I cannot say I noticed his jacket

or his wrists. I was too busy noticing his utter disdain.'

'Disdain is his forte for sure. That and looking down his nose.' Max looked down his and crossed his eyes, simply to hear her laugh again. Each one felt like rebuilding another section of the bridge back to friendship. It was staggering how much he had missed it. Missed her, truth be told. Effie, it turned out, was the sunshine in his darkness. 'And talking of jackets... I doubt Sir Percival needed extra padding. He seemed to fill his more than adequately... With pudding, I suspect.' A low blow, when despite the jealousy Max actually liked the man, but he wanted to gauge the depth of her feelings towards him, hoping he was worrying for nothing.

As if he was ever going to dare tell her how he felt.

'Percy is lovely. Pudding and all.' Not at all what Max wanted to hear. 'Anyway—the methods I use are fairly new and are not used extensively in antiquarian circles. I have been tremendously inspired by the work of the late William Cunnington, a great man who believed in respecting the past by treating the site with integrity. I am not averse to using a pickaxe or a shovel, because both have very obvious advantages, especially when it comes to removing several feet of soil.

However, like Cunnington, I prefer to use more precise tools like my trowel when I get close to the artefacts. In a clumsy excavation, many delicate or small finds can so easily be missed or destroyed in haste. In fact, I dread to think how many important treasures have been needlessly and thoughtlessly discarded at important sites like Pompeii or Stonehenge. We cannot let that happen at Rivenhall.'

'It won't. Rivenhall is mine.' But all of a sudden he knew he wanted to share it. 'And only you get to say how it is dug.'

'That's very noble of you.' She smiled and then hid it behind her hand to stifle a yawn, then, to compound his misery, stretched. 'As is sitting here in the small hours while I waffle on when you must clearly be desperate for your bed.' Only if she were in it with him. 'We have an early start tomorrow.'

'Breakfast at seven.' He swallowed hard in case he drooled when she stood and the candlelight worked its magic with her nightgown again. He seared the image on his mind to keep for ever. 'Then we are under strict orders from Eleanor not to return to the house till at least one.'

He followed her to the door. 'I am so humbled by Eleanor's efforts on my behalf today. And yours. Thank you. It means the world.'

'You are very welcome.'

He watched her lace-covered hand reach for the handle before she paused and turned around, leaning her back against the door. 'Can I ask you a question, Max?'

Please God, don't let it be about the mirror. 'Ask away...' The candles picked out the flecks of gold in her irises while the darkness rendered the brown almost black. Both seemed to hold the power to hypnotise him.

'I know things have been awkward between us of late and I understand why...' Was that regret? It certainly looked like it from where he was standing. Unless he was willing it to be regret and therefore entirely probable, he was misreading things. Even so, a tiny shoot of hope sprung eternal. 'But what made you change your mind this morning?'

He had anticipated this question and given it a great deal of thought during the frequent moments when his eyes had glazed over at the particularly baffling antiquarian discussions throughout the day. Except the glib, bland, hastily glossing-over response he had planned was not what came out of his mouth. 'I wanted to be different.'

'From what?'

'All the other men...in the past...who ran away or put you down or tried to diminish what and who you are, Effie… I couldn't bear to be one of them.'

'Oh…' Her expression was confused for a second, as if she had not been expecting that response at all. Which made two of them. Telling the truth made him feel nervous and exposed. What if more leaked out? Would she run? 'That is actually very sweet of you.'

'Can miserable, reclusive, angry-at-the-world curmudgeons be sweet?'

'Difficult to answer as the only one I know is you. Perhaps you are softening?' She gave him a half-smile—part-irony, part-shy. Wholly bewitching. 'Or perhaps I am growing on you?'

'Perhaps…' It was funny. He had never felt like this when he had been with Miranda. There had been lust, of course. But not friendship or understanding. He'd never known what she was thinking or feeling, and perhaps that had been what had drawn him then. With her it had been fraught. Unsettled. Unfulfilling. Even superficial. Yet with Effie, it felt like a warm eiderdown wrapping him in reassuring comfort. Different. Better. Right…

She made no move to turn back towards the door and gazed at him expectantly although Max couldn't for the life of him think of anything else to say that did not involve admitting she had more than grown on him. She had taken root and taken over. Made his heart beat and his days something to look forward to. Because despite the bizarreness of the situation, the complicated charade and the house filled with strangers, he realised with a start he was looking forward to tomorrow entirely owing to the fact she would be in all of it.

'I suppose I should go…'

'I suppose you should.'

'Unless…' She chewed her bottom lip again and then shook her head. 'Never mind… Ignore me. I am being silly…' Now she was obviously awkward—not uncomfortable awkward, but hesitant.

It was ridiculous to allow the tiny shoot of hope to grow bigger, yet it was. 'Unless what?'

'I am galloping ahead of myself… I am useless at this sort of thing. I can never accurately gauge people's emotions until it is too late and I have gone too far… And it was obvious you regretted the last one…'

His heart was hammering in his chest now. Every signal she was sending him was positive. Or at least he thought they were. Before the burns, he wouldn't have been so uncertain. Wouldn't have dithered. The old Max would have grabbed this opportunity with both hands and to hell with the consequences. He'd have taken the risk—but the new Max had so much more to lose and simply wasn't brave enough.

Her teeth worried her plump lip again and she couldn't meet his eyes, except briefly, too briefly, and he was sure they flicked to his mouth.

'I am reading too much into what you just said and... I mean, you *are* different, Max. You have always been different from everyone else. You seem to be able to tolerate me for a start. And what you are doing for me now speaks volumes, but... I should be happy with that... I am happy with that, but... What I mean is there is different and then there is *different*...' Her gaze was now riveted to a spot on the floor, her hands busily fidgeting among the lace. 'Really, I should go. And let sleeping dogs lie... Shouldn't I?'

Of its own accord, his finger reached out to tilt up her chin. In case he had completely misread things, he needed to see her eyes before he dared to dream. Needed to hear the words. 'Unless what, Effie? Ask your question.'

'I know I am odd and not quite what any man expects or wants from a woman... But I was wondering if you would like to try...' She turned her face to the side and he realised she was blushing now, too. 'Lord, this is mortifying. That I have to *ask* should tell me all I need to know... Which in itself makes it apparent that of course you wouldn't like to kiss me again...' All the air rushed out of his lungs and the ground felt unsteady in the very best way. 'I'm sorry, Max—I should never have...'

He pressed his lips to hers greedily and to his complete delight she melted instantly against him, winding her arms around his neck as she sighed into his mouth. It was all the encouragement he needed.

There was no possibility of this kiss being soft and unhurried. Too many emotions had been stirred up this last week and he had temporarily lost the ability to mask them. There were too many of them coursing through his body now to dawdle or hold back. Utter despair had turned to overwhelming relief. Longing to lust. Grief to joy. Elation. Surprise. Affection... No... Something else, something big and complicated and frankly terrifying—except he wasn't terrified. Not in the slightest. He was glad for it. Giddy with it.

She was kissing him!

With all the enthusiasm and passion she displayed in everything she cared about.

Max filled his hands with her curves, revelling in the feel of her naked body beneath the thin material of her siren's nightgown. Apparently misplaced jealousy made him possessive and desperate to stake his claim on her and brand her as his. He deepened the kiss and she matched him, her tongue tangling with his as her fingers wove themselves into his hair and anchored him firmly in place. He could feel her pebbled nipples through the unwelcome barrier of his shirt. The rapid rise and fall of her bosom as she pressed herself against him. The throaty, wanton sigh when he finally gave in and cupped her breasts was like an hallelujah. She wanted this. Wanted him and that indeed was everything.

Then all at once she placed the flat of her hands on his shoulders and pushed them apart. Her eyes wide. Kiss-swollen lips parted. Her breathing erratic and laboured as she stared at him. For a moment, he was terrified she already regretted it, until her fingers touched her lips and miraculously she smiled. A sultry, seductive and wholly feminine expression he had never seen on her before.

'That was…rather lovely.'

'Yes, it was.' He found himself smiling back.

'Enlightening…'

'Very.' He had certainly never experienced a kiss like it. But then again, he had never kissed a woman he loved heart and soul before, so it was no wonder. And wonderful.

She reached behind clumsily to open the door, still facing him. 'My very first second kiss.'

The first of many if he had anything to say about it. 'It bodes well for the third.'

'Yes, it does… Will that be happening tomorrow?' She clamped her mouth shut in the way she so often did when her thoughts escaped before she had time to stop them and he laughed.

'I think I can guarantee it—Miss Never-been-kissed-twice-before.'

She smiled again, a little shyly, a little expectantly, as she slowly retreated across the landing to her bedchamber, her pretty eyes never once leaving his. 'Goodnight, Max.'

'Goodnight, Effie… Sleep tight.'

It was only after she had closed the door that her words permeated his lust-addled brain.

I can never accurately gauge people's emotions until it is too late and I have gone too far… And it was obvious you regretted the last one…'

Had he been the one to get it all wrong all along?

Chapter Twenty-One

Dig Day 803: one brooch, fourteen shards of pottery—or perhaps it was thirteen? Or even sixteen...

It had been an odd day. So odd that even at this late hour she wasn't entirely sure what to make of it. There were so many things to think about. So much indecision it was all sending her mad. She didn't have all the answers—but what she did know with complete certainty was that she needed Max.

'Of course, Miranda was the worst kind of seductress.' After two evenings left to their own devices while the men played billiards, they had exhausted all conversation about the charade they were performing for the antiquarians and had resorted to discussing the one thing that inextricably bound them.

Him.

'Such a practised flirt never walked the earth before. All those calculated, heated glances, the rehearsed grace, the confident allure and that classical, effortless beauty... She was used to men dissolving in a puddle at her feet. She had been declared an Incomparable two Seasons before and wielded that title with brutal and well-aimed precision. Every man wanted her, so it was hardly a surprise she snared my brother. He didn't stand a chance against all her obvious charms.'

It was all well and good hating Miranda on principle, but that didn't help Effie's cause on a practical level. If Miranda was the sort of woman he went for, she had little in her own arsenal to compete with the memory. Effie wasn't a seductress or an Incomparable or in possession of classical and effortless beauty. She knew she was considered pretty, as that had been a frequent compliment over the years before her odd personality and manner sent the gentleman who had hastily bestowed the compliment running the obligatory mile to get away from her.

She certainly wasn't graceful, was woefully incapable of flirting and the less said about her lack of grace the better. It didn't bode well for her quest to convince Max they should be more than friends. 'He must have loved her a great deal.'

Eleanor scoffed and shook her head. 'He might think he did, but that wasn't love. It was lust. With a healthy dash of one-upmanship. Pure and simple.' Eleanor drained the last dregs of her fourth sherry and waved the empty glass around. 'The trouble with my brother is he has always been competitive. He cannot stop himself. Miranda was *the* prize every bachelor in London wanted to win and he made it his mission to hoist the trophy. And the fool had no clue she made it easy for him because he was a trophy, too. The handsome, decorated naval hero who just happened to be in line to inherit all this alongside an earldom.'

She stifled a yawn and leaned closer. 'It all happened too fast, if you ask me.'

'Really?'

'He was given extended shore leave while his ship was in dry dock at Portsmouth, fresh from the Battle of Vis and sporting a shiny new victor's medal to make the ladies swoon, and he arrived in London to a hero's welcome. Obviously, that set him a notch above all her battalions of eager suitors and she played him like a fiddle. It was a whirlwind romance.' The whirlwind was a little slurred, but Effie was in no mood to judge. Poor Eleanor had performed a minor miracle in their absence today and had served a veritable banquet for dinner. It was a testament to her strong character she wasn't swigging the stuff directly from the bottle. Something Effie was sorely tempted to do to simply calm her nerves.

'How fast a whirlwind was it?' Not that Effie really needed to know. She was intimidated enough by the seductive Miranda already without knowing how swiftly she had captured Max's heart.

'Fast. He proposed after only three weeks.' Effie had known him for a good seven and had only achieved two kisses. Or one kiss and an over-excited bumping of faces in a confined space. And she still had no earthly idea where she stood. 'The pair of them were the talk of the ballrooms, which suited her very well and wherever he went the men slapped him on the back and congratulated him on his impressive conquest. Then he got deployed to the Americas and she got to play the tragically stoic heroine as she waved him off from the dock. Miranda wept such pretty tears while she waved that exquisite silk handkerchief. I always distrusted that about her. When I cry, my entire face collapses. I look as though I've been smashed in the face with a shovel.'

'So do I.'

'And there is no shame in that, Effie. Those are real tears. Everything about Miranda was fake. Calculated. With my cynical hat on, I would even go as far as saying she'd been out for two Seasons and, with no wealthy duke on the horizon, the sands of time were running out. There is only so long one can be an Incomparable before the bloom fades from the rose.'

'There is?' The world of ballrooms and Seasons and society was a mystery to her. Her academic father had also thought them frivolous and with no mother figure in her life, or even a distant Nithercott aunt somewhere, there was nobody around to organise one. All she had been to were a couple of faculty dances at Cambridge and the local assembly. Neither of which she had bothered attending in years because she had nobody to attend them with.

'She was four and twenty! That is *old* for a debutante.' Which made Effie positively ancient by comparison. Yet another blow to her fragile confidence. How exactly was she supposed to compete with all that?

Eleanor yawned again as the clock chimed midnight. 'I suppose we should call it a night. The gentlemen are clearly having too much boisterous fun to be rejoining us any time soon and I have to be up at the crack of dawn. And so do you. But we can chalk today up as a success though, can't we?'

'Indeed. A resounding success.' Effie supposed she should mark it up as a triumph. After

a long day of digging Percy was beside himself
for finding the brooch, Lord Denby was clearly
impressed with everything despite his naturally
pessimistic character and, because his crony was,
so was Lord Whittlesey, therefore Effie should
have been delighted the eminent antiquarians
all agreed she—or rather Max—had discovered
something amazing. Doubting Denby had also
sent her sketches of the shield to the printers by
express to ensure they were added to the article
alongside an additional couple of paragraphs—
ostensibly hastily written by Max as well—to
ensure everything was included before they published it for the world. But she was too distracted
to give much of a care, truth be told. Distracted by
all her racing thoughts and feelings. All churned
up by that phenomenal kiss yesterday and vehemently refusing to go away.

She and Max hadn't discussed it. There hadn't
been either the time or the opportunity, entirely
thanks to the visiting antiquarians who had mo-
nopolised them since breakfast. It had been hard
to concentrate on the task at hand when her mind
was so full of him and desperately wondering if
there was, or could ever be, a them.

What exactly did that kiss mean?

Because to her it already meant something more
than lust. It had made her begin to crave things

from Max which went beyond a kiss and her over-active mind was determined to plan the next few years rather than the next few hours. Racing ahead again before reality could catch it up.

'Only another full day to get through and we can wave them off from the doorstep.' The sands of time were clearly running out for Effie, too. She would leave hot on the heels of the antiquarians and, at this rate, without the promised third kiss she had been craving since last night or any clue how Max felt about her. 'And we'll be reading your work in that funny-sounding journal and you'll be the talk of the antiquarian world.'

'Well, Max will.' A sacrifice she had accepted for the sake of knowledge when she had signed his name instead of hers. That didn't make it any easier to swallow and the blatant unfairness of the world still galled.

'But you will know it is yours and so do we. Perhaps in a few years, when times have changed, you will get the credit you deserve. Max will tell them the truth when the time comes, so you do not need to worry on that score. He might have abysmal taste in fiancées, but he is an honourable man to his core.'

He was. And a frustratingly difficult one to read.

Effie saw Eleanor to her door and then retreated into her own room to wait. No matter what time the dratted game of billiards finished, or how exhausted she felt from a day spent largely on edge, she needed to talk to Max alone to assess the lay of the land. She needed to know where she stood, although after her conversation with his sister, the spectre of Miranda now hovered ominously. How exactly was she supposed to compete with that?

She stared at her reflection in the dressing table mirror and tried to ignore her racing pulse.

What was Max thinking?

Hard to say. He had been perfectly pleasant all day. He'd placed a lingering kiss on the back of her head when she had arrived a tad flustered at breakfast—but as he was doing a splendid job of pretending to be her fiancé, he could have been acting. He had also been most solicitous during the long hours they had all spent digging, including her in conversations which two of the other gentlemen naturally excluded her from, helping her in and out of the trenches and offering her reassuring smiles throughout. But again, as her pretend fiancé he would do all those things, too, and in isolation they did not mean he was really as happy about everything as he looked.

As Eleanor had quite rightly pointed out—lust wasn't love. And once again, her overactive imagination was running ahead of itself. Love did not happen overnight—unless you happened to be an

Incomparable named Miranda—and it certainly was not something she could ask him about if she ever got him alone. Such declarations had to be offered freely, not prised out, and if she admitted she was falling hopelessly in love with him, he would probably baulk. She would most definitely *not* bring that up if she ever cornered him alone again.

It was so frustrating! Twice, they had almost been alone. The first time he had leaned towards her, clearly about to say something about them or the kiss or both, but Percy had interrupted. The second time, he had caught her hand in the hallway, then a moment later Lord Denby had spirited him away. They had also shared a couple of meaningful glances over dinner, although Effie had no clue as to their real meaning. But when he had suggested the gentlemen did not abandon the ladies tonight and gazed at her, he had been boisterously cajoled into another game of billiards by Percy who declared that when a fellow had rinsed all the others of their coin the night before and then refused to give them the opportunity to win it back, it was very poor form. Obviously, Max had relented—what other choice did he have? But that did leave her and their potential third kiss in limbo.

She stared at her hair, still elaborately dressed and tamed by what felt like a thousand pins.

Would a woman waiting to be kissed still have her hair styled so formally after two hours of waiting? Probably not. Nor would a woman on the cusp of thirty try to entice a gentleman to kiss her looking like the nervous dolt staring back at her now. Effie wanted to appear both confident and alluring like the fiancée who had captured his heart in just three short weeks. Max liked her hair down—at least she assumed he did because he had made short work of the loose bedtime plait last night before he had fisted his hands in it possessively.

Maybe she should take it down? Her scalp would certainly be happy if she did. All those pins were digging into it now and her head felt as heavy as her aching, needy breasts. She pulled out the pins and watched it tumble around her shoulders. If that wasn't a blatant invitation, she didn't know what was and, seeing as at this stage she was prepared to do almost anything to move things rapidly forward, she didn't care if it was too obvious a gesture. Obvious was confident and confident, if Miranda was any gauge, was alluring.

But had she pushed him into the second kiss?

The question which had been niggling the most since she had shut her door last night made her pause again to consider it. The simple answer was most definitely—she had had ample opportunities to leave his bedchamber at the end and had taken none of them. But he had seemed to enjoy it regardless. He had been as breathless as she when she had ended it—it had been she who had necessarily ended it for certain, not he, because she couldn't trust herself not to take things too far and scare him off. But she had felt his obvious desire through her nightgown pretty much from the outset. Surely he couldn't fake that? Everything she had read about the male anatomy suggested such a feat wasn't possible. Therefore she decided to trust the science and assume the kiss had affected him as much as it had affected her. He felt lust at least, if not affection, and that was a start.

However, the first time they had kissed he had seemed as overwhelmed by it as she was and then he had dismissed it as a heat-of-the-moment bumping of faces born out of the excitement of finding the shield. Maybe his passionate reaction this time stemmed from the sheer relief of getting through the first day of their charade without issue? And while he might well have said he *would* kiss her a third time today, after sleeping on it he could well have changed his mind.

But if he wasn't averse to indulging in a third kiss, which she sincerely hoped he wasn't, should she broach the subject of all the other things she had lain awake thinking about then incessantly pondered still or was it too soon? All-encompassing new feelings, desire, outright curiosity—and the future. Would such things scare the daylights out of him? She'd never had anyone to ask.

Common sense told her of course it was too soon even though she might feel the moment was right. What did she know about such things anyway? She usually got this sort of stuff wrong as her extensive lack of real friends and woeful shortage of eager beaus was testament to. Just because she was feeling all of these heady, thrilling and all-consuming things, just because she was tumbling head over heels into love, did not mean he was. In fact, so early into their ever-changing relationship and only two actual kisses in, there was every chance he hadn't given any of it much thought. Max was clearly an expert in kissing and she certainly wasn't his first. Therefore, it stood to reason that what they had shared thus far wasn't the least bit significant as far as he was concerned.

Besides, and to give him the benefit of the doubt for his potential lack of similar angst, he'd had his hands full since yesterday pretending to be something he wasn't. He'd been too busy charming Lord Denby into agreeing that her roundhouse was indeed a roundhouse, that one could clearly discern the remains of the long-rotted-away post holes in compacted mud and that the amazing finds which had emerged from the site so far indicated the Celtic dwelling was considerably older than the Roman ruins nearby.

And he was doing all that for her. Which suggested he must care in some way, although it was which way he cared that consumed her. She sincerely doubted Miranda would have needed to ask. Or needed any reassurance of her abilities to snare him. She would have known—or perhaps assumed, as Eleanor had intimated. Maybe that was what was needed here?

Perhaps if she behaved a little more like the sort of woman Max was obviously drawn to—the confident, flirty, effortless seductress rather than the clueless oddity with her head buried in a hole—then she might convince him to be similarly besotted with her.

How hard could it be to be a seductress anyway?

She had the basic equipment if the compliments were anything to go by and she had certainly read enough romantic books to be able to mimic some of the techniques from the pages. She could start right this second by using this time to rehearse her words. Not questions which demanded answers but assumptions which told him in no uncertain terms that a third heated kiss and everything beyond was a foregone conclusion.

Hello, Max... I've been waiting for you.

Too bold?

Hello, Max... I couldn't sleep.

Which sounded as though that was his fault—which might be good. Or it might come across as pathetic and whiny. It was probably all in the tone and the facial expressions. She practised a few sultry looks in the mirror and, when she found one she liked which involved her twirling her finger in her hair, she rehearsed her lines again, dropping her voice to a breathy whisper.

Hello, Max...

Perfect!

Ambiguous, but hinting at promise...except... Drat it! She'd knotted her finger in her messy hair! Thank goodness this was just a rehearsal as the calculated Miranda would have known she should have brushed the tangled mess first before fiddling with it.

Effie had only just unknotted her finger and grabbed the brush when she heard his feet on the stairs, then practically jumped out of her skin as nerves took over. This was it! There was no more time to procrastinate. No more time to prepare herself. It was time to make him fall in love with her.

Wide-eyed, she took a last look at her reflection in the mirror and her heart sank at the ridiculous state of her hair. What had she been thinking to take out all the pins and destroy a perfectly lovely hairstyle?

In desperation, she gathered it all up and twisted it into a knot, then blindly rummaged for her hairpins. She jabbed a few in, but when they stubbornly refused to work resorted to her trusty old faithful. He had said he preferred her pencil and so a pencil it would have to be! She cast her eyes frantically about for the slippers she had kicked off the second she had entered the room, but when she located only one realised she had no choice but to go to him barefoot.

Bare feet and a pencil! Heaven help her if those were the only weapons she had in her seductress's arsenal! At this rate, they'd never bump faces again.

She heard his door click shut and realised she was in grave danger of losing the moment. If she left it any longer, he'd be in bed and that certainly wouldn't be proper.

Proper!

As if anything about this was proper.

She inhaled deeply before wrenching open her door and inhaled once again before she knocked on his. To her surprise, it opened straight away, almost as if he'd expected her.

'Hello, Max. I've been waiting for sleep and couldn't.'

She cringed and immediately prayed for death as his handsome face scrunched in confusion.

'Couldn't what?'

'It doesn't matter.' The confident seductress had clearly been shot in the paddock before the race. 'I just thought we should discuss…um… your evening… Make sure we are presenting a united front.'

'I am glad you are awake. I've been wanting to speak to you about last night.' His suddenly serious expression killed all her last hopes of seduction stone dead. 'Come in for a second.' *Just a second.* Disappointment settled in her stomach. 'This is not a conversation for the hallway.'

Effie stepped in on leaden feet, urgently rehearsing her nonchalant face in her head. If he was going to break her heart, she'd be damned if she allowed him to see it. He closed the door and leaned his back against it.

'What did you mean when you said it was *obvious* I regretted the last kiss?'

'The bumping of faces?' She had not expected him to start with that question. Or any question to be frank when she was expecting a polite let down.

He winced. 'I said that, didn't I?'

'You also called it a big mistake.'

'Not my finest hour. But in my defence you had just knocked me sideways and I was…' He sighed as he turned away and then gazed at her sheepishly though the heavy curtain of his hair. 'I didn't mean it, Effie. Any of it. That first kiss was special. Last night's was spectacular.'

'Oh…' She had no earthly idea where this was going.

'And I would very much like to do it again… Right this second, in fact…in case you were wondering.'

Chapter Twenty-Two

Two beautiful big brown eyes...

It had been an odd day. So odd that even at this late hour he wasn't entirely sure what to make of it. There were so many things to think about. So much indecision it was all sending him mad. He didn't have all the answers—but what he did know, with complete certainty, was that he needed Effie.

She looked so lovely in the candlelight, bare toes just poking out from under the hem of her unbelievably distracting coral evening gown, nothing but a pencil holding up her hair and blinking back at him as if he'd just spoken to her in a foreign language rather than admitting he was desperate to kiss her. 'May I?'

To his utter delight she answered by launching herself at him, knocking him back against the door as her lips greedily found his. It was this honesty he adored about her. There was no artifice about Effie. No deception. No games. She wanted to kiss him and he desperately wanted her to. It was strange—a few short weeks ago he had been convinced no woman would ever want to kiss him again and he had mourned all those faceless, voiceless, soulless women as if he known each one personally, yet now he couldn't care less because none of them interested him. Why would they when the only woman he could ever imagine kissing again was the one currently in his arms? He'd craved this all day, which was no mean feat when one considered the day he'd had, but it was true. She had possessed him, thoroughly bewitched him, and despite the war currently being waged in his head he had counted every second just waiting for the chance to hold her again.

He felt her hands burrow beneath his coat and smiled against her mouth. He hadn't misread her desire yesterday. She was as desperate for the contact as he was and he felt gloriously alive again. Perhaps not entirely whole, not at all his old self, but not the shadow he had been when he had come here to Rivenhall completely broken. Something was shifting. He was changing. But she was here and nothing else mattered.

Which was a dangerous game while her passionate exuberance was scrambling his wits and driving his body mad with longing.

Not ready to put a sensible stop to it yet, he poured his heart and soul into the kiss, wrapping his arms tightly around her and not entirely sure if he would ever let go. Almost immediately, things got out of hand and he revelled in that, too. She ground her hips against his arousal, moaning as his lips found her ear. Her neck. Her shoulder. At some point, he must have lifted her and reversed their positions, because Effie's legs wrapped themselves around his waist as he held her suspended from the ground using only the door and the hard press of his body, losing himself entirely in the moment. Losing himself in her. The urge to tear the buttons from his falls and plunge himself deep inside of her was the only thing which brought him up short.

He tore his lips away and rested his forehead against hers, gulping for air, his body aching for release and his head whirling like a frantic spinning top.

'Did I do something wrong, Max?'

The bark of laughter came out of nowhere. 'No, Miss Naive. You did everything right. Too right—when I am desperately trying to be a gentleman and about to fail miserably.'

'Oh.' She was pleased with herself. He could hear it in her voice and he liked that, too. No games. No lies. Just Effie.

He gently lowered her to the ground and stepped back, trying and failing not to notice how scandalously wanton she looked with her lips all swollen, those sultry dark eyes molten and one sleeve hanging off her shoulder as her straining breasts rose and fell against the silk. Thank the lord the pencil had held or he'd be completely done for, although it looked precarious. 'Perhaps we should talk for a little while.'

'About what?'

'About…' He considered suggesting something inane to do with the antiquarians or the dig, but knew there were more important things which needed to be said. 'About me.' Max exhaled loudly to calm himself, feeling more vulnerable than he had since those first months in his sickbed after his world had fallen apart. 'Because I have all these confusing thoughts suddenly crashing about in my mind and I cannot make head nor tail of them. And seeing as you are the cleverest person I have ever met, I was hoping you could help me make sense of them because I have to face them, Effie. I don't want to, but I know I must.'

'All right…' Her concern was instant and genuine. 'We should probably sit in that case…' She wandered to the bed and was about to lower herself on to it when he held up his hand.

'Not there! Have a care, woman! How am I supposed to have any sort of rational, let alone important conversation with you sat on my bed looking like temptation incarnate?'

She smiled as if he had just given her the most beautiful compliment and took herself to the *chaise* near the window instead. 'Is this better?'

'Only slightly, but it will have to do.'

Max propped a hip on his mattress and racked his brains as to where he should start. 'Because I kept catching him staring, I told Percy about my burns this morning and he said the strangest thing...' It was probably the wrong place entirely, but as his insightful comment had come directly after Effie's outburst about Max regretting their first kiss, it joined with it to plague him and make him question everything he thought he believed. 'It was quite philosophical, actually—he said he didn't doubt an experience like that put everything else into perspective... And it set me to wondering, because I used to be level-headed. I used to be pragmatic and philosophical and optimistic, but I have no clue exactly where my perspective on things went because I am no longer sure I have any.'

'Hardly a surprise. There is nothing like a traumatic event to shift perspective on its axis. It is hard to be any of those things when fate deals you a blow. After Rupert died, I was so lost and distraught, I didn't know which way was up or what I was going to do. I'd put all my eggs in one basket, mapped out my life and had no contingency plan. It took a while to find my feet again and to find a new path. That was the power of one single traumatic event. You were dealt a succession of blows, Max—the burns, the loss of your ship, your crew, your career, your father and your fiancée. And perhaps even your dreams. All in quick succession. Each one of those has the power to tear the ground from under the feet. Combined, I should imagine they are devastating and each would need adequate time to heal.'

He hadn't thought of it like that. There had been a series of separate catastrophes, some inextricably linked to be sure, but all bundled together into one indigestible mass. Yet in the last few weeks, it had felt as if a fog was lifting and he no longer saw the mass as much as sensed there were separate components to his grief. And she was right about that, too. It was grief which had overwhelmed him. For so many things he hadn't known where to start mourning them all. 'I've started to contemplate the future again.' The truth tumbled out. Truth he had not realised until he vocalised it.

'That's good. Does it involve the sea?'

How did she know him so well? 'I think so… Not the navy any longer. I was done with that before the fire.' Another truth he had not seen coming. 'Ships, I think… Cargo, perhaps. Or passengers. Maybe both. It's hazy. Not properly formed. Starting small…' Some of the tangled thoughts began to unravel and he felt strangely lighter.

'From little acorns…' She smiled wistfully. 'That's wonderful, Max.'

'It's terrifying. I am not sure I am ready to go back out into the world.'

'You are more ready than you were when I first met you almost two months ago.'

'True…'

'And I dare say Eleanor would corroborate that by confirming you are much more ready than you were a year ago.'

That was also true. A year ago he had been in a very dark place. He wasn't in that infinite pit any longer. More a hole a little deeper than one of Effie's trenches—but he could see some light now. Quite a bit of it. One of the brightest shining beacons was sat right in front of him. How could he sail the seas and leave her behind? Yet another tangled thought to swirl among the mess. 'It's probably all too soon.'

'Why?'

'Because I still can't see the wood for the trees. Still can't make much sense of it all.'

'Scientifically speaking, the best way to work through a difficult problem is to break it into chunks and go through it systematically. Start at the beginning and work from there.' She settled back, her cheek propped against her hand. 'Perhaps it is time to re-evaluate some of those things and look at them with fresh eyes? The fire happened, what, a year and a half ago? Do you have misgivings about what you did?'

'No. I wish it hadn't happened, but it did and I had to do what needed to be done to save the ship and the crew. We were all in the thick of it.'

'And after that?'

'Six months of blurriness. Pain, laudanum and stupor.'

'Then do you recall where you were a year ago?'

'Eleanor's house. Feeling very alone and very sorry for myself.'

'Why?'

He slanted her a disbelieving look. 'All of the above.'

'That's not true, is it? Your sister told me once the worst was past and the threat of death was gone, you were full of fight and optimistic about your recovery. What changed?'

'I saw myself.' A lie. That had come after and he suspected Effie had worked that out already. 'Miranda…'

'Do you want to tell me about it?'

No. But how could he ever move forward if he didn't? 'Nelson was an ugly bugger. A great man, but nowhere near as pretty as his portraits would have you believe. He'd lost most of his teeth to scurvy, so his face had caved in. He was blinded when a shell exploded and, aside from ruining the look of that eye, it also ripped his entire eyebrow off and took a chunk out of his forehead. His arm was missing and he had more nicks and scars on his face than a face should carry, but both his wife and Emma Hamilton still loved him to distraction. He wore those scars like medals—proud badges of honour—and nothing kept him down. That inspired me. I assumed my face would heal, my stunning fiancée would still marry me even with a few battle scars and I'd be back sailing the high seas in no time. But Miranda recoiled in horror the first time she saw me.' He'd tried to hold her hand. Had needed to know everything was going to be all right. 'I assumed it was because it was all such a mess…the wounds were still open, some were festering, it must have been disgusting.'

'You hadn't seen it, then?'

'No... Unbeknown to me, Eleanor had forbidden anyone from giving me a mirror in case I was so horrified by what I saw, I wouldn't be able to cope.' He felt his throat constrict at the memories he had tried so hard, but never entirely been able, to bury. 'As time went on, they healed and the threat of infection was over, but Miranda still recoiled. I could see I disgusted her, but...' He felt the bile rise at the memory. She had made him feel hideous.

'You still gave her the benefit of the doubt.'

'I thought things would improve. Clung to that thought. My father died then. We had never been particularly close because he was a difficult man as I'm sure my uncle would testify. He tried on several occasions to heal the breach between them, but my father would have none of it. I have no idea what they fought over, but I do know he never forgave me for running away to sea rather than going to university and training to be the Earl I was destined to become. We rarely saw one another when I came home on leave. I preferred to stay at my sister's house and he preferred to avoid me when I did. We never ever sorted it out or mended the breach between us either...even when I was on the brink of death myself. I recall he visited me twice and both times he was adamant none of it would have happened if I'd obeyed him as I was supposed to… And then it was too late. I was still too ill to attend the funeral and while Eleanor went, she asked Miranda to sit with me. And it all came out. She was dreading the prospect of marrying me, even admitted gazing upon my face made her feel physically sick. She claimed she needed time and, because I still foolishly hoped she would come around, I offered her a termination of our engagement.'

'An offer she gratefully accepted.'

'She did—but not before assuring me that she probably *did* only need time and that it was more a postponement than a termination. And that once my scars had healed… I demanded a mirror that same day because I wanted to know how long they would actually take to fully heal and…well…'

'You realised they were always going to be there. How did that make you feel?'

'Hideous. Ashamed.' Should he tell her about the young mother? 'Shortly after that, Eleanor bullied me into getting some fresh air. It was early. We crossed the road from her house to the empty park and we fed the ducks. A woman arrived with her son to do the same. She took one look at me and hastily covered the child's face to shield him from the sight.'

'Oh, Max…' He saw tears glisten in her eyes. 'People can be awful.'

'It was the last straw. I suppose I lost all hope of everything then.'

'That is always easier.' She shot him a wry smile at his obvious consternation. A sure sign she was about to give him a swift kick up the backside. 'Admit it, Max, giving up is always easier than daring to dream. Expecting disappointment is easier than hoping for happiness. Accepting shallow Miranda's or that stupid, thoughtless woman in the park's assessment of what you were gave you the excuse to give up.'

'Are you suggesting I took the easy way out?'

'No...I'm suggesting you took the natural path—the fragile human path first as we all do when hope seems lost—but that now you are ready and able to brave another. That is human nature, too. When we get knocked down, inevitably we have to get back up. History is peppered with examples. Would you like me to recite some?'

'Don't you dare.' Now he was smiling, too. He'd just told her that he had scared a woman in a park and repulsed his fiancée and he was smiling. Clearly it was a day for the miraculous. 'Perhaps time really does heal all wounds?'

He watched her gaze wander to the sheet covering the big mirror and seriously considered shutting her down before she dared ask what he knew she was going to, but didn't. 'What do you see now when you look at your reflection?'

'I try to avoid it.'

'I know…' She walked towards him and held out her hand. 'But you cannot avoid it for ever.'

She tugged him to the mirror and then ripped away the sheet, forcing him to stare at his own reflection while she gazed up at his face. 'Do you want to know what I see?'

She didn't wait for his answer.

'I see a man who has survived the worst and lived to tell the tale. I see a man who put his entire crew before himself and sent every one of them home to their families alive. I see a man who is lost, but is trying to find his way again. A man who loves his sister even though she drives him mad. Who digs trenches for a peculiar stranger who he allows to trespass on his land. One who insists on accompanying a woman home to keep her safe. Who claims he wants to be left alone, but actively seeks me out. A man who can predict the weather and charm the most toffee-nosed snob into his way of thinking. Who carries a few scars that I no longer notice because I only see the hero who lies beneath them, who thinks too deeply and cares too much what others think of him.' In the mirror, he watched her smile the same sultry smile she had allowed him to see last night after their kiss. 'A man who wears his breeches too well and, in my humble opinion, fills his coats better than any other. Whose eyes dance with mischief. A man who isn't the least bit intimidated by a woman who is far cleverer than him…'

'I wouldn't go that far…'

Lilacs and roses enveloped him before she reached out to trace the ugly disfigurement on his cheek and he forced himself not to flinch or pull away, while he anxiously watched their reflections to see if she was tempted to. Then felt humbled and elated and overwhelmed that she didn't.

'I see the man I want to kiss again—because his kisses are divine and they make me feel like a woman rather than an oddity. And nobody has ever made me feel like that before, Max…only you.'

It was more a whisper than a kiss, but more potent because of it. Her lips brushed over his, then slowly worked their way across his scar to his neck. Her teeth nipped his ear while her fingers wove their way into his hair and when she kissed his mouth again it was achingly soft, but bold and sensual. 'I've been thinking about this all day… You… Me… All alone.' She took both his hands and placed them on her body and the question he hadn't dared ask suddenly blurted out.

'Do you see a man who you might consider for ever with?'

She paused and turned towards the mirror to gaze at his reflection while he gazed at hers. 'That depends…on what you see when you look at me.'

If she was expecting a long speech, she was about to be disappointed. There was only one answer he could give at this significant and pivotal moment, and that was the truth. 'I see the woman I love, Effie.'

And then he saw exactly what she was feeling in the unfathomable depths of her eyes before she said the words he so desperately needed to hear. 'Then for ever sounds perfect…because I love you, too, Max. I think I always have.'

Chapter Twenty-Three

Dig Day 804: you learn something new every day...

He kissed her, but this kiss was entirely different. She could feel all his emotion and all his love because he poured it all into it until she felt breathless. And then, when he stopped, she could see the passion in his eyes. The need. The absolute noble frustration.

'What's the matter?'

'I'm still desperately trying to be a gentleman.' His dark eyes were serious and full of longing. The question implicit.

'There is no need. I am not very good at playing hard to get... I've never really had cause to practise it. If you want me, I am yours.'

His gaze heated. 'I can wait. I am happy to wait.'

'I'm almost thirty. I think I have waited long enough. And I am dying of curiosity. And lust... It has been torture all day... My body feels so ripe and needy... I've read about it. Extensively. But reading about it isn't like actually experiencing it, is it? And...' Should she be admitting all this? 'What I mean is... I have so many questions...' He placed his finger over her lips.

'Breathe, Effie.' The wretch was smiling, on the cusp of laughing at him. 'Then for the love of God shut up so I can start answering all of them.'

He kissed her again, then lifted her into his arms and carried her to the bed. He sat next to her on the mattress and simply stared. 'There's something I've wanted to do for the longest time. Something that I've imagined at least a thousand times... Something I dream about incessantly... Something very, *very*...intimate.' His voice had dropped to a sultry whisper. The intense and carnal way he gazed at her made her pulse quicken and every tiny nerve in her body tingle in anticipation.

'What?'

'I can't explain it. I have to just do it... May I?'

She nodded and intently watched his hand as it came towards her, excited and perhaps a little anxious at the unexpected and unknown. Except it didn't head to her breasts or her gown as

she expected. It went to her hair. 'This pencil…
is the single most erotic thing I have ever seen.'
He sighed as he slowly pulled it from her hair and
watched the tangled mess fall about her shoulders.
'That's it. I am thoroughly seduced.'

'That's all it took?' She found herself laughing. 'I've been worrying myself silly all day about
how to go about seducing you tonight and all I
needed was a pencil?'

He tumbled her back on to the mattress. 'A pair
of mismatched shoes or those fetching breeches
would have worked, too—but that damn pencil has haunted me for weeks.' His dancing eyes
turned serious then and his mouth brushed over
hers. 'Are you sure about this, Effie?'

'For once, I do not have a single nagging question in my mind.' She traced her finger over his
mouth and down his throat, then boldly began
to undo his cravat. He stiffened, but did not pull
away, and her full heart wept for him and the way
the callous Miranda had made him feel.

Suddenly, he sat bolt upright 'Perhaps now is a
good time to turn off the lamps…' Effie stopped
him as he reached over.

'I want to see you, Max. All of you. Don't you
want to see me?'

She watched him swallow and nod, saw his
anxiousness and indecision and decided there and

then he needed her to take the lead to help him banish his demons. She moved to sit before him on the mattress and lifted up her hair in invitation. 'Undo my laces, Max.'

She felt his fingers fumble and smiled to herself. His nerves empowered her. If he was seduced by a mere pencil, then he was about to receive a shock. How wonderful would it be to have this complicated, damaged and intrinsically lovely man so overcome with desire he couldn't think straight?

As the bodice loosened, she allowed it to slip from her shoulders, then stood to make him watch her send it falling to the floor. His gaze swept the length of her, then settled on where her hands undid her stays before following the tiny garment where she tossed it to the floor. The gauzy shift which went with the gown left little to the imagination. She knew that because she had thought as much as she had donned it earlier. Max's sharp intake of breath confirmed it. No doubt he could see the dark shadow of her nipples, but in case he missed it, or was being too gentlemanly to look, she glanced down and watched his eyes follow. Watched his jaw clench. Heard his ragged breath as those eyes darkened with unmistakable desire.

To torture him, she bent to kiss him, letting her tongue leisurely entwine with his while she held his hands to prevent him from touching her. Only when she couldn't bear it any longer did she step back and slowly peel the translucent linen from her shoulders, until her bare breasts were fully revealed, closely followed by the rest of her.

'Oh, Effie...' His sigh was like a benediction. His appreciative gaze like a caress. But she knew he needed to be half-mad before he fully forgot his scars and gave himself completely to her as she intended to give herself to him.

She kissed him again and lost herself in it, revelling in the feel of his hands on her naked skin. Max was lost, too. So lost he hadn't noticed she had unbuttoned his waistcoat until she pushed it from his shoulders. Beneath her palms she could feel his heart beating, and it sped up when she began to untuck his shirt.

'It looks like Africa... The scar...' His voice was awkward again. Self-conscious.

'Useful, then—for a sailor. If you ever happen to be going that way.'

'I suppose.' He smiled and shook his head. 'Sometimes you say the damnedest things.'

'I'm odd, remember. What do you expect?'

'Always the unexpected with you.' He lifted his arms and allowed her to drag the soft linen over his head, then held his breath.

As did she.

She wasn't entirely sure what she had expected to see—but it wasn't this. The muscles across his shoulders and in his arms were beautifully defined, like a Roman statue, but carved out of flesh instead of marble. The light dusting of dark hair across his chest narrowed to an arrow which bisected his navel and disappeared beneath the waistband of his breeches. Breeches which did little now to disguise the impressive bulge beneath them.

Because she couldn't help herself, she ran her palms over his skin, feeling those distracting muscles bunch and tense beneath her touch, only because he was awaiting her judgement. She allowed her eyes to focus on the scar. It was one continuous mass which started on his left cheek, down that side of his neck and bloomed over his shoulder before petering out towards the bottom of his ribs. She trailed her fingertips across it. It felt different from the rest of him. Tighter and textured, but not unpleasant. 'Is this the part where I am supposed to recoil in horror?'

He nodded. 'Hideous, isn't it?'

'I never ever believed I would have something in common with Nelson, but I don't see hideous. I see the bravery it took to get them and the determination it took not to allow them to kill you like the doctors assumed.' She traced the outline with the pad of one finger. 'And it is shaped like Africa, which is fortuitous.'

'How so?'

She allowed the finger to follow the intriguing arrow of hair down his abdomen to the first button on his falls before smiling up at him saucily. 'Because I've always found maps fascinating, but have to confess I find what's under here more fascinating. I've never seen a real naked man in the flesh.'

'Then allow me to be your first.' Confident, flirty Max was back with a vengeance. 'Although I must also insist I am your last.' His hands made short work of the buttons.

'What if we have sons?'

'They don't count...' Then he cupped her cheek and gazed deeply into her eyes. 'And while we are on the subject of children, would you like me to be careful tonight?'

Her womb seemed to sigh inside her. 'I would prefer you to be careless... Outrageously careless.'

'Even if it means you might have to marry me straight away?'

'Especially if it means I have to marry you straight away. There are only two things in this world I've always wanted—and apparently only you have to power to grant them both.'

'Marriage?'

'Love—although I had convinced myself that was never on the cards before I met you. And a family. A place where an oddity like me always belongs. I actually hate being lonely, Max.' She watched his expression cloud with sympathy and understanding.

'That was the real reason you were marrying Rupert, wasn't it? You wanted to belong.'

'He wanted an heir and I wanted all the things other women—normal women—take for granted. Because I am still a woman regardless of my big brain.'

'That, madam, I am well aware of.' His eyes raked her naked body, the blatant appreciation in them making her skin tingle. 'And for the record, I've always been aware of it. Big brain and all.' He bent to kiss her forehead. 'Although to be honest, and perhaps this makes me an oddity, too, but I have always found your excessive intelligence attractive. I love your mind as well as your body.' His finger grazed the skin of her neck before tracing the outer edge of her nipple. 'Well, all right then…' He sat back and bent to tug off his boots. 'Outrageously careless it is. Prepare to be ravished, Miss Naked As The Day You Were Born.'

'How exactly do you plan to ravish me when you are still wearing your breeches?'

He kissed her again, laughing before he finally

gave her a peek under those breeches and thoroughly enjoyed watching her eyes widen as she tentatively explored the shape of him. 'It's a bit different from the diagrams...'

'Book learning will only take you so far, Effie.' His voice was unsteady. Staccato. His eyes fluttered closed and he gasped as she traced the obviously sensitive tip, then he groaned and hauled her into his arms, tumbling them both back on the bed. Then exacted sweet revenge for the way she had tortured him only moments ago by trailing hot kisses along her jaw and throat and between the valley between her breasts.

Then down over her belly. His clever lips followed the path of his hands along the curve of her hip, the sensitive flesh of her inner thigh, all the way down to her toes which he reverently kissed one by one before working his way diligently back up again.

She moaned aloud when he teased her taut nipple with his tongue, then practically growled when he finally sucked it into his mouth and did unspeakably wicked things to it. She could feel his hardness against her belly and instinctively moved her hips to receive it, only to hear the throaty rumble of his laugh deep in his chest when he purposely moved out of the way to deny her. 'Not yet, love.'

'But, Max… I'm ready…' Her body was screaming for release. Aching for him. 'So ready…'

'Shhh…' His touch whispered between her legs and she melted. So soft but so deadly, the pleasure so intense she was certain she couldn't bear it. Yet each time she thought she might die from the wanting, he took her higher until she was begging him to take mercy on her and fill her body with his.

'I've read about this…'

'Of course you have.' He was propped on one arm, staring down at her through hooded eyes as she writhed uncontrollably under his lazy, decadent touch. 'And what did you learn?'

'That it really didn't feel this good when I tried it myself…' She shouldn't have said that, but she wasn't thinking straight. Never should have admitted that because he stopped what he was doing to stare at her. Then the wholly male smile which slowly transformed his expression seemed more intrigued than amused. And aroused. Very aroused.

'Then you should probably brace yourself, because I can guarantee this will feel better.'

And it did. He used his mouth and tongue to love her instead, pushing her to the edge of an invisible cliff which made her fists grip the sheets to steady herself and her hips buck as her body simultaneous welcomed the onslaught and fought against it. Then he was filling her. Slowly, achingly slowly, edging himself inside, kissing her mouth and her eyelids and whispering her name. Telling her that he loved her. That he would always love her.

There wasn't any of the pain or discomfort she had read about, only rightness, as if she had been specifically designed just for him and him for her. With absolutely no thought at all, her body knew how to move against him and she stopped fighting the pleasure. She accepted it all, allowing it to build in waves, possess her, take control of her completely, until all there was, all that mattered, was Max and the blinding stars he showed her when they fell off that imaginary cliff together.

Chapter Twenty-Four

Five stolen kisses...

Max couldn't wait for the day to end so he could spend another night with Effie. Unfortunately, as it was the antiquarians' last day at Rivenhall before they left first thing the next morning, all three of them were keen to maximise their remaining time. It was past six and Lord Percival was still digging, deep in a baffling conversation about something to do with blasted Tacitus with the woman of his dreams and clearly in no immediate hurry to stop.

Not that he was jealous.

After last night, he was in no doubt she was as besotted with him as he was with her, which was a blasted miracle he still couldn't quite get over, but one he was determined to enjoy for as long as he had breath in his body. But he wanted this interminable visit done so they could just get on with for ever. Now that he had a future, he wanted to start it. They had plans to formulate. Vows to take. Dark-haired, ridiculously clever babies to make. Things he couldn't begin to do with a bunch of irritating academics in his house. He'd barely managed to steal a few stolen kisses from Effie since breakfast. All of them much too short.

At least Lord Denby and Lord Whittlesey had finally called it a day. Both were headed back towards the house with buried treasure in their pockets which Max had graciously donated after Effie had assured him she already had enough axe and spear heads from the site and wouldn't miss them.

'I hate to chivvy the pair of you on—but Eleanor will have my guts for garters if I don't get you back in time to change for dinner.'

'It's all right for you, old chap.' Sir Percival stared wistfully at the ruins before sighing. 'You take all this for granted. You get to come back here tomorrow with your charming fiancée and dig to your heart's content whereas I am still desperately waiting for a second invitation to come back here to Rivenhall.'

'You are welcome any time, Percy.' Effie clearly had a soft spot for the man. 'And I can keep you regularly apprised of the dig via letter.

Once Max goes back to sea, I shall be glad of the distraction and the company.'

It was a throwaway comment.

Not intended as a dig or barb, but it wounded him all the same, because after they had made love they had talked for hours and she had let him wax lyrical about all his forgotten dreams of building up his own fleet of ships and not once did she try to talk him out of it or ask what his prolonged and continued absences would mean for them.

She had just accepted them.

Selflessly.

Because she loved him and knew he loved the sea.

But as much as he loved it, it had suddenly lost a great deal of its appeal. The last thing he wanted to do was to have to wave her goodbye and not see her for potentially months on end. Effie hated to be lonely. He knew that now because she had entrusted him with the truth only moments before she entrusted him with her body. Yet here he was, offering her an equally as lonely future while he went off to chase his own dreams and left her to her own devices.

He watched Percy help her out of the trench and purposefully lagged behind them on the way back to the house, much too busy pondering this new revelation in just a few scant days of nothing but revelations to pay much attention to their conversation. The pair of them were halfway up the stairs before he had the wherewithal to call her back, claiming some domestic pretence so that the devoted Percy wouldn't follow her, and because he did not want to waste a second, tugged her into the closest room.

'I've decided I'm staying here.'

She frowned. 'All right... But Eleanor is going to expect you to at least change before dinner.'

'Not here in the drawing room. I meant I am staying *here*. At Rivenhall. Indefinitely. I do not need to go back to sea.'

'But you love the sea.'

'I love you more and I never want to have to wave goodbye to you from the dock.' Just picturing it made his heart ache.

'I am not Miranda, Max... My affection for you will not wane in your absence.'

He shook his head, grasped her hand. 'This has nothing to do with her. I *know* you are nothing like her.' Was that what this was about? Was he worried history might repeat itself? That she might regret shackling herself to him, too, and think better of it? Philosophically, everything he had had with Miranda had begun to unravel the moment he had sailed away.

He cast his mind back to that fateful day in Portsmouth. Saw Miranda on the dock next to his sister. Saw the charts and orders on his desk in the cabin. His crew nudging him and congratulating him on such a bonny catch. Saw the vast horizon that had always called to him and it all became very clear. He suddenly remembered how eager he had been to be gone and on to the next adventure. The adventure had always been more important then. More important than anything or anyone else.

And it wasn't now.

He'd been a fool not to have seen it before.

'I shall be waiting for you when you get back, Max… I promise.'

'Which is exactly the problem! I don't want you waiting for me, I want you with me, woman! Sailing away from you wouldn't be like sailing away from Miranda. I was ready to go then. In fact, I was eager to go. I'd been on land too long and the ocean was calling me.'

'It's still calling you.'

'It is… But my heart is calling louder. Sailing away from you would be like cutting off my arm. I couldn't bear it.'

'I don't want you giving up your dreams for me, Max. We'll find a compromise to make it work.' She smiled in reassurance but he saw the sadness in her eyes. 'Perhaps I could take an active part in the business? Run your offices at the port? Be closer for when you get home...' The compromise would be all hers and he couldn't bear that. Effie would drive herself mad not exercising her mind with complicated purpose. She could balance the books and whatever else needed doing in her sleep. Then what? Embroidery? Knitting bonnets for their babies? A lifetime of only being his wife? His chattel? He wouldn't do that to her either. She was never made to fit in a traditional mould.

'I don't expect you to give up your dreams either, Effie, to traipse around following me and mine. That's hardly fair either. I'd much rather stay here and be part of your life. Digging is your calling and I make an excellent assistant...'

'Having you and our family is more important.' She seemed sincere—yet she still deserved more.

'But it is your dream to have your work published.'

'As validation, Max. To prove to myself there was some reason I was given this odd brain which the world tries to continually prevent me from using. At some point, I will have exhausted all of Rivenhall's secrets and I shall have to find something new to occupy my mind. I've always known that. Digging is the latest of many obsessions.

How do you think I came to be fluent in Greek or Norse or Saxon? I pick up a new distraction and completely exhaust it. Digging was the one that helped me to get over my bereavements and cope with the prospect of eternal spinsterhood. I made it my dream. I can find another, Max. One that doesn't impede on our future...' Her lovely eyes clouded. 'I would feel awful knowing you had given up your lifelong dream of the sea for me. You are worth more than just swinging a pick-axe—no matter how much I might enjoy watching you swing one.'

'I don't want you to be the one who has to make all the sacrifices and I certainly do not want to have to keep saying goodbye! I could still buy ships—just not sail in them.'

Something which would leave an empty hole inside. He knew that, just as he knew Effie would always have a part of her missing if she gave up uncovering the past and digging up treasure. They were both free spirits. It was who they were. Both adventurers in their own way.

'You'd hate that. I'd hate it, too. Unless we? No...' She shook her head, rolling her eyes in that self-deprecating manner he had come to adore. 'Ignore me... It's probably a stupid idea...'

'You have an idea?' Of course she did. Effie always had an idea. A solution. A hypothesis. No problem was too big for the alluring genius he was going to marry.

'I'd drive you mad… Although…' He watched the myriad emotions skitter across her lovely features as the cogs of her brilliant mind turned and she considered and discounted things. Asked herself questions which she typically answered just as quickly. 'It might work… I'd certainly enjoy it… And you'd also get to…'

'Would you and your big brain mind including me in this discussion?'

'It's a silly idea… Certainly unconventional… What I mean is…' She suddenly gazed into his narrowed eyes and smiled. And loudly inhaled before blowing it out. 'How would you feel about doing *both* together? A proper compromise.'

'I'm all for compromise if it means I never have to part with you. What do you have in mind, Miss Knowledgeable and Wise?'

'Part of the year we could stay here at Rivenhall so I could dig it up while you look ruggedly handsome wielding that pickaxe, and the other part…' she slanted him a hopeful glance '…we could…perhaps…sail the seven seas together.'

The idea had merit. Glorious, logical, ridiculous merit. 'You would be prepared to go to sea? To leave all the comforts of home behind? All your books and holes in the ground? To live in a cabin?'

'I'd live in a burrow as long as it was with you! And who says I have to leave all my books behind?' The golden flecks in her whisky eyes positively gleamed. 'Just think of all the things I could learn, Max. All the new places I could visit. All the new history I could discover. The languages. The culture.' Then those beguiling eyes clouded once more as they sought his for reassurance. 'Unless it's not the done thing for a woman to go to sea?'

'It's not the done thing in the navy—' He felt the corners of his mouth curl up as the weight on his shoulders lifted. 'But I wouldn't be in the navy! And who cares what the done thing is anyway? They'll be my ships and I get to say who sails in them.' He allowed her unconventional proposal to sink in and marinade and decided he approved of it in every possible way. He liked being at Rivenhall and he liked digging with Effie. If they had a family, and he would move hell and high water to make that dream come true for her, then he would need to have solid roots somewhere. He loved the sea, but did not want to leave her. Her dream and his dream. Shared dreams. Dreams he couldn't wait to live. 'I'm game if you are.'

She beamed and the world felt brighter, their future exciting. The old thrill of adventure burning as bright as it ever had—except better. Because he had her.

'Then we have the foundations of a plan...'

'Which knowing your brain, will doubtless be fully fledged before the dinner is done.'

The big clock chimed the hour in the hallway, reminding them both that the meal was imminent. They both stared at it and sighed.

Effie traced a button on his waistcoat. 'As much as I don't want to, I need to bathe and change for dinner. Eleanor has spent hours planning this final meal on my behalf.' Max wound his finger around one of the stray tendrils which had fallen out of her pencil, trying, and failing, not to think of her in the bath. 'We could discuss it all later. Shall I visit you tonight?'

'I was rather hoping you would...although doubtless, I'll be stuck playing blasted billiards with your antiquarians till midnight.'

'You know I will wait up.'

'No... Go to bed. I'll wake you when I'm done... And I'll enjoy it.'

She shot him a wicked glance out of the corner of her eye as he escorted her back into the hallway. 'Make sure you do. I shall leave my door scandalously unlocked because, as you already know, I am incapable of playing hard to get where you are concerned. But I should warn you, it is a warm night...'

'What has that got to do with it?'

She leaned close to whisper, her warm breath tormenting his ear, 'I cannot guarantee I will be wearing a nightgown.'

All his blood seemed to pool in his groin. 'Until midnight, then, Miss Nithercott.' He kissed her hand, thoroughly enjoying their flirting and the havoc she was playing with his body. 'I shall count the seconds—alongside the panelling and the billiard balls, of course.'

Max watched her disappear up the stairs and turned towards his study, then stopped dead when he encountered Lord Percival staring at him open mouthed.

'Did I hear you say Miss Nithercott?' His blood ran cold. 'As in Miss Euphemia Nithercott?'

'It's not what you think, Percy.'

'The Miss Nithercott who submits paper after paper to the Society? The one Lord Whittlesey has banned?' Max could tell by his wide eyes that the man had heard a great deal more of their conversation than just her name and was rapidly piecing it all together. 'She is not Miss Jones... You are not really engaged... This is all a ruse!'

'Not entirely.'

'Are you really Lord Rivenhall, sir? Or is that an alias, too? Is this whole thing a deception?'

'Of course I am Rivenhall and Effie really is

my fiancée—or at least she is now. And the dig is real. All the finds are real. The only deception is the name on the paper, and in her defence, she had no choice.'

'She wrote the paper!'

'Well, of course she wrote the paper. I cannot write for toffee! I'm a sailor, not an antiquarian. I can barely string two long sentences together because my schooling stopped at twelve! But Effie knew you would never publish the damn thing if it came from her, so we put my name on it instead! That hardly matters in the grand scheme of things.'

Perhaps he could appeal to Sir Percival's better nature. The man adored Effie. The pair of them were as thick as thieves. Too ridiculously intelligent peas in a pod. 'You said yourself you had never read an essay so thorough, so compelling or so well written.'

'That was before I knew it was plagiarised!'

'How can it be plagiarised when Effie wrote it?'

'Because you are attempting to take the credit for it, sir!'

'Out of necessity because your stupid Society refuses to consider anything written by a woman.'

'*Archaeologia* is a respected publication, Lord Rivenhall. It cannot be party to a fraud. This is a travesty! I have to tell Lord Denby.'

And just like that, one of her two dreams would be shattered simply because Max had opened his big mouth.

'Then put Effie's name on it and it won't be a fraud. Then Denby and his minion will definitely not publish it for sure and the entire world of antiquity will be denied her discovery! That, sir, is the travesty.'

'She was to be denied anyway if it was to be published in your name.'

'And isn't that the greatest travesty of all?'

Effie awoke with a start to the sun shining through her bedchamber window and an empty space next to her in the bed. She could see by the covers he hadn't been there and wished she knew why he hadn't come.

The last thing she remembered was the raucous sounds of what appeared to be a very drunken game of billiards downstairs shortly after the clock struck twelve. After that she must have dozed off and there was every chance he had stuck his head in, seen her sleeping soundly and decided to leave her to rest.

Even though he had promised he would wake her and even though she was scandalously naked and had brushed her hair one hundred times and left it loose. Now she was still outrageously naked, but her shimmering curtain of *beguiling* hair probably now resembled a bird's nest.

She took one look at the clock and was horrified to see it was already eight. With the antiquarians leaving at nine, breakfast was probably already in full swing and she was in grave danger of missing it as well as the elusive Max. She shrugged on her unused nightgown quickly, called for the maid and tried not to read anything untoward into his absence. He loved her. She was sure of it. He wouldn't be having second thoughts. Would he?

Downstairs, there was still no sign of him. Nor his sister. But their three guests were all seated in the breakfast room unattended, so she hastily abandoned her plans to hunt for her lost lover and joined them at the table.

'I am sorry for my tardiness, gentlemen. I am afraid I overslept.'

'It seems to be a common problem this morning as your fiancé is yet to make an appearance, too.' Although not half as condescending as he had been upon his first arrival, it was still apparent Lord Denby had taken Max's absence as a slight. 'Mrs Baxter has said he was called to urgent estate business, but would be here as soon as he could.'

Estate business? As far as Effie was aware,

Max hadn't involved himself at all in any estate business yet, which threw up a hundred questions as to what was really afoot. 'I am sure he will be here presently. Running Rivenhall does take up a great deal of his time.'

Eleanor burst through the door smiling, but Effie couldn't help noticing it was forced. She looked drawn. Pale. As if something had happened and the prospect made Effie panic further. 'Hello, Eleanor…' Their eyes locked across the room. 'Are you…*well*?'

'Perfectly.' She waved it away in typical Eleanor fashion. 'Everything is sorted now. Max is on his way.' She sat beside Lord Denby and snapped open her napkin. 'Tenants! Do you have them, my lord?'

'Indeed I do, madam. Many.' He made it sound like a brag.

'Then you will appreciate what a chore they can be sometimes. How are the kippers, Percy? To your satisfaction.'

An oddly reticent Percy nodded. 'Splendid as always, Eleanor.' But an odd look passed between them which did nothing to ease Effie's nerves. 'The carriage leaves in forty minutes.' A strange thing to say for no apparent reason. 'On the stroke of nine.'

'Excellent…excellent. Then everything is on

time.' Smithson passed the older woman some tea and she gulped it down and then glared at Effie as if she expected her to make all the conversation.

'It is a shame you cannot stay a little longer, gentlemen.'

'Indeed it is,' said Lord Whittlesey, 'but Sir Percival has to be at the printers before they close tonight to oversea the final proofs of *Archaeologia*, so alas our journey is going to be arduous. He delayed the presses in view of Lord Rivenhall's discovery.'

'Did my sketches make it to the engravers in time?'

'I sent them by express yesterday morning to ensure they accompanied the article. Our members will doubtless appreciate their inclusion.' Lord Denby gave her what she assumed was his version of a smile. 'These past few days have been most enlightening.' Indeed they had. For all manner of reasons. 'I cannot remember when I have been so impressed with a fresh discovery. Roundhouses! Who knew?'

The next half an hour crawled past slowly. Eleanor kept glancing towards the door. Percy barely said a word and Max failed to materialise. The gentlemen were in the process of leaving the table when he finally strode into the room and Effie swore she saw both his sister and Percy physically sag with relief.

'Sorry I am late, everyone!' He looked tired. Rumpled. As if he had slept in his clothes. 'Tenants! What a palaver.'

'You are just in time to wave the antiquarians off, Max.' Eleanor's smile was as brittle as spun sugar. 'I was beginning to think you wouldn't make it.'

'Well, I did.' His eyes flicked to Effie's then and they were filled with apology. 'Better late than never.'

As he pulled out his sister's chair so they could wave off their guests, she noticed his fingers were covered in ink. Then Smithson hurried in and skidded to a stop directly in front of them. 'The carriage is loaded, my lord.'

'Is all the luggage on board?'

'Indeed it is, my lord. Including the small case Lord Percival *accidentally* left in his bedchamber.'

'Capital.' Max came to Effie's chair next and solicitously pulled it out before taking her hand and wrapping it tightly around his and squeezing it in reassurance, although lord only knew what he was reassuring her of.

The three of them stood on the porch as the antiquarians climbed into the coach, and they stayed there waving, fake smiles glued in place until it disappeared down the drive. The second it did, Eleanor slumped against a column. 'Smithson! Bring some sherry. No, make that brandy! I don't care if it is nine o'clock, my poor nerves are shot.'

'Would somebody please tell me what's going on?'

'It was nothing. A little hiccup. I fixed it.' Max frowned as his sister punched his arm.

'Oh, you fixed it, did you? That would be the reason I have been up all night, my eyes are crossed and my poor nerves are shot to pieces! Not to mention the not-inconsequential detail that if you hadn't broken things in the first place they wouldn't have needed fixing!'

'Please tell me what has happened?'

'Percy discovered you were Miss Nithercott.'

'Thanks to your big mouth! And because of plagiarism, fraud and the stupid rules of that silly Society he belongs to, he wasn't going to publish your paper, Effie!'

Max saw her face drop and smiled. 'But he is now. Because I rewrote it.'

'*You* rewrote it!' Eleanor whacked him again.

'All right… I wrote the additional words while Eleanor dictated them, although frankly and do not tell the upright Sir Percy, they are still mostly yours, Effie, because I had to plagiarise them.

Neither of us knew what half of it meant. It took us all night.'

'You should have woken me.'

'I didn't dare. The only way I could convince him to publish the new article was if it all came from my pen. He was adamant Lord Denby would have his guts for garters if he allowed a woman's work to slip through the net… Society might crumble after all… Although to be fair to him he did think the stupid rules were old fashioned and he did think your article was one of the best things he had ever read. And we were both disgusted that you weren't going to get the credit for it—so I changed a few things. Wrote it from a different perspective.'

'I don't follow.'

'After a long and heated discussion about those blasted rules, we both came to the conclusion they say the Society will not accept articles written by a woman—but that does not mean they cannot publish articles *about* a woman. So now, instead of giving me all the credit for the discovery, the paper tells the truth.'

'The truth?'

'That I merely wielded the pickaxe and you were the brains. I submitted the article as your humble assistant, Effie. It will go to press tonight and before Lord Denby can stop it, it will have been distributed to every antiquarian from here to John O'Groats.'

'I get all the credit?'

'Every last bit. I've even committed to doing a talk at your dratted Society on the subject next month in London in front of a baying, staring crowd, where I will also reiterate your brilliance and denounce I had any hand in it beyond that of pickaxe-wielding minion who just did as he was told.' He smiled smugly at her stunned face. 'You can kiss me now.'

'That's the nicest thing anyone has ever done for me.' What a wonderful man she had! 'But you don't have to do a talk, Max. The article is enough—no, more than enough for me. My work is being published! That is all I ever wanted.'

'I know. But it's time to cast off my widower's weeds and stop hiding from the world.' He tapped his lips. 'I am still waiting.'

Eleanor beamed and hugged her tight. 'Congratulations! Max told me you are engaged! I couldn't be happier for you both. And he's taking you to sea! That is so romantic!' She sighed and clutched her heart.

'Where she can be my blasted assistant for a change. For six months of every year...after she's worked her way up the ranks and learned the ropes, of course, the way I did. You can't learn to be a sailor by reading. Just as you cannot become an antiquarian until you've done the drudge work.'

'You expect your fiancée to begin as a cabin boy?'

'She's a clever thing.' He pretended to ponder it, his sinfully talented mouth struggling to contain his smile. 'I suppose she can come aboard as an ordinary seaman and I'll only make her swab the decks on alternate Tuesdays.' He turned to Effie, love, desire and mischief dancing an apt sailor's jig in his beautiful dark eyes. 'Meanwhile— Miss Not A Nithercott For Much Longer, thank the lord—I still seem to be waiting for that kiss. And as your occasional Captain…' he tugged her into his arms and pulled the pencil out of the hair she had worn expressly for him and always would '…but never your lord and master…and in case that big brain of yours was wondering…after the night I've had, that's an order.'

* * * * *

COMING SOON!

MILLS & BOON

Coming next month

THEIR MARRIAGE OF INCONVENIENCE
Sophia James

The ground was torn out from beneath her feet. If she had been braver, she might have spoken up for the kiss, for the dance, for the safety. But her courage had completely deserted her and lay shattered at her feet in tiny bits of shame. She stayed quiet because any admission would undo her.

'I think that you are a woman who clings to the best chance for herself and is able to turn facts on their heads with an ease that is disturbing. I also think you could probably give the best courtesans in London a run for their money with your expertise in kissing.'

She blushed and hated herself for doing so.

'Then if pretence is a skill, Mr Morgan, you are equally as good in the art as I am.'

He moved at that. 'Really?' One finger carefully traced its way down her cheek across her throat and on to the flesh above her bodice. She felt her skin raise in response. 'In my experience pretence does not usually look like this.'

He brushed his hand across her lips like a feather, barely there. Breathing out, she tipped her head back and waited and when his lips came down across her own she shut her eyes and only felt, shock burning its way through her body, warming all the coldness that had been there for ever.

She couldn't stop him even despite the words, the accusations, the anger. This was more than all of that put together and if lust could make her feel complete then who was she to bring it to a halt. Simeon would never love her, she knew that, or trust her, but this was another language entirely and one which, apparently, they both could speak fluently.

Her hand cradled his neck and she leant in, wanting what he offered with every fibre of her being. She knew that she had him when his breath hitched in surrender, only the two of them in a world of silence.

It was unlike any kiss he had given her before because this one held an element of desperation, an anchor offering a safe harbour just for this small piece of time, caught to each other by consequence just before a storm.

Continue reading
THEIR MARRIAGE OF INCONVENIENCE
Sophia James

Available next month
www.millsandboon.co.uk

LET'S TALK

Romance